Trip strode quickly across the deck, practically running Hoshi over in his haste to get to the com. "Tucker to the bridge. I've got a visual on an object that looks remarkably like a—"

The deck underneath Trip roared, then buckled upward.

The ship shuddered a second time, lifting him up into the air and then dropping him back down again, face first.

Someone moaned behind him. He turned and saw Hoshi sitting up, holding her forehead. Trip helped her to her feet.

"You all right?" he asked.

She nodded. A diagnostic cable slid past him, heading toward the far wall.

Then Trip heard it—a slow hissing sound, like air leaking out of a bicycle tire.

A chill ran down his spine as he realized what was happening.

"Hull breach!" he said.

ENTERPRISE™

DAEDALUS

DAVE STERN

**Based on *Star Trek*®
created by Gene Roddenberry
Enterprise™ created by Rick Berman & Brannon Braga**

POCKET BOOKS
New York London Toronto Sydney Singapore

An *Original* Publication of POCKET BOOKS

POCKET BOOKS, a division of Simon & Schuster, Inc.
1230 Avenue of the Americas, New York, NY 10020

This book is published by Pocket Books, a division of Simon & Schuster, Inc., under exclusive license from Paramount Pictures.

ISBN: 0-7434-7118-0

First Pocket Books printing December 2003

10 9 8 7 6 5 4 3 2 1

POCKET and colophon are registered trademarks of Simon & Schuster, Inc.

Manufactured in the United States of America

For information regarding special discounts for bulk purchases, please contact Simon & Schuster Special Sales at 1-800-456-6798 or business@simonandschuster.com

To Maddy and Boo
For leading me to strange new worlds . . .

The events take place just prior to
Captain Archer being taken by
the Tellarite bounty hunter Skalaar on
March 21, 2153.

One

"COMMANDER?"

Trip looked up from the intermix chamber, where he'd been monitoring the composition of the matter-antimatter stream. Engineer Second Class K. P. Ryan—tall, lanky, usually quiet to the point of reclusive—stood on the access ladder below him.

"Ryan. What's up?"

"You have a moment? It's about the cell-ship."

Trip—Commander Charles Tucker III, chief engineer aboard the *Starship Enterprise*—frowned. He had a systems status meeting with the captain in a few minutes, and he was already running behind schedule.

But the cell-ship . . .

Analyzing the captured Suliban vessel had been a priority for Trip over the last several months. First on his own, then with key members of his department—including Ryan—Trip had turned the cell-ship virtually inside out, trying to plumb the secrets of the Suliban's superior technology.

"What about the cell-ship?" Trip asked.

"Their warp drive. The propulsion system." Ryan's eyes gleamed with excitement. He looked more animated than Trip had ever seen him. "I think I've figured it out."

"You're kidding."

"No, sir." Now Ryan actually smiled. "I'm not."

"Sonuvagun." Trip set down his diagnostic spanner on top of the intermix chamber. "Come on. Show me."

Ryan led him out of engineering and down to Launch Bay Two. The cell-ship sat in the far corner—looking like nothing so much as a multi-sided dice cube precariously balanced on one edge, perhaps a third as big as one of *Enterprise*'s shuttlepods. Its forward hatch was open, and portions of the hull had been removed, exposing layers of exotic-looking circuitry. Cables of varying thickness and color—most of them supplying power, but some more diagnostic in nature—ran from various nodes in the circuitry to a diagnostic station nearby. One of those nodes was the warp-drive module—a rectangular box roughly the size and shape of an old orange crate—which had been pulled out from the instrument panel and now lay on top of the cockpit console.

Trip hadn't gotten very far in analyzing that module—but one thing was clear. Unlike *Enter-*

prise, which used a series of controlled matter/antimatter explosions to achieve warp velocity, the Suliban drive depended on an exotic series of reactions between charged particle streams—the exact composition of which had defied decipherment.

At least until now.

"We've been doing a black-box analysis on the module the last few days," Ryan said. "Feeding different particle streams in, measuring the energy that comes out."

"Yeah," Trip said impatiently. He knew that—he was the one who'd started the black-box analysis a week ago. The last few days he'd had to spend most of his free time in engineering, though, so he'd handed over that analysis to others. "Go on."

"At approximately"—Ryan consulted the display screen—"fifteen hundred hours we input a series of discrete ion streams into the warp module. The power output was negligible—until I had an idea. Alternate the charge on each succeeding stream—follow a positive stream with a negative, then another positive, and so on. And if you—"

"Hold on a minute." Trip felt suddenly lightheaded. "Are you trying to tell me the Suliban ship runs off an ion drive?"

Ryan smiled. "Yes, sir. I think so."

Trip kept his gaze neutral.

But inside, his mind—and his heart—were racing.

An ion drive.

3

Daedalus.

Ryan was still talking, Trip realized.

". . . somehow prevent the streams from crossing until the last possible second—then all that pent-up energy gets released at once. I think that's what the Suliban drive does—the ions come together like real streams do, to make a river."

"Cascading," Trip said softly. "The word you're looking for is *cascading.*"

"A cascading ion drive." Ryan nodded. "That sounds about right. Of course, we can't be certain that's exactly what we're dealing with here—it is a black box, after all, but . . ."

Ryan continued talking, but Trip no longer heard him. He was hearing another voice in his mind, a voice coming from fourteen years and billions of kilometers in the past.

Victor Brodesser's voice, as the most controversial scientist Earth had produced in a dozen generations stood up from behind his desk and reached forward to shake Trip's hand.

"Welcome to the Daedalus Project, Mister Tucker." Brodesser—in his early sixties, a broad, barrel-chested man with a massive shock of wild gray hair that made him look every inch the mad scientist his reputation made him out to be—had a fierce grip. "We're here to make history."

And they had. Just not in the way Brodesser had hoped.

* * *

"Commander?"

Trip realized Ryan had asked him a question.

"Sorry, K.P. Say again?"

"With your permission—I'd like to follow this full-time. If these power curves hold, and we could gather enough data—maybe we could even reverse-engineer the drive. . . ."

Ryan's voice trailed off. The young engineer looked at Trip, and frowned.

"Is something the matter, sir? I suppose I should have called you down when I started to get results, but—"

Underneath the ensign's worry, Trip could sense a hint of anger and suddenly realized what was going on. Ryan thought he was jealous of the ensign's discovery.

"Hey, no, no, Ensign. Everything's fine. Just . . . preoccupied with something, that's all."

"About the cell-ship?"

"No," Trip answered, wondering if he should tell Ryan about *Daedalus*. No. He needed a conversation with the captain first. And—there was no need to shoulder Ryan with the burdens of the past just now.

"Listen, this is good work, Ensign. Good work. You absolutely deserve to be the one following up on it."

"Thank you, sir."

"Now, full-time . . . I don't know about that. But

for the next few days I'll switch you off the maintenance roster. You'll have to make up those shifts, though . . . down the line."

"Yes, sir. Thank you, sir."

Ryan smiled so broadly his teeth showed.

Trip couldn't help but smile back.

The companel sounded.

"Archer to Tucker. Archer to Commander Tucker."

The smile froze on Trip's face.

The status meeting.

Trip strode quickly to the nearest companel.

"Tucker here, sir. Be there in a minute. Just finishing up a little something in Launch Bay Two."

"The Suliban ship?"

"Yes, sir."

"Good. That's one of the things we'll need to discuss. When you get here."

"On my way, sir."

Trip closed the channel and turned back to Ryan.

"Keep me posted, K.P. Progress reports every day."

"Yes, sir."

Trip would be studying those reports carefully—and certainly dropping by frequently to check up on Ryan's progress in person.

He'd put his heart and soul into *Daedalus*. Even after all this time . . . it would be nice to see that work—not to mention Brodesser's belief in the ion drive—validated. Even if the professor himself was no longer around to see it happen.

Still, as he headed for the turbolift, the ion drive wasn't uppermost in his mind.

Trip was wondering why in the world Captain Archer wanted to talk about the Suliban ship at the status meeting.

The captain, Sub-Commander T'Pol, the ship's armory officer, Lieutenant Malcolm Reed, and—to Trip's surprise—ship's physician Doctor Phlox, who almost never attended these status meetings—were gathered around the situation room table as Trip entered.

T'Pol was in the middle of a heated speech—heated for her, anyway; after serving with the Vulcan this long Trip had come to recognize the cutting tone her voice took on when she felt particularly strong about making her point—and Trip waited for her to finish before making his presence known.

". . . so my preference remains a continued series of long-range scans, rather than the uncertain—and potentially catastrophic—alternative Lieutenant Reed proposes, which would—"

"Now, hold on a minute, Sub-Commander." Malcolm Reed—who was also the ship's tactical officer—frowned. "I grant you that by using the cloaked vessel we take a chance, but catastrophic? Surely that's a bit of an exaggeration—"

"On the contrary, Lieutenant, *catastrophic* describes precisely the consequences almost certain to result should our presence be detected by the inhabitants of—"

"All right. T'Pol, Malcolm—please." Archer's own voice had an edge. "I think both of you have made your positions clear on this. Now—"

Trip cleared his throat. "Excuse me—Captain?"

Archer looked up at him and smiled. "Ah—Commander Tucker, isn't it? Join us, please."

Everyone around the table—everyone except T'Pol, of course—laughed.

"Sorry about being late, sir. But"—he looked around the table, from Reed to T'Pol to Doctor Phlox, and then back at the Captain—"cloaked vessel? I have to guess you mean the cell-ship, but . . . would someone please fill me in on what else I missed?"

"We are talking about the cell-ship" Archer nodded. "As to what else is going on . . . T'Pol? If you wouldn't mind bringing Commander Tucker here up to speed . . ."

"Certainly." T'Pol shifted in her chair and spoke directly to Trip. "As you may or may not be aware, several days ago we entered the K'Pellis Cluster, an aggregation of previously unexplored stellar systems. Almost immediately sensors detected a massive gravitational anomaly within one of those systems. We have been conducting intensive studies of the anomaly since that initial contact—and have agreed a series of close-up observations are in order."

Trip got it instantly. "And you want to use the cell-ship to do that."

Reed spoke up. "Yes."

"But cloaked—why?"

"I will show you." T'Pol touched a button on the table in front of her, and the display set in the center of the table came to life. From left to right it showed a blinking white oval, a band of much smaller, irregularly shaped objects, and two circles, one much larger than the other.

"This is the Cole One-twenty-eight system—which the anomaly here"—she pointed to the blinking oval—"is located in. The system also contains an extensive asteroid belt"—she pointed to the band of irregular objects—"a single Minshara-class planet"—to the smaller of the two circles—"and a yellow sun, point-six-hundred-seventy-six on the K'uda luminosity spectrum."

She looked up at Trip.

"The planet is inhabited. A bipedal, humanoid race—"

"With, I might add, an unusual amount of genotypical similarity to Earth humans," Phlox interjected. "If the preliminary data holds up, in fact, we're looking at an almost ninety-nine point nine percent congruity between these aliens and your species. Which is remarkable, considering the distance between Earth and this world. Wouldn't you agree, Sub-Commander?"

T'Pol raised an eyebrow. "*Remarkable* is a very strong word, Doctor. I would characterize the preliminary data as 'of interest.'"

"Ah. Remarkable, of interest—we're talking about the same thing. A—noteworthy situation, hmm?" Phlox smiled. "Forgive the interruption. Please—continue."

She did so—Trip noting that however you wanted to characterize the data, it at least explained Phlox's presence at the situation table.

"This race, Commander Tucker, has minimal space-flight capabilities. Based on intercepted E-M transmissions, they are at least a century away from warp flight capability. Should they detect our presence, it would undoubtedly have far-ranging consequences for the development of their civilization. Potentially"—she inclined her head in Lieutenant Reed's direction—"catastrophic in nature."

Reed rolled his eyes.

Archer held up a hand before the lieutenant could start in again.

"Well . . . hold on a minute," Trip said. "I still don't see why you need the cloaked ship." He pointed to the display. "You've got the asteroid belt between your anomaly here and the planet."

"This civilization has ships in the asteroid belt," T'Pol said. "Most likely performing mining operations."

"Most likely with limited scanning ability," Trip countered. "If we know where those ships are, I'd bet we can get *Enterprise* in and out without being detected—and you'd have plenty of time to run your scans. . . ."

His voice trailed off as he noticed Reed shaking his head.

"She needs a week," Malcolm said.

"At minimum. And there are dozens of ships in the belt," T'Pol said. "Too many for us to remain hidden that long."

"Which is why I suggested cloaking the cell-ship," Reed said. "That way—"

T'Pol shook her head. "If the cloak should malfunction . . ."

"Trip," Archer asked. "What do you think? Can you get the cloak up and working again—and guarantee it won't fail?"

Trip let out a long, slow whistle. They'd used the cell-ship's cloak on one previous occasion—a life-or-death occasion—and though it had ultimately done what they required of it, its function had been . . . well, intermittent at best.

Trip had also ended up cloaking his own hand for the better part of a week while working with the cloak. One of the most unsettling experiences of his life—looking down and seeing your hand gone from the wrist up, made doubly unsettling by the fact that even though he couldn't see the hand, he could still feel it.

Still . . .

"*Guarantee* is a pretty strong word, Captain. But I tell you what—I wouldn't mind taking another crack at it. A couple days of solid work and I'll be able to let you know one way or another."

"Commander," T'Pol said. "With all due respect—one can be certain that the Suliban did not develop their cloaking technology in a 'couple of days.' To think that you will be able to decipher the principles behind it in that span of time—"

"I don't need to understand the principles," Trip said. "I just need to get it working."

"If we do not understand the principles on which the cloak is built, we cannot be sure of its reliability."

Archer nodded. "A fair point."

Trip frowned. "Well . . . maybe. But you don't necessarily have to know how something works to use it, Captain. I mean, half the people on this ship couldn't fix the impulse engines, let alone the warp drive. Am I right?"

Archer nodded again, and smiled. "You're right. So is T'Pol. Which is why"—the captain leaned forward in his chair—"I'll ask her to assist you in repairing the cloak. That way she can be assured of its reliability before we decide whether or not to undertake the survey."

"Of course, sir," T'Pol said.

"Yes, sir," Trip chimed in, biting down hard on his lip to avoid showing his irritation. He would far prefer to work on the cloak himself, having done a lot of work with that module already, all of which was in his head and only in his head, so he would have to spend a good chunk of time bringing T'Pol up to speed on where he was before moving forward on his analysis.

He looked up and saw Archer smiling at him—as if the captain could read his thoughts.

"We'll get on it right away," Trip said, returning his commander's grin with as much sincerity as he could muster.

"Good." Archer looked around the table. "Now, if we're all done here—"

"A moment, Captain." Doctor Phlox, who had remained silent during the entire discussion, spoke up.

"I would like to remind everyone of the unfortunate consequences of Commander Tucker's previous attempts at working with the cloaking device. The 'missing hand' episode, as I have come to think of it."

"You don't have to remind me," Trip said.

"But that is precisely what I wish to do," Phlox said, his voice growing suddenly earnest. Even after all this time serving with the doctor, that was the one thing about him that Trip still had a hard time getting used to—how Phlox could go from irreverent to dead serious within the space of a single breath. "We found no long-lasting health consequences as a result of that incident, but it seems to me that Sub-Commander T'Pol's point is worth repeating and even amplifying. Playing with technology—"

"I'm not playing," Trip said forcefully.

Phlox nodded. "An unfortunate choice of words. Forgive me. *Experimenting* with technology without fully understanding its ramifications is a situation rife with—shall we say, catastrophic potential—especially aboard the cramped confines of a starship. I would urge extreme caution."

"Point well taken, Doctor. Trip, T'Pol . . ." Archer took them both in with a single glance.

"We'll bear that in mind, Captain," Trip said.

"Yes, sir," T'Pol concurred.

"All right, then. I'll want a progress report tomorrow by eighteen hundred hours—we should make a decision by that time the following day." Archer looked around the table again, then stood.

"Dismissed."

But Trip had another matter he wanted to discuss with the captain.

He followed Archer into his ready room.

"Commander Tucker," the captain said as he sat down at his workstation. "Let me guess—you'd prefer to work on the cloak alone."

Trip smiled. "Sure would. But that's not what I wanted to talk to you about."

"Oh?" Archer activated his monitor and began scrolling through his incoming messages. "What's on your mind?"

"Ryan's made a very interesting discovery—about the warp drive on the cell-ship."

"Uh-huh. Go on." Archer was half-listening—as absorbed in scrolling through the information on his monitor as he was in what Trip had to say.

"Captain." Trip leaned over Archer's shoulder. "Preliminary indications are that it's an ion drive."

"Really? An ion drive?" The captain still didn't look up from the screen.

"I think so, sir. Of a type very similar to the one we used in *Daedalus.*"

Archer's fingers, in the middle of keying in a response to one of the on-screen messages, froze in midair.

The captain spun around in his seat to face Trip.

"And this is a functional ion drive?"

"Well . . . that's what we need to confirm," Trip said. "I told Ryan he could go at it full-tilt over the next few days—that'll have to wait until we finish up with the cloak now, of course—but even so, I'd like to get him access to the *Daedalus* files—Brodesser's files—as soon as possible. With your permission of course, sir."

The captain drummed his fingers on his desk.

"*Daedalus,*" he said, wearing a faraway look. Trip knew what the captain was thinking about: Archer had lost friends as well—good friends—when *Daedalus* exploded. "That was a long time ago, Trip. . . ."

"Fourteen years."

"Fourteen years. That long . . ." Archer shook his head. "You think about what people would be like now . . . what they might have done."

Trip nodded. He certainly did.

"Brodesser and Duvall—if the drive had worked, *Daedalus* would have beat us out here by more than a decade. They would have half the quadrant mapped out by now. Both of them would be as famous as Zephram Cochrane."

The captain was talking in general terms—"out here" meaning "unexplored space"—but in point of fact, from what Trip remembered of the mission profile, K'Pellis and the surrounding sector had actually been in *Daedalus's* initial destination matrix.

"So the drive on the Suliban ship is similar to . . ." The captain frowned. "What was it called?"

"The cascading ion drive," Trip said. "Cid."

"That's right—how could I forget? El Cid. Like the story."

Trip looked at the captain.

And once again, he saw Brodesser.

"The cascading ion drive," Brodesser had said that first day Trip had walked into his office. "I've spent the last five years of my life working on it. Here."

Brodesser turned the display on his desk so that Trip could see it.

The monitor was filled with line after line of

equations. Trip couldn't make heads or tails out of half of them.

"You'll note"—Brodesser pointed at one of the last few lines on the screen—"the maximum speed the drive is capable of achieving."

That line was one of the ones Trip could understand.

"Warp seven-point-six." He blinked just to make sure he'd read it right. "Seven-point-six? The Vulcans aren't even there yet. Don't expect to be there for another hundred years."

"That's right," Brodesser said. "It would be nice to address them from a position of superiority for once—wouldn't it?"

"Sure would," Trip said.

The two of them shared a smile.

"You'll need to get clearance from Starfleet to open up those old records on *Daedalus.*"

The sound of Archer's voice brought Trip back to the here and now.

The captain had risen from his seat and was now standing by the ready room's sole window, his back to Trip. "Compose a request for me, and I'll forward it on."

"Will do."

Archer turned around then, and shook his head. "*Daedalus.* An ion drive. It's a small universe, after all."

"That it is, sir."

"It'd be nice to remove some of the clouds hanging over that project."

"Just what I was thinking."

"You'll be careful, though? You'll make sure Ryan's careful?"

"I'll watch him like a hawk."

"All right, then. Dismissed."

Trip headed back down to Launch Bay Two to break the good news—and the bad—to Ensign Ryan.

Two

"COMMANDER?"

"Hang on a minute." Trip leaned over the cell-ship console, cracked his knuckles, and keyed in one final line of code. There.

"That should do it," he said, watching the program run. "Disengage the last of the start-up subroutines, let us maintain full power to the cloaking device." Which had been the problem the last time they'd used the cell-ship—to rescue the captain and Malcolm from the wrong end of a noose. The cloak kept failing at the most inopportune moments because the ship's computer automatically assigned other systems priority over it. Not anymore. Not if Trip was good at his job. Which he liked to think that he was.

"Whenever you're ready, Sub-Commander."

He looked up at T'Pol.

Ensign Ryan was leaning over her shoulder.

"As I was trying to tell you," T'Pol said, "you have a visitor."

Ryan nodded. "Just a quick question, sir. Won't take a moment."

Trip frowned.

This was Ryan's third "quick question" of the day. To go along with the half-dozen from last night Trip had found waiting on his computer this morning. Not that he minded enthusiasm—which was all Ryan had displayed ever since Trip had gotten permission to show him the *Daedalus* material.

But there was a time and a place for everything—and right now, with Trip working full-time on the Suliban cloak, was neither. A point he thought he'd made clear to Ryan last night. Not clear enough, though, apparently.

"Come with me a minute," Trip said, taking the ensign's arm. He led Ryan halfway across the Launch Bay floor, out of earshot from T'Pol. At least, Trip assumed they were out of earshot. The more he learned about Vulcans, though, the less he discovered he knew.

"Mister Ryan—what does the phrase *not today* mean to you?"

"Sorry, sir, I know we talked, but this—"

"We did talk." Trip folded his arms across his chest. "What didn't I make clear?"

"Actually it's the files that aren't clear, sir," Ryan said, misunderstanding Trip's question. "The cascading protocol Brodesser outlines is not the same as the one we talked about this morning."

Trip sighed. "The papers don't reflect some of the last-minute changes the professor—excuse me—made. Just do the best you can for now, K.P.," he told Ryan. "After T'Pol and I have finished, I'll be happy to go over the equations with you."

"Yes, sir. Sorry about being a nuisance."

"It's all right, Ensign," Trip said—

And at that instant, as those words left his mouth, another memory from that long-ago year he'd spent working with Victor Brodesser came rushing back.

He was standing in the corridor in front of the door to Brodesser's quarters, about to touch the entry panel, when the door slid open. Trip started to apologize about the lateness of the hour, and the professor cut him off.

"It's all right, Lieutenant," Brodesser had said. "Come in, please."

The time was twenty-two hundred hours exactly—Trip remembered because he'd been in the operations room, about to go off-duty when he'd received a summons from Brodesser, a text message at his station.

Lieutenant Tucker:
Please see me tonight, before you turn in.
—Brodesser

His heart had sunk immediately on seeing that message. He knew why Brodesser wanted to see him. He was replacing Trip as operations manager because of the arguments they'd been having the last few weeks. Brodesser had decided to put someone else in charge of the launch, someone less contentious, someone whom he felt more sympatico with.

A year of my life, Trip remembered thinking. *A year of my life down the drain, because I couldn't keep my big mouth shut.*

Trip had followed Brodesser into his quarters. They'd made idle chitchat for a while, until Trip couldn't stand the suspense any longer and had spoken up.

"It's all right, sir," he'd said. "You don't have to dance around the subject. It's your ship—your project. You have to do what you think is best."

Brodesser frowned. "What are you talking about, Lieutenant?"

"Why you wanted to see me," Trip said. "To make the change. Remove me as operations manager."

"To remove you—" Brodesser shook his head. "Why would I want to do that?"

"Because of the cascading protocol."

"The cascading protocol? What about it?"

"I know I've been pushing pretty hard for a change, but I think I'm right. I know I'm right," Trip said, bulling ahead full speed, damn the torpedoes, damn the consequences. Brodesser had taken him on as operations manager to focus on the big picture, and that was what he was going to do. "I know it costs us acceleration time, but we need a bigger safety margin, especially during the initial engine ramp-up. And that's why—"

"You're right," Brodesser interrupted. "I thought about it, I looked at the equations again, and I decided to make a change. That's why I asked you to stop by."

Trip opened his mouth, then shut it again. For the last few months he'd been arguing for a slow-down of the initial cascade reaction. Brodesser had fought him almost every step of the way—until tonight. The eve of the launch.

"Come with me, and I'll show you what we've done."

Still in somewhat of a daze, Trip followed the man into his office.

It looked exactly as it had that afternoon he'd joined *Daedalus*. The long desk, piled high with scraps of paper (one of Brodesser's quirks, Trip had discovered—the man preferred working on hardcopy to typing on the screen), the photos of a young girl Trip now knew to be the professor's granddaughter, Alicia (perhaps the only other thing in his life that gave Brodesser pleasure be-sides his work), the model of *Daedalus* as the pro-fessor had originally envisioned the ship . . . all those seemed just as they had that first day.

One thing was new, though.

A single, oversize, leather-bound book propped up, front cover faced outward, on a small shelf behind Brodesser's desk. *The Song of El Cid*. A gift from the project's senior staff—including Trip—to the professor.

Trip couldn't remember who had first made a connection between Cid the drive and *El Cid* the poem—but not more than a month into the project, that was what everyone working on translating Brodesser's concepts into reality was calling the cascading ion drive. "El Cid," or simply "Cid"—as in "El Cid was a bear today," or "the buffers on Cid are acting up," and so on, and so on.

When they'd finished construction on the main drive chamber two months before, the staff could think of no better present to give Brodesser than a copy of the poem itself—signed, of course, by all the staff.

That moment—when Brodesser unwrapped the book and began flipping through the pages, reading the inscriptions each engineer had written—was the only time Trip had ever seen the professor speechless, or even slightly subdued.

Until now.

"Here." Brodesser picked up a stack of paper from his desk. "I've been talking to Mister Cooney, and here's how we're reprogramming the initiation sequence. It's going to cut down on our velocity—but I think we'll still hit warp six."

Trip took the sheaf of paper Brodesser held out

to him, and flipped through it. The professor had indeed done what Trip suggested—slowed down the initial cascade reaction. Not to the degree that Trip had recommended—he would like to see another five percent reduction, but still . . .

It was a significant change. How much of a difference would that last five percent make?

"It should do the trick—don't you think?"

Trip looked up.

Brodesser was staring at him expectantly, waiting for a response, looking—for the first time since Trip had known him—every one of his sixty-odd years.

He's exhausted, Trip realized. And no wonder . . . the strain of running a project this size at his age, not just overseeing the design and construction and personnel associated with *Daedalus* but fighting the political battles with fleet brass, many of who were convinced *Daedalus* was a dead end, that it was using up resources better spent at the Warp Five complex . . .

It had to be killing him.

Trip handed Brodesser back the sheaf of papers.

"I think we're in pretty good shape now, sir," he said.

"Excellent." The professor smiled. The expression lit up his face, made him look twenty years younger.

It was the last time Trip saw him in person, in the flesh.

Some twelve hours later Brodesser and everyone else aboard *Daedalus* was dead.

And the only concrete memento Trip had of that year of his life was the leather-bound copy of *El Cid*—which he convinced the professor's granddaughter to let him take. That book had traveled with him on every subsequent posting he'd had.

Right now it lay on the table next to his bunk. Last night, for the first time since coming aboard *Enterprise*, Trip had taken it out, looked over the words that he'd inscribed on the inside front cover:

Professor:
Thanks for the best year of my life—so far.

And smiled then, as he always did, remembering the debate he'd had with himself about that inscription, whether or not to add those last two words, afraid that they might somehow offend Brodesser.

He'd been young back then, all right. No recriminations about the inscription, not after seeing the look on the professor's face as he read over it, Trip thought, but there were plenty of others. He allowed himself the luxury of basking in them until far too late in the evening.

"Sir?"
Trip blinked.

Ryan was talking to him.

"I just wanted to say again—I'm sorry if I've been a little bit of a nuisance these past couple days. It's just that the whole *Daedalus* story—Cid, and everything—I didn't know any of it before, and I'm just—"

"Easy, Ryan." Trip put a hand on the ensign's shoulder. "Don't worry about being a nuisance. But do me a favor, though—all right?"

"Sure. I mean, yes, sir."

"Wait until tomorrow for the next round of questions."

Ryan smiled. "Yes, sir."

Trip turned and marched back to the cell-ship.

T'Pol was sitting in front of the display, her fingers flying across the console.

"What are you doing?" Trip asked.

"I am taking the liberty of rewriting some of your code," T'Pol said. "The syntax is unnecessarily complex."

Trip took a deep breath.

"I thought we were in a hurry," he said. "The code will work fine as is."

"Commander Tucker," T'Pol said, and her voice took on a scolding tone that reminded him suddenly of his mother. "If there is not enough time to do a job properly, then there is not enough time to do that job."

"Ooookay." Trip rubbed his brow and began counting to ten.

He got to five and stopped.

"You know what, Sub-Commander," Trip began, his voice rising. "If you want to . . ."

He bit his lip to keep from continuing.

She looked up. "Yes?"

Trip sighed. "Never mind."

"Trip. T'Pol."

He turned and saw the captain walking toward them.

"How's it going?" Archer asked.

"Fine," Trip said. He forced a smile. "Just dandy."

"We are making good progress," T'Pol said.

"What's that you're doing there?"

"Rewriting Commander Tucker's code."

"I see." Archer looked at Trip. His eyes twinkled in amusement. "And you Commander—what are you up to?"

Trip opened his mouth to speak, and shut it again. Another saying he often associated with his mother came to mind.

"If you don't have something nice to say, don't say anything at all."

He forced a smile, and shrugged.

"Just—ah—waiting to make myself useful. Sir."

"Glad to hear it." The captain nodded. "I may have just the thing."

"Sir?"

"Let's head up to the situation room," Archer said. "T'Pol, you, too. We can talk on the way."

* * *

They had a problem, Archer explained. That problem was the Denari. That, Hoshi—Ensign Hoshi, the ship's communications officer—had discovered, was what the inhabitants of Cole 128's Minshara-class world called themselves, and their planet.

They were about to launch a new observational platform.

"Once the platform is up and running, they'll be able to detect *Enterprise*—and any ship that enters the system," Archer said.

"Based on com traffic from within the system, that could happen any moment now," Hoshi added.

"Can you be more precise than 'any moment now'?" T'Pol asked.

Hoshi shook her head. "No. I've got hundreds of E-M intercepts, in fourteen different languages, running through the translator. But it's slow going."

"Which means we have to make a choice based on what we know now," Archer said. The captain spoke to everyone around the situation table—Trip, T'Pol, Hoshi, Reed, and Ensign Mayweather, the ship's helmsman. "Go, or no go. Explore the anomaly or leave it be. T'Pol, it's largely your call."

"I am forced to modify my earlier statements, Captain. Based on further analysis by the science department, I now believe we must explore the anomaly—at a proximity only the cell-ship can afford us." She spoke with what was as close to passion as Trip had ever heard in her voice. "This phenomenon is literally a once-in-a-lifetime occurrence."

"All right, then." Archer nodded. "So where are we with the cloaking device?"

Trip spoke first. "In good shape, I think. The new code should keep it up and running without any malfunctions."

"Sub-Commander? You agree?"

"I do. The code looks as if it will work," she said. "Of course, it will need testing."

"How long will that take?"

Trip and T'Pol spoke at once.

"A day should be sufficient," she said.

"Two hours, give or take," he responded.

They looked at each other.

"Two hours is about what we have, T'Pol," the captain said. "Can you live with that?"

T'Pol frowned, and thought a moment.

"Yes. I believe so. However, it will involve designing a very specific testing routine." She stood up. "With your permission, sir, I will get to work immediately."

Archer nodded. "Go. Trip, Malcolm—let's prep the cell-ship for launch in two hours. Travis, you'll plot a course for *Enterprise* to the edge of the anomaly. Call on whoever else you need for assistance. Is that clear?"

Heads nodded around the table.

"All right, then. Dismissed."

Half a minute later Trip and Archer were the only ones left around the table.

"I thought I said dismissed."

"That you did." Trip smiled. "Just wanted to tell you—better make it three hours. For that launch."

"That's just what I was going to tell Travis."

"You're ahead of the game," Trip said.

Archer nodded. "That's why I'm the captain."

Trip smiled, and headed for the turbolift.

Three

LAUNCH BAY TWO was a madhouse.

Shuttlepod One was moving slowly across the deck, being slid out of launch position to make way for the Suliban ship. T'Pol was hunched over the cell-ship console, running her testing routines. Trip disconnected diagnostic cables as she worked. Hoshi had brought a specially designed Universal Translator module (just in case) and stood next to Reed, watching him as he stretched over T'Pol's shoulder to retrofit it to the Suliban communications array.

Trip had already decided he wasn't going to feed it power unless another hour magically appeared in the launch window. No way was he going to put anything in the cell-ship that might draw juice from the cloaking device.

The companel sounded.

"Ensign Duel to Commander Tucker."

Trip crawled out from under the cell-ship and opened the channel.

"Tucker here. Go ahead."

"Sir, I need some instructions here. We are modifying sensor equipment for installation in the cell-ship—"

"Hold on a minute." Trip frowned. This was the first he'd heard of modified sensor equipment. He turned to call out to T'Pol, to see if she knew anything about it—

And found her standing right at his shoulder.

"Excuse me a moment," she said, and stepped past him. "Ensign Duel, this is Sub-Commander T'Pol. I will join you shortly. Out."

She closed the channel.

"Modified sensor equipment?" Trip asked. "Are you sure that's a good idea, Sub-Commander? The cloak needs all the power—"

"The sensor equipment will be remotely powered," she said. "The interface, however, needs to be modified to allow it to work in tandem with the Suliban scanners."

Trip frowned again. What she was saying made sense, but still—he didn't like the idea of all this additional gear in the cell-ship. Maybe T'Pol had been right. Maybe they did need a full day of testing.

The com sounded again.

"Archer to Commander Tucker."

"Excuse me a minute," Trip said to T'Pol, and opened a channel again.

"Tucker here, Captain."

"Trip—we're ready to go here. How close are you?"

He looked at T'Pol.

"Fifteen minutes," she said.

"You hear that, Captain?"

"Yes, I did," his voice came back.

"About the same for me, sir," Trip added.

"All right," the captain said. "I'm ordering Travis to move closer to the anomaly now. I want to be able to drop the cell-ship and go. We're picking up a lot of activity near that orbital platform. Malcolm still down there?"

"Yes, sir. Hold on a minute."

"No need for that, Trip. Just send him up here."

Trip turned and saw Reed stepping out of the cockpit. Malcolm gave a thumbs-up and headed out the bay doors.

"He's on his way," Trip said.

"All right. Let me know as soon as you're ready to launch. Archer out."

Trip punched the channel closed.

"Commander?" Trip turned and saw that Hoshi had taken Reed's place inside the cell-ship. She was frowning. "I think I switched on the sensors by accident."

"Give me a minute," Trip said. He turned to T'Pol. "You want me to finish testing the code?"

"The test is finished," she said. "The new code checks out fine. I'm going to assist Ensign Duel with the sensor equipment. We'll return in fifteen minutes, and launch then."

"We'll be ready," Trip said.

T'Pol walked across the deck and through the entrance doors, squeezing by Lieutenant O'Neill, who was just entering with a case full of ration packs. Enough for T'Pol and Ensign Duel—who would join her for the testing—to last out the week in the cell-ship.

She set the case down next to the cell-ship and turned to go.

Trip felt *Enterprise* surge beneath him. Moving on impulse, heading toward the gravitational anomaly.

Moving on a sudden impulse himself, Trip spun around and walked to the nearest port. He wanted a view of this anomaly—this once-in-a-lifetime sight, if T'Pol was to be believed.

And as Trip approached the window, he slowed, and decided she was.

The anomaly was beautiful.

At first glance it looked like a miniature nebula—a haze of colorful gases, strewn haphazardly in space.

But as *Enterprise* drew steadily closer, as the distance between them and the anomaly shrank, Trip became aware that the cloud of gases had motion to them, spin—as if they were being drawn slowly inward, to the center of the anomaly. Like a whirlpool.

He frowned.

In the black space between the anomaly and *Enterprise,* he had seen something. A flash of metal.

"Commander—the sensors?"

He turned and saw Hoshi, her arms crossed, waiting a few feet back from the cell-ship, now being set down in launch position.

"One more minute," he told Hoshi, and turned back to the window. He squinted into the distance and looked carefully.

There it was again. Definitely man-made—spinning, just as the gas clouds in the anomaly were, vaguely circular in shape . . .

Trip's heart thudded in his chest.

It looked a lot like a gravitic mine.

Not that the Denari would be capable of constructing such an object, but still . . .

The resemblance was remarkable.

The object flew past, a few hundred meters to starboard.

Trip watched it fade into the distance, then looked ahead again.

He saw another flash of metal, heading straight their way.

A different one of his mother's favorite sayings came to mind:

Better safe than sorry.

Trip strode quickly across the deck, practically running Hoshi over in his haste to get to the com.

"Commander, what—"

"Sorry, Hoshi," Trip said, and slapped a channel open. "Tucker to the bridge. Travis, please check your starboard sensor readings. I've got a visual on an object that looks remarkably like a—"

The deck underneath Trip roared and buckled upward.

He fell forward, into the wall, and then backward onto the deck.

The ship shuddered a second time, lifting him up into the air and then dropping him back down again, face first.

Trip tasted blood in his mouth—a cut lip.

He staggered to his feet.

Someone moaned behind him. He turned and saw Hoshi sitting up, holding her forehead. Trip helped her to her feet.

"You all right?" he asked.

She nodded. Trip looked around the bay, so crowded just minutes before, and realized that the two of them were the only ones left here.

A diagnostic cable slid past him, heading toward the far wall.

Trip blinked to make sure he wasn't seeing things. But there it was, a cable slithering away from him under its own power, like a thing alive.

As he watched, a second cable followed the first.

A ration pack headed off in that cable's wake.

Then Trip heard it—a slow hissing sound, like air leaking out of a bicycle tire.

A chill ran down his spine as he realized what was happening.

"Hull breach!" he said, turning toward Hoshi. "Grab on to—"

A huge, sucking roar suddenly filled the launch bay—like a thousand vacuums being switched on at once.

The case of rations flew past Trip and smacked against the far wall. It spilled open—dozens of packs disappeared through the breach into the empty vacuum of space beyond.

Trip felt himself being dragged in that direction as well.

He struggled to stay on his feet, to find something to hold on to. His eyes fell on the cell-ship and the sole remaining diagnostic cable still attached to it.

He reached out and grabbed it—and at that same instant heard a noise. Someone yelling, he realized . . .

And turned just in time to see Hoshi sliding past him, tumbling head over heels toward the breach.

He lunged forward and grabbed her hand.

"It's all right!" he yelled. "I've got you!"

She nodded wordlessly and shut her eyes against the wind.

They were still moving toward the breach.

Trip glanced behind and saw the cable was stretching—fraying—pulling away from the cell-ship.

Hold, damn you, he willed silently.

It snapped.

The two of them flew toward the far wall, and the breach.

Next to him, Hoshi grabbed a recessed handle on one of the storage lockers.

Trip stretched out a hand, trying to follow suit.

Too far.

He slid past the lockers.

His fingers closed on Hoshi's ankle. He held on tight—literally, for dear life.

He looked up at Hoshi and saw her eyes closed, her teeth gritted in effort, both hands hanging on to the handle.

He saw something else, too.

Her grip was slipping.

"I can't hold on!" she yelled.

"You have to!" Trip shouted back. "Just a little longer!"

The pressure should begin to equalize somewhat in a few more seconds—enough so that the rush of air would lessen, the pull on them—and everything else in the launch bay—would die down a little, long enough to seal the breach.

Hoshi's right hand slipped—her shoulder slammed into the deck.

She screamed out in pain, and surprise.

Trip lost his grip on her ankle, found it again, and lost it a second time.

His index finger caught in the upper sole of her shoe.

He scrambled to get a grip with the rest of his hand, but the other fingers simply couldn't get purchase. This was ridiculous, he thought as his body literally lifted off the ground as it was sucked toward the breach.

One finger was all that was keeping him from joining the parade of debris floating out behind *Enterprise*.

His eyes widened then, as he saw Hoshi's shoe slipping from her foot.

"Hoshi! Your shoe!" he yelled—and even as she turned to look, Trip realized something important.

He'd actually heard his voice.

Which meant the pressure was beginning to equalize. The rush of air being sucked out into space was lessening.

He let go of Hoshi and dragged himself across the floor.

It was cold—ungodly cold in the bay now.

He sucked air into his lungs—what little there was of it.

His vision swam.

Hoshi lay on the ground, wheezing for breath.

He crawled past her and ripped open the nearest survival locker.

Oxygen mask—a single one, for him. No time to give Hoshi a second—he had to seal the breach, or they'd both be dead within thirty seconds.

He reached deeper into the survival locker. There. The emergency kit.

He found a duranium patch and sealed the hull.

Within seconds the bay began automatically pressurizing.

He got an oxygen mask for Hoshi. Placed it over her mouth, let her breathe in slowly, in and out, in and out, until she was strong enough to get to her feet.

She grimaced as she tried to walk.

"My ankle—I think it's twisted." She hobbled forward a few steps and rested against one of the control consoles. It was her right ankle that was hurt, Trip saw—the one he'd been holding on to for dear life.

"That must have been me," he said. "Sorry."

"It's all right." She smiled. "Better that than the alternative."

The com sounded.

"Launch Bay, report. Reed to Tucker, report. We've picked up a hull breach down there—are you all right?"

Trip crossed the bay and punched open a channel to the bridge.

"We're all right, Malcolm. Breach is sealed. What's the situation up there?"

"We're in a bad way, Commander. Whatever that explosion was—"

"Looked like a gravitic mine. I saw two of them. You'd better tell the captain to back out of here slowly and carefully—there may be more around."

"We won't be doing any maneuvering for a while yet, I'm afraid. We've got a hole ten feet wide in the armory, and the sensor arrays are going to be off-line for a few minutes. No casualties, but we're pretty well blind right now."

Blind, and listing a little to starboard, Trip realized. Something was wrong with the artificial gravity as well.

Damn, damn, and damn. He had to get back to engineering.

The light coming through the deck windows changed.

Trip turned and saw that even after the explosion, *Enterprise* had kept moving, was at that very second passing through the clouds of gas on the fringes of the gravitational anomaly.

Colors swirled past the window. The ship suddenly lurched forward—

Caught by the anomaly? he wondered.

And in that second the world turned inside-out.

Trip didn't know how else to describe what he felt—it was as if he were being disassembled and put back together, over and over and over again. It wasn't at all like the feeling he got going through the transporter, this was—well, not worse, but different—a whole new level of unsettling.

And suddenly—just as quickly as it had come on—the feeling was gone.

Trip shook his head, tried to clear it.

Hoshi was looking at him with a vaguely disturbed expression on her face. "What was that?"

"I have absolutely no clue," he said, shaking his head again. "Come on. Let's get out of here, see if we can lend a hand."

He put an arm around Hoshi's waist and walked her toward the exit door.

First on his list was getting the sensors back online—the last thing they wanted to do was be flying blind right now. Where there was one mine, there were probably others—not to mention the nearby asteroid belt, the gravitational anomaly—

Trip was so involved in running through worst-case scenarios in his head that he almost walked straight into the door.

For some reason it hadn't opened at their approach.

"Huh," Trip said. "Hold on a minute."

He guided Hoshi to the wall, then turned around, walked ten paces, and started toward the door again. Same result.

"Commander?" she asked. "What's the problem?"

"Door sensor must be damaged. Probably during the hull breach." Trip opened the panel next to her and found the manual release. The door slid open.

But Trip stayed right where he was.

A foot past the entrance the corridor was blocked by a solid steel wall.

"What is that?" Hoshi said. "Where did that door come from?"

"Not a door." Trip shook his head. "An emergency bulkhead. Designed to seal off the launch bay from the rest of the ship in case of a hull breach."

"But we sealed the breach."

"Obviously that message hasn't gotten through to the computer yet." Trip frowned, realizing that with the damage they'd sustained, it probably wouldn't get through for a little longer yet. Possibly longer than a little while.

For the foreseeable future, the two of them were trapped right here.

He turned back towards Hoshi—

And at that moment klaxons started ringing all across the ship.

Four

HE AND HOSHI EXCHANGED a puzzled glance.

"Those are the tactical alert Klaxons, aren't they?" she asked.

"That they are." Malcolm's specially designed tactical-alert Klaxons—when they sounded, everyone aboard *Enterprise* knew that a very specific state of emergency existed. More precisely, that the ship was under attack.

"There's no reason for them to be going off now," Trip said. "Must be a false alarm."

"Must be," Hoshi agreed.

Had to be, Trip thought. They couldn't be under attack.

Could they?

The Klaxons suddenly cut off—just as Malcolm had designed them to. Ten seconds after first sounding, if Trip remembered right.

But if that part of the system was working . . .

Trip frowned and walked back to the companel.

"Tucker to bridge. Malcolm, come in."

No response.

"Tucker to bridge. Travis? What's going on up there?"

Still nothing.

The com suddenly crackled and sprang to life.

"Mayweather here Commander sorry can't talk right now we've got two dozen hostiles approaching at warp 2 from the next system over we'll be back asap."

The com fell silent again.

Trip looked back over at Hoshi.

"Tell me I'm not going crazy. You heard that, right?"

She nodded. "I heard it—it just doesn't make any sense. Two dozen hostiles from the next system—approaching at warp 2? That's impossible. The Denari don't have warp drive. And we didn't pick up any other signs of civilization out there."

"We missed something, then," Trip said.

"Either that, or these hostiles—whoever they are—they have cloaking devices, too."

"Maybe. Two dozen ships, Travis said." Trip shook his head. "They had to come from somewhere."

A loud clanging suddenly rang out in the bay—something metal, banging against the hull of the ship.

"What was that?" Hoshi asked.

Trip frowned. "We might have run into part of

the debris from the breach—or the explosion that hit the armory—"

The clanging sounded again, from farther up the hull.

Suddenly Trip had a bad feeling in his stomach—a horrible, sinking feeling—that he knew exactly what that clanging was.

He strode back to the launch bay window and pressed his face up against the port.

Directly to his left, a ship had landed on *Enterprise*'s hull. A small ship—roughly twice the size of one of their shuttlepods. One of the hostiles.

"Commander?"

He turned back to her and shook his head "We're being boarded."

Hoshi went white as a ghost.

Trip craned his neck, trying to get a better look at the hostile. Drive configuration looked standard, but he could tell little about the weaponry or crew complement from where he was. Not that it mattered. With the armory damaged, torpedoes off-line, phase pistols unavailable . . .

There was nothing they could do to stop the intruders.

The com sounded again.

"Launch Bay—do you read?"

"Travis?"

"It's the captain, Trip. We're being boarded."

"I know, sir. Who are they?"

"Denari—we picked up com traffic as they approached. They're not responding to our hails, though."

"Denari?" Trip looked over at Hoshi. "But I thought—"

"We all thought. Doesn't matter now. Can you—"

The com suddenly went dead.

"Captain?"

No response.

"Captain!"

Another clanging—louder than before.

Trip looked up.

The stars were gone.

All he could see through the launch bay window was metal—the underside of another Denari vessel, right outside the bay.

The light above the airlock began flashing. The Denari were going to force their way in. It shouldn't take them more than thirty seconds, Trip figured, based on the level of technology he was seeing now. Thirty seconds, and then . . .

He didn't know what then. But the fact that the Denari weren't responding to hails was not a good sign. *Hostile* was exactly the right word to describe them—and the way they were behaving. Trip didn't know why—maybe this was all some big misunderstanding, maybe once the captain had a chance to sit down and talk to them face-to-face everything would turn out fine, but still . . .

This was not the moment to be seeking explanations.

His eyes went to the cell-ship—prepped and ready to go. With the cloak fully operative.

And he made a decision.

"We're getting out of here," he said, striding back over to Hoshi.

"What?"

"We're getting out of here," Trip repeated.

He helped her into the cell ship and sat her down.

"See if you can bring sensors on-line. I'll be right back."

He didn't even wait for Hoshi's response, just turned and ran to the nearest storage locker. He grabbed a first-aid kit, as many ration packs as he could carry, and dumped them all on the cell-ship floor, as out of the way as he could put them in the cramped interior.

Then he ran for the upper deck control room, taking the gangway steps two and three at a time.

He reached the control station, and set the bay doors to open in ninety seconds. The instant he punched the "execute" command, a computerized voice filled the air.

"Please clear the Launch Bay. Ninety seconds to bay doors opening. Please clear the Launch Bay. Eighty-five seconds to . . ."

Trip stood, about to head back down the gangway to the cell-ship, and saw the light on the airlock suddenly stop flashing. At that same instant there was a muffled bang that echoed throughout the bay.

The Denari had broken through the outer hull.

The airlock door began to slide open.

Trip reached down and killed the bay lights.

The Denari entered Launch Bay Two.

He counted fifteen, all in white EVA suits, all with weapons drawn and at the ready.

They moved carefully out onto the deck and spread out in formation.

Humanoid, bipedal for sure, facial structure very similar to human, from what he could see of them from his vantage point behind the console.

Out of the corner of his eye, he caught a flicker of movement on the bay floor. Right where he'd left the cell-ship.

For a second his heart sank. It had to be Hoshi, leaving the Suliban vessel.

But when he turned to look there was nothing there.

Literally.

The cell-ship was gone.

No, he realized a split second later. Not gone.

Cloaked.

Trip almost laughed out loud. *Nice move, Hoshi,* he thought. Cloaking the ship—the Denari wouldn't even know it was there. Which meant the two of them still had a chance at a clean escape.

All he had to do was get back down there to pilot the ship.

"Sixty-five seconds to bay doors opening.

Please clear the Launch Bay. Sixty seconds to bay doors opening . . ."

The Denari soldiers were looking all around now, seeking the source of the voice. Probably wondering what it was saying, as well.

Trip certainly wasn't going to tell them.

Moving as quietly as he could, he slid out from behind the console. Hugging the floor, he started down the gangway . . .

Just as one of the Denari soldiers reached the bottom and started climbing up.

Trip scrambled back into the control room and ducked out of sight.

"Fifty seconds to bay doors opening. Please clear the launch bay. Forty-five seconds to bay doors opening . . ."

Footsteps sounded as the Denari soldier climbed the ladder. Then those footsteps stopped.

Trip risked another peek over the edge of the console.

The Denari still stood in the exact same spot at the top of the gangway, hands on hips, his back to Trip.

Then he did a hundred eighty degree spin and started walking right toward the control room.

Trip ducked back out of sight.

"Thirty-five seconds to bay doors opening. Please clear the launch bay. Thirty seconds to bay doors opening—"

His mind raced. It would be suicide to show

himself. Even if he somehow managed to surprise and overpower this soldier, the commotion would draw every other Denari in the bay right to him. There'd be no way to reach the cell-ship in time.

But he was out of time anyway. He didn't see that he had any choice. It was either go now or not at all.

The soldier's footsteps grew closer.

"Twenty seconds to bay doors opening. Please clear the launch bay. Fifteen seconds to—"

The soldier stepped around the corner of the console.

All he had to do was look down and he'd see Trip.

Trip gathered himself, ready to attack. . . .

And his eyes fell on the panel he'd used to dim the lights.

The soldier looked down.

Surprise, Trip thought, and slammed the lights back on, full intensity.

Trip caught a glimpse of the face behind the mask—a remarkably human looking face, at which point Phlox's words ("an almost ninety-nine point nine percent congruity between species") came rushing back to him—and then the soldier blinked.

And in that split second, Trip sprang out of hiding and drove his shoulder square into the Denari. The soldier staggered backward.

Trip jumped past him and onto the gangway.

"Bay doors will open in ten—nine—"

He slid the last fifteen feet down the gangway and ran for the spot he'd last seen the cell-ship.

Come on, Hoshi. Decloak. Or I'm not going to be able to find you, either.

He was also, more likely than not, going to run headfirst into the hull.

"Seven—six—"

A Denari soldier stepped right into his path, weapon raised.

And then the cell-ship appeared.

"Four—three—"

Hoshi leaned out of the hatchway and threw a ration pack right at the Denari soldier. It caught him square in the back of the head, and he stumbled forward.

Trip vaulted past him and through the hatchway.

"Two—one—"

The door closed behind him.

The bay doors opened.

And then, with a sudden, gut-wrenching swiftness, they fell down and out of *Enterprise*, into the vast empty space beyond.

Five

TRIP SCRAMBLED UP into his seat and grabbed the controls.

"I didn't think you were going to make it," Hoshi said.

"I was sure I wasn't. Thanks." He fired the aft thrusters, sending them shooting forward, away from *Enterprise*. "Nice arm back there, by the way."

"Thanks."

"And the cloak." He smiled. "That was brilliant."

She smiled back.

The tactical display beeped.

Trip looked down and saw they'd been spotted. A half-dozen Denari ships had broken off their assault on *Enterprise* and started after them.

"Here we go," he said, reaching down and switching on the cloak.

At almost the exact same instant, he activated the braking thrusters.

The Denari ships shot past them, then slowed in obvious confusion.

Trip smiled. You had to give it to the Suliban—or rather, their mysterious benefactors. The cell-ship could stop on a dime.

He punched the thrusters. The cell-ship rose straight up, giving them a bird's-eye view of the Denari ships circling the area where the cell-ship had cloaked, still trying to find their quarry.

It also gave them a bird's-eye view of *Enterprise*, under siege.

Denari vessels swarmed all over the starship's hull. Two dozen of them, at least—maybe closer to three dozen. A lot of ships. A lot of soldiers. He'd counted fifteen in the launch bay—assuming every Denari vessel was similarly manned, that made over three hundred armed soldiers attacking *Enterprise*.

It wasn't going to be much of a fight.

He turned to Hoshi. "We have to get help."

"Starfleet, you mean?"

"Starfleet, or the Vulcans—whoever. What can we do?"

She shook her head. "I'm not sure. The nearest beacon is too far off to reach with this. I could try to modify the transmitter"—she nodded toward the Suliban communications array—"to send a wide-band distress signal, but that'll take some time."

"All right." Trip studied the Suliban tactical display a moment. "We're right near the asteroid belt. We should be able to find a place to set down there. Let you work in relative peace and quiet."

He punched in a course.

But they hadn't been traveling for more than ten seconds when the console emitted a soft beep.

"Something directly ahead of us," Trip said, and consulted tactical again. Something small—not much bigger than a soccer ball.

He switched the display to visual, and frowned.

It was a gravitic mine—identical to the one that had hit *Enterprise*.

The console beeped again.

Trip switched his display back to tactical and found another mine a few kilometers aft. And a third, a few kilometers beyond that.

He eased off on the thrusters and swept the entire area for mines.

And let out a long, slow whistle.

"Sir?" Hoshi asked.

"This whole area of space," he said, shaking his head. "It's a minefield. There must be hundreds of them—thousands maybe."

Enterprise, he realized, was lucky to have hit just one.

But why hadn't they picked the mines up on sensors before this? He could see how one or two could slip past unnoticed, but this many? It was impossible.

Something strange was going on here.

He studied the tactical display carefully. The

area was riddled with debris—wreckage from ships that hadn't been as fortunate as *Enterprise*, he supposed—and he slowed thrusters again to avoid hitting any of it.

Tactical showed him something else as well— the minefield had a definite shape to it. A funnel, with the narrow end pointing directly toward the asteroid belt.

They were heading directly down that funnel. The closer they got to the belt, the more mines they'd encounter.

This was definitely not the way to go.

"I'm gonna head out the way we came," Trip said. "See if we can find another approach into the asteroid belt—"

A sudden explosion rocked the ship.

Hoshi glanced over at him nervously.

"Sir?"

"Debris," he said. "Set off the mine nearest us. A kilometer to starboard."

He checked diagnostics. The ship checked out fine.

Still, they didn't want that to happen again.

"Let's hold here a minute while we recalibrate the sensors," he said. "We'll—"

The ship shook again.

"That wasn't a mine," Hoshi said.

"Definitely not." Trip checked tactical.

The half-dozen Denari ships chasing them were on the move again. Heading right toward the spot where the mine had exploded, and firing as they went.

"Smart," Trip said, nodding his head in admiration. "They saw the explosion. They think we set off the mine."

"So they're firing blindly," Hoshi said.

Trip nodded. "Yeah. But coming a little too close for my taste. Hang on a second—I'm gonna bring shields on-line."

He punched in a half-dozen commands, then hit the execute key.

Nothing happened.

Another explosion shook the ship. Minor damage that time, he saw on tactical. One of the thrusters was slightly damaged.

Trip keyed in the shield power-up sequence again. Still nothing.

What was wrong?

He glanced down at the console, looking for answers on the diagnostic screen. Something on tactical caught his eye.

The Denari ships were moving toward them arrayed in a spread formation—blocking their way out of the minefield. Trapping them.

Without shields the odds of moving either forward or back without getting blown to pieces were slim and none.

Trip shook his head.

"I don't understand." Now that he thought about it, he shouldn't even have to activate the shields. They were supposed to come on automatically in the event of—

"Oh." He exhaled loudly. "We rewrote the code."

Hoshi turned in her seat to face him. "What?"

"We rewrote the code," Trip said. "To keep other systems from stealing power from the cloak."

"Including the shields?" Hoshi asked.

"Including the shields." He sighed again. "It seemed like a good idea at the time."

"What do we do now?" Hoshi asked.

Trip shook his head slowly.

"Give me a minute," he said, and considered his options. Which boiled down to two:

Sit here for an hour, rewrite the code yet again, and hope the Denari didn't nail them with a lucky shot . . .

Or drop the cloak and hope shields powered up before the alien ships could target them.

Dangers and definite advantages associated with each choice. Trip wondered if this was how Captain Archer felt all the time, sitting in the command chair on the bridge, all eyes on him, waiting for a decision.

He leaned forward, hands poised over the console.

"Commander?" Hoshi asked.

"Hang on," he said, and shut down the cloak.

At that same instant he brought the shields online.

And just in time. A nanosecond later light exploded all around them. Phased-energy weapons, just like the ones on *Enterprise*—he recognized the characteristic flash. Five shots, five direct hits, according to the tactical display.

The Denari were good—not good as in lucky, but good as in very, very well-trained. Military.

Best to get out of their range, and cloaked again, as quickly as possible.

He hit the thrusters full throttle, heading straight for a gap between the two nearest Denari ships. They swerved almost instantaneously, trying to close the gap, firing as they moved.

Light flashed again—and again, the cell-ship absorbed the blast with no damage.

The cell-ship streaked past the Denari and back out into open space.

Safe at last, Trip thought—and then the console beeped again, and he saw half a dozen more ships on the way, moving as close to warp as they could get without breaking through the light-speed barrier. Their paths showed up on tactical like flashes of light—thousands of kilometers away one second and on top of them the next, arming weapons and preparing to fire, and—

Trip activated the cloak. He veered sharply aft, and then down, cutting the thrusters as he did so to eliminate any exhaust trail.

The Denari ships peeled off in different directions, trying their best to follow. One whizzed by, less than a kilometer away, so close that Trip could read the hull markings—well, not read them, he couldn't read Denari, but he could see the markings plain as day—and then it was gone.

The cell-ship hung a moment in space, motionless.

Then Trip activated thrusters and turned them back toward the asteroid belt.

On their way they passed *Enterprise* one final time.

More Denari ships had arrived, were circling the larger vessel, firing at parts of the ship where—Trip supposed—their troops were encountering resistance. Not that they could be having too much trouble crushing whatever fight was left in *Enterprise*—he couldn't count the number of Denari vessels now clinging to the starship's hull.

For the first time, too, he saw the gaping hole at the bottom of the saucer section—at the armory, where the mine had exploded.

Through the windows ringing D-deck, he caught scattered glimpses of weapons fire.

And the bridge was completely dark.

Trip started to run through scenarios in his head of what might have happened—what might be happening—to Captain Archer and the rest of the crew. Malcolm. T'Pol. Travis.

Then he stopped himself.

No point in wondering, really. The main thing was this:

Enterprise was lost.

He fired thrusters and banked away from the depressing scene.

Two hours into the belt Trip finally felt comfortable looking for a place to land. A place to shut off the cloak and let Hoshi work uninterrupted on the communications system.

He chose an unremarkable asteroid big enough to land on, but not so big as to announce itself as an obvious destination, and set them down, slowly and gently, on its surface, in between two towering, finger-shaped stone formations.

Then, and only then, did he power off the cloak.

"All right," he said, turning to Hoshi, "you might as well . . ."

Get started, he'd been about to say.

But she was a step ahead of him.

She already had the com schematic up on her display, and a panel from the communications array itself partially disassembled on the console to her left.

"You need any help?"

She shook her head. "No, sir. Not at the moment. Maybe down the line."

"Fair enough. Just let me know."

Trip decided to make himself useful another way, to rewrite the Suliban code yet again in order to avoid having the same problem with the shields crop up later—but the second he'd brought that code up on screen, he suddenly realized how exhausted he was.

So he shut the panel down and sat back in his seat. Stretched out his legs and tried to get comfortable.

Forty winks would do him just fine, he decided, and closed his eyes.

A soft beeping woke him up.

For a second he didn't know where he was. Not in his quarters aboard *Enterprise*, but . . .

The cell-ship.

He sat up and saw Hoshi peering at the ship's status read-out, a frown on her face, and he remembered. The mine, the hull breach, the Denari—

"I was just about to wake you," Hoshi said. "It's been making that noise for the last few minutes."

She pointed at the console.

Trip rubbed the sleep from his eyes and sat forward to see what was happening. Something was wrong, he saw that immediately, but what . . .

"Oh, no," he said, and blinked.

I'm dreaming, Trip told himself. *That's it, I'm still asleep, and I'm dreaming. Because otherwise . . .*

"What's wrong?" Hoshi asked. "What's happening?"

"What's happening?" He shook his head. "We're losing oxygen, that's what's happening. The question is why."

He brought the diagnostic screen up on his display and almost immediately found the problem.

There was a hole in the cell-ship hull.

A minuscule hole—not much bigger than a pinprick. Right along the main hatch. He had no idea when it had happened.

"What?" Hoshi asked. "What's the matter?"

"We've got a leak," Trip said.

"So let's fix it."

"With what?"

"Isn't there some kind of emergency kit here—like the one on *Enterprise?*"

"Not that I know of."

"So what do we do?"

"You keep working," Trip said. "Let me try a few things."

And he did.

He tried activating the shields, to see if the seal they made around the ship might somehow act to slow down the rate of atmosphere loss.

It didn't.

He tried the same thing with the cloak, with the same results.

He tore the ship apart, looking for something that might act as a temporary patch on the leak. No luck.

Finally he sat back down with a resigned thud.

At least the hole wasn't getting any bigger—whatever material the hull was made of, it was strong enough to withstand a lot of pressure. The ship wasn't going to fall apart around them, that was clear.

No, theirs was going to be a slow, lingering death as their oxygen supply finished leaking out into space. Which, according to the diagnostic, was going to happen in about six hours, at the current rate of loss. Of course, they'd start feeling the effects long before that—shortness of breath, dizziness, hallucinations . . .

Hoshi stopped work and looked over at him.

"Nothing?" she asked.

"Nothing." He nodded at the communications array, which was now in several pieces around her. "How far off are you from being able to send that wideband signal?"

Hoshi shook her head. "Pretty far. A solid day's work."

"Can you send anything at all?"

"What'd you have in mind?"

Trip sighed. "An S.O.S."

"But the Denari—they'll pick it right up. They'll . . ." She looked at him then, and understood. "You're saying we surrender. After all that we went through to escape?"

"I know," Trip said. "I just don't see that we have any other options."

It was Hoshi's turn to sit back and look frustrated.

"There has to be something else we can do," she said.

"You let me know."

They sat a long time in silence.

Finally Hoshi leaned forward and began picking up pieces of the communications array.

"It'll take me a couple of hours, at least."

"No rush." Trip opened a ration pack and settled back in his seat. "I'm not going anywhere."

Six

It actually took closer to three hours to put the array back together.

But only fifteen minutes for them to get a response to the S.O.S.

A response in the form of a ship, heading right for them.

A big ship, the tactical display told Trip. Traveling sublight, about twenty minutes away.

"Signal coming in," Hoshi said. She leaned over the console and hit a switch.

Nonsense syllables filled the ship. At least they sounded like nonsense to Trip—Hoshi listened intently a moment, then gave a nod.

"It's one of the Denari languages," she said.

"You understand it?"

"Enough to know we need this."

She reached overhead and tapped on the Univeral Translator module Reed had installed.

Trip powered it up.

The nonsense syllables suddenly changed to English. A man, talking.

"... Kairn of the Guild ship *Eclipse*. Unidentified vessel, you have trespassed into a war zone. Stand down all weapons systems, defensive and offensive, and await further instructions."

Trip looked over at Hoshi.

"Unidentified vessel—they don't know who we are."

"Word must not have gotten through to them about *Enterprise*. The attack, our escape . . ."

"Maybe," Trip said. He consulted the display again. According to the read-out, the ship approaching had sublight drive only. A fusion reactor, deuterium-tritium based, putting out much less energy than he'd expect to see, with those numbers the engine had to be operating at less than seventy percent efficiency. . . .

Their technology, he realized, was a considerable step down from that possessed by the ships that had attacked *Enterprise*.

War zone, the speaker—Kairn—had said.

Which might explain the technological disparity. This ship might be on the other side.

Trip smiled. Maybe they were going to get out of this after all.

"Let them know we're out here and that we can understand them," he told Hoshi.

She nodded. "Should I tell them who we are—where we're from?"

"No. As little information as you can get away with right now." More out of strategic consideration that any possible concerns over technological contamination—the Denari who attacked *Enterprise* had warp drive and obviously knew about the existence of other races, so it was a near-impossibility that the people in this ship were any different.

Hoshi spoke into the translator.

"Denari vessel, this is the cell-ship . . . *T'Pol.* We have a hull breach and are in need of immediate assistance. Over."

They listened to static a moment.

"Cell-ship *T'Pol?*" Trip looked over at Hoshi, a smile on his face.

She smiled back. "Spur of the moment."

The speaker came to life.

"This is Marshal Kairn of the *Eclipse.* Cell-ship *T'Pol,* stand by to be boarded. Out."

Trip looked over at Hoshi and didn't know whether to laugh or cry. All that trouble to escape, and they end up being boarded anyway.

He looked down at the status display. The ship should be in visual range just about . . . now.

And there it was.

It looked exactly like one of the old Fleet mining ships, massive, solid-looking, half again the size of *Enterprise,* its surface pitted and scarred by what looked like weapons fire. He caught a quick glimpse of its underside, which had been retrofitted with some sort of weapons—they reminded him of pulse-cannons—and then the vessel passed overhead and out of sight.

"That's an antique," Hoshi said.

"Sure is." Trip nodded. An antique with a fusion engine that seemed to be crying out for just the kind of loving care it was his business to provide. A rough scenario was already unfolding in his mind—barter his services in exchange for materials to repair the hull, and modify the communications array. And along the way garner a little information about this war Kairn referred to, find out why the Denari—the other Denari, the ones that had attacked *Enterprise*—had shot first, and saved the questions for later.

The asteroid beneath them trembled slightly—the mining ship, he saw on tactical, setting down just behind them.

Hoshi finished programming two translator modules and passed him one. A minute later he heard metal clanging on metal. Then the sound of a seal being formed.

Trip stood and faced the airlock.

The hatch slid open.

He was looking down a long, dark tunnel—a collapsible tunnel, he saw, made out of some type of material that looked frighteningly fragile—thin enough that a strong wind could tear it apart. The air coming down that tunnel from the other ship had a slight chill to it, and carried the hint of a strange, almost metallic scent that for some reason raised the hairs on Trip's arm. An alien smell, for lack of a better word—like nothing he'd ever come across before. He wrinkled his nose and glanced at Hoshi, still in her chair, and saw that she was making a face, too.

Trip turned back to the tunnel. A single steel ring, an uncoiled corkscrew of metal that reminded him of a child's toy, was the structure's only visible means of support. Making their way toward them, using the unwound coils of the ring like stepping stones in a pond, were two men.

No. Not men—Denari. Though Trip saw nothing that made him want to modify his earlier appraisal—they were indistinguishable, as far as he could tell, from humans. Skin a little paler perhaps, their faces longer, features set closer together, but otherwise . . .

The one in the lead was tall, and thin, with dark circles under his eyes, and a hard set to his mouth. He wore a green and orange uniform gone ragged and threadbare at the knees. A prisoner of war, Trip thought, thinking of the Suliban refugees they'd rescued from the Tandaran detention complex. This man was no prisoner, though—he carried a weapon that looked remarkably like a phase pistol on his belt, and another, more exotic-looking firearm in a shoulder sling.

The second man was much the same in appearance, gaunt, unshaven, dirty-looking, long pale hair pulled back in a ponytail. His weapon was unholstered, and he held it pointed at Trip as he approached.

The first man stopped five feet from the entrance to the cell-ship and stared.

Trip cleared his throat.

"I'm Commander Tucker. Marshal Kairn?"

"No." The man looked behind Trip, into the cell-ship. "Who's back there?"

"My crewman—Ensign Hoshi. She's injured."

The man frowned. "Tell her to stand and move into view."

"That's a little tough for her to do," Trip began. "Her ankle—"

"Tell her to stand." The man in the lead raised his weapon as well. "Now."

Trip glared, but didn't see much use in fighting. "Hoshi?"

"I heard, Commander." She hobbled forward and leaned on the hatch just behind him.

"Satisfied?" Trip asked the man.

He nodded. "You're not Denari."

"No. We're human—from a planet called Earth. Quite a long ways off."

"You have warp drive, then."

It wasn't a question.

"That's right."

"On that?" The man frowned and looked behind Trip into the cell-ship. Trip knew what the frown was for—he was obviously finding it hard to believe that a vessel the size of the Suliban ship could carry a warp engine.

Trip decided not to disabuse him of that notion—not just yet, anyway.

"This isn't our main vessel," he hedged. "This is a shuttle. Our main ship—*Enterprise*—was attacked just as we entered this system."

"I don't doubt it. Sadir keeps a pretty close eye on this part of the Belt." He frowned. "How'd you get here?"

Again, Trip hedged. He told the story, but left out any mention of the cloak.

The man listened impassively. When Trip finished, he frowned.

"Step aside. I need to take a look at your vessel."

Trip slid up against the hatchway as the alien stepped past and peered through the hatch.

Even if Trip had designs on disarming him, it would have been impossible. The second man kept his weapon—and his eyes—focused on Trip the entire time his companion was inside the cellship. All of about five seconds.

When the first man turned around to face Trip, there was a hint of a smile on his face.

"It's even smaller than it looks."

"It wasn't built to be a pleasure craft."

"Obviously. It has weapons, though?"

"A minimal complement."

"Describe them."

Trip did.

"I'd ask about food supplies, but even if you stuffed that thing full with provisions, it wouldn't amount to much."

Trip nodded. "You're right. We don't have much."

"Your message said something about a hull breach. . . ."

"A slow leak in the mainframe. We could use help in—"

"Open a channel." He waved his weapon at the control panel. "I need to talk to the Marshal."

Trip nodded to Hoshi, who did as the man had asked.

"This is Commander Tucker, on the cell-ship."

"This is Kairn, on the *Eclipse*. Royce?"

"Two of them. No food, or weapons to speak of, but some very advanced technology here."

"Thank you. Commander Tucker?"

"Right here, too."

"You ask for help. What can you offer in return?"

"I'm an engineer," he said. "I fix things. I could work on your ship."

"I have people to work on my ship. I'm more interested in your technology than your repair skills."

"We can talk about that," Trip said. "But—"

"Then come aboard," Kairn replied, cutting him off. "And we'll meet."

"What about our ship?"

"We'll take that on board as well."

Trip frowned. Things were moving a little too quickly for his taste. He might not mind trading this Kairn some technology, once he knew a little more about the situation he'd landed in, but he certainly did not want *Eclipse* to take the cell-ship on board. That would leave them pretty close to powerless.

"Marshal," he said. "I'm happy to come aboard to talk with you, but I'd like my crewman to stay with our ship for right now. I think we can—"

"*Eclipse* can't stay here," Kairn interrupted again. "Sadir's ships patrol this area constantly."

"Who is this Sadir you keep talking about?"

"I'll answer all your questions aboard *Eclipse*."

"But—"

"Tucker, you and your shipmate can either come aboard or not. It's your choice. Kairn out."

The channel closed.

"Like he said." The man who had been doing all the talking—Royce—holstered his weapon. "You can either follow us or not. I don't expect you'll get a similar offer from the next ship that shows up."

And with that, he turned his back on them and, along with his silent partner, started heading back down the tunnel, toward *Eclipse*.

Trip watched him go.

"Sir?" Hoshi said. "What do you want to do?"

"What do I want to do?" Trip shook his head.

What he wanted to do was rescue *Enterprise*. A little down time then might be nice—give him a chance to figure out the Suliban cloak, the ion drive, the cell-ship's weapons systems . . .

For that matter, he wouldn't mind a good long look at a Vulcan warp drive engine. . . .

And a second day—and night—on Risa, another chance at the kind of shore leave that he and Malcolm had had so rudely interrupted before . . .

Unfortunately, this decision was not about what he wanted. It was about what they had to do. Either let *Eclipse* take off without them, and hope someone else answered the distress signal in the next five hours (though like both Kairn and Royce had just said, if another ship did show, it would probably be one of Sadir's), or follow Royce and the other man down the tunnel, and let them take the cell-ship aboard *Eclipse* . . . which meant effectively surrendering control over their own fate.

He didn't like either choice.

But the second option, as problematic as it was, gave them the best shot at getting *Enterprise* back.

He turned back to Hoshi.

"I don't see as we have much choice," he said. "We'll meet with this Kairn."

And hope, Trip added silently, that they didn't end up in exactly the same situation as he feared Archer and the rest of *Enterprise*'s crew were in right now.

The cold (and that strange, metallic scent Trip had noticed before) got stronger the closer he got to *Eclipse*.

Trip still couldn't place the smell. But he had

other things on his mind now. Like helping Hoshi avoid falling through the all-too-thin material that the airlock tunnel was made from.

She'd taken a couple practice steps, to see if she could make it down the tunnel on her own, but it had become immediately clear her ankle was too badly sprained for that.

So Trip—after slinging the medkit, stuffed full with ration packs, over his shoulder—had eased her through the hatch, and started down the passageway between their vessels. Which hadn't seemed that long a trip when they started it, but was taking on the feel of an epic journey, as he stepped carefully onto the next of the tunnel's unwound coils, half-carrying, half-dragging Hoshi right along with him.

"I could try again, sir. A few steps. My ankle might have loosened up."

"No. It's all right. We're almost there." Trip looked ahead and frowned. "More than halfway, at least."

"I'm sorry about this."

"Not your fault. Mine, actually. Remember?"

"You want to take a break?"

"No. I'm all right." If he stopped, Trip wasn't sure he'd be able to start up again. "It's just that you're heavier than you look."

Hoshi frowned. "I think that's a compliment."

"Then take it that way." He took another step then, and almost slipped.

"Commander. Are you sure you don't want that break?"

"Okay. Maybe you're right." She was, of course. He was tired. "Let's stop a minute."

He eased his arm out from around her waist. She balanced against the coil's vertical surface.

Trip used a hand to brush away the sweat from his forehead. His clothes were drenched with it already.

He was going to want a long, hot shower when they got aboard *Eclipse*.

"Should have brought a spare uniform, too," he muttered.

"Excuse me?"

"Nothing." Trip stretched his neck. "Come on. Let's get going."

They started off again.

"Something just occurred to me," Hoshi said, a few steps on. "If they're going to take the cell-ship on board . . ."

"Yeah?"

"We could have just stayed in it. Avoided this whole exercise."

"Fine time to think of that," Trip muttered. He supposed it was true—though he'd lay odds that they would have had a heckuva bumpy ride. An old mining ship like this—probably had nothing even halfway as sophisticated as *Enterprise*'s grappler. They would have to use tools designed for moving digging equipment back and forth from *Eclipse*'s hold to an asteroid's surface.

Which he should have thought about before, Trip realized.

Those kind of tools were not exactly designed to be delicate. He shuddered involuntarily, imagining the cell-ship being lifted off the asteroid's surface and crushed in the process.

Being rescued wouldn't do them any good at all if their ship was mangled in the process.

He wondered if it was too late to call the whole thing off and take his chances with Sadir.

All at once Hoshi stiffened.

"Sir . . ." She nodded her head toward *Eclipse*'s airlock.

Trip looked up and saw two things.

They were about a dozen feet away from the Denari ship.

Where a monster was waiting for them.

All right, *monster* was an exaggeration. The figure before them was a man—albeit a ridiculously tall, ridiculously thin one (he made Royce look positively overfed), whose complete lack of hair (on his head and his face) only added to his formidable appearance.

He waved them hurriedly forward, a look of impatience on his face.

"Hurry," he said. "Sadir's ships. Hurry."

Trip and Hoshi exchanged a quick glance. Despite his size, the man's vocabulary was that of a child. The look on his face, too . . .

Something was wrong with him.

"Hurry," he said again.

Despite the man's formidable appearance, Trip couldn't help but be annoyed.

"Give us a hand, why don't you, if you're in such a rush?"

To Trip's surprise, he did just that.

Both hands, in fact. The man bounded through the airlock, onto the coils, and practically yanked Hoshi free from him and plunked her down onto the deck of the Denari ship before Trip could get out a word of protest.

All he could do, in fact, was follow. Seconds later he was climbing up on deck next to the two of them.

"Watch out," the man said, interrupting his thoughts.

Before Trip could ask why, he pulled a lever on the panel in front of him. A hissing noise came from directly behind Trip, and he turned just in time, as a transparent panel slid across the open hatchway—sealing off the tunnel and missing him by inches.

"Hey!" Trip glared at him.

The man—still absorbed in working the panel before him—didn't even look up.

The tunnel, Trip saw now, had detached from the cell-ship—a second later, with an audible clang, it had fully retracted into *Eclipse's* hull. Trip caught a glimpse of a metal arm extending from *Eclipse* toward the cell-ship, and then a second panel—this one solid steel—slid across the hatchway, cutting off his view.

Probably for the best—Trip did not necessarily want to watch that arm lift the cell-ship.

The man turned his back on them then, to close the panel.

Which was when Trip got his first look at the scar.

It ran from the top of the man's skull to the base of his neck—a thick, ugly dark red line. An old scar, long since healed.

There was a second scar underneath it as well—a much smaller one, circular in shape. Like a period underneath an exclamation mark. Trip couldn't help but wonder if the two were indicative of some underlying damage. If that underlying damage had something to do with the way the man spoke.

The giant turned then and saw him staring. He locked eyes with Trip at that second, almost daring him to say something.

"Ferik."

That was a woman's voice—coming from a speaker just above them, and to the right.

"Trant," the man—Ferik, Trip assumed—replied, looking past them and turning toward the far end of the airlock.

Trip looked with him and saw a woman's face peering in through a clear panel at the three of them.

Her eyes betrayed a keen, questioning intelligence, and even through the panel, they were the deepest, most piercing shade of blue he had ever seen.

Trant, he gathered. Her eyes met his, and she inclined her head in greeting.

"Commander Tucker. Please prepare for decontamination."

Trip frowned.

"Hold on a second, there," he said, stepping towards her. "Interspecies contamination is as close to impossible as you can get, so I don't think—"

"The risk is negligible," she interrupted. "But still present. I prefer my risks at the zero mark."

A metal panel slid in front of the glass, cutting off her face from view.

"Fifteen seconds," she said. "Please stand facing the wall to your right."

With a shrug of resignation Trip did as she said. Hoshi followed suit, as did Ferik.

"What exactly does this decontamination procedure involve?"

The giant attempted a smile.

"Don't fear," he said. "Harmless. Painless."

"The decontamination procedure is an ionizing radiation burst." The woman's voice again, from the speaker. "As Ferik said—painless. In five seconds. Four. Three . . ."

Trip steeled himself as she counted down. At least this doctor wasn't making them strip for decon procedures, the way Phlox did. At least—

A blue light filled the chamber.

And every inch of Trip's skin erupted in pain.

Seven

"HOLD STILL, COMMANDER. One more minute."

The doctor—Trant—leaned over him and retaped one of the diagnostic sensors to his forehead where it had come loose. Then she turned and watched the monitor on the far wall of the medical ward.

Trip watched, too. Not the monitor—he had no way of knowing what any of the readings meant, though he was impressed by the number of gauges and dials his bodily functions were apparently causing to spin—but the doctor. Trant. He could tell from the expression on her face that she was as puzzled right now as she'd been over an hour ago, when she had rushed in to the decon chamber.

The pain had been fleeting—it stopped the instant the rays did, thank goodness—but Trant had insisted on getting a complete set of readings from him and Hoshi, who had been affected exactly the same way Trip had by the decontamination rays.

The doctor shook her head and shut down the monitors.

"I must admit, I'm completely baffled. Nothing like this has ever happened before—to any of us."

"None of you are human," Trip pointed out. He nodded to the sensors taped to his forehead and neck. "Can I—"

"Yes, please. If you would."

He began detaching the diagnostics from his body. Ferik, who had followed them to the medical ward, took the sensors from him and hung them back in place next to the monitor.

Trant, meanwhile, was doing the same to the sensors Hoshi had worn.

Again, Trip watched her.

She was somewhere around his age, he guessed, as thin and pale as the other Denari, hair pulled back up underneath a scrub hat so he had no way of judging either its color or length. She had an attractive, angular face to go with those piercing blue eyes, a green and orange uniform— like the others—and a calm, reassuring manner. Trip liked her immediately.

"From what I can tell so far, there's a marked similarity between our underlying biological structures," Trant said, hanging up the last of Hoshi's sensors. "I'll study these readings closer to see what I can found out about why the decontamination rays affected you both as they did. In

the meantime," she said, lifting Hoshi's leg
slightly, "let's see about this ankle."

"It's just a sprain."

"Probably. But we'll want to make sure there's
no damage to the underlying tissue. I have an
X-ray machine, but . . ." She frowned. "I'm not
sure we should risk a repeat of what happened
before."

"We have something that might do," Trip offered. "Hold on a second."

He swung down from his cot and went to get
the medkit, just inside the ward entrance. He
swung it up on the table, reached inside for the
diagnostic sensor—

And a hand clamped down on his arm.

Ferik.

The man's strength was unbelievable.

Trip felt as if he were caught in a steel vise.

"There's no need for that," Trip said.

Ferik didn't blink.

"Your hand," he said. "What you have. Show
me."

Trip drew his arm out and handed Ferik the diagnostic sensor. The man looked it over, frowning.

"What is this?"

"Medical equipment. For Trant."

The doctor, who had had her back to them, suddenly turned and saw what was happening.

"Ferik. No," she called. "It's all right."

The man released his grip.

He and Trant exchanged a look that Trip couldn't make heads or tails out of.

Rubbing his arm where Ferik had grabbed it—Trip was sure he'd have a huge bruise there tomorrow—he brought the sensor to Trant.

She turned it over in her hand, studying it carefully, front and back.

"It's a diagnostic tool," Trip said. "If you hit the main button there—"

Trant did as he said, and a moment later, nodded to herself. "Yes. I see."

She ran the sensor along Hoshi's ankle.

"Just a sprain, if I'm reading this right." Trant smiled. "The swelling should go down in a few days."

"Thank you," Hoshi said.

"We'll tape it up, though. Just to be sure."

She handed the sensor back to Trip. "That's a remarkable piece of equipment."

Trip was about to respond when the door to the medical ward opened, and three men strode inside.

Two Trip recognized immediately—Royce and his silent partner from before. The third, who took another step forward now, had a much more commanding presence. The way he carried himself, his uniform, which, if no less threadbare than those of Royce and the other man, was cleaner, more spit-and-polish. His hair was a shock of silver-grey clipped close to his skull; a military cut, for a military man.

"Marshal Kairn," Trip said.

"That's right. Tucker?"

"One and the same."

"Welcome aboard *Eclipse*." Kairn looked past Trip to the doctor. "I understand there was a bit of an incident in the decontamination chamber."

"A bit," Trip said.

Trant stepped forward and explained.

"No lasting harm, though?"

"No. We're fine," Trip said, indicating himself and Hoshi.

"Good. I apologize nonetheless. That's obviously not the kind of welcome we intended."

"Apology accepted."

"I thought you would like to know—your ship is aboard, down in our launch bay. And quite safe."

"Thank you."

"That's a very unique design—the drive configuration, the shape." Kairn studied him closely. "I don't think I've ever seen anything quite like it."

Trip's eyes narrowed.

The way Kairn said that bothered him.

How closely had he seen the cell-ship? In his shoes, Trip suddenly realized, he would have examined it very thoroughly indeed.

Another problem with accepting *Eclipse*'s "hospitality," one he hadn't thought all the way through before coming aboard.

"It's unique, all right," Trip said, certain that telling the marshal it was actually a twenty-fourth century design would be a violation of some sort of Starfleet protocol. "Though fixing the breach is still just a matter of welding in a patch."

"That sounds like something we could help you with."

"We'd appreciate it."

Kairn looked noncommittal.

"You were attacked outside the asteroid belt, Royce tells me. By Sadir's ships."

"I'm not sure who was doing the shooting, to tell you the truth," Trip said. "But that's where it happened."

"It had to be Sadir." Kairn went on then to describe, in precise detail, the ships that had boarded *Enterprise*.

"That's them all right," Trip said. "And you're at war with this Sadir?"

"We are."

"Mind if I ask why?"

"It's quite simple. He overthrew our planet's elected government and set himself up as dictator. We fight to see him taken down."

"We being—"

"The Guild. Miners, mostly—the people who worked, and lived, in the asteroid belt. Some refugees from Denari itself—members of the Presidium."

Trip frowned.

"Our elected government. One of us—myself, Royce, perhaps the doctor"—he nodded toward

Trant—"will be happy to give you more background on the war later. Now, if you wouldn't mind answering a question for me . . ."

"Sure," Trip said, his guard going up a notch (in his experience, when military types like Kairn started to act casual was precisely the time to stay well up on your toes). "Go right ahead."

"I have to admit being a little puzzled, Tucker. From what I've seen of your ship, your technology is obviously superior to Sadir's. So how is it you find yourselves"—he spread his hands to take in the empty room—"in this position?"

Trip sighed, and, as quickly as he could, relayed the story of what had happened to them over the last few days—*Enterprise*'s discovery of the anomaly, their arrival in the Denari system, the mine, the attack by Sadir's vessels, their subsequent escape on the cell-ship, leading up to their rescue by *Eclipse*. He left out only the cloak—he had a gut feeling that if the marshal even suspected something like it existed, he'd stop at nothing—literally, nothing—to get that device for his own.

"An unfortunate series of events," Kairn said, when he'd finished.

"*Unfortunate* is the word, all right." And inexplicable. Reviewing the events of the last few hours only made it harder for Trip to understand how *Enterprise*'s sensors could have missed detecting Sadir's warp-capable ships, how they could have so badly misread the level of the Denari civilization's technology.

"And this hull breach, the last of them. Which is what you want our help with."

"That's right."

Kairn nodded. "You seem like a plain-speaking man, Tucker."

"No point in beating around the bush, my daddy always said."

Kairn looked puzzled.

"In wasting time," Trip said. "It's an Earth expression."

"I see. Colorful use of the language."

The marshal exchanged an amused glance with Royce.

"I won't beat around the bush either, then," Kairn said. "We are at a distinct disadvantage in this war, Commander. For one simple reason— Sadir has a warp drive, and we do not."

Trip nodded, keeping his face from betraying the sudden sinking feeling in his stomach.

He knew what was coming next, and it wasn't going to be pretty.

"Commander Tucker, we'll fix your ship," Kairn said. "We'll go well beyond that. I don't know what it is you people from Earth value. What you value personally. But if we have it here on *Eclipse*—if we can go someplace and get it—it's yours. In exchange for a working warp drive."

Trip sighed. "Listen. In the first place . . . you can't just drop a warp engine into a ship and expect it to go. You need to strengthen the hull, upgrade your power relays—"

"We've seen Sadir's ships. We know the kind of changes that need to be made."

"You can't make changes, you need whole new ships."

"All right, we need whole new ships," Kairn said. "We can build ships. What we need is the technology."

Trip sighed. "I can't help you," he said.

Kairn's eyes blazed. Royce and the other man, who'd stayed by the entrance to the medical ward, moved closer.

"Can't—or won't? You said you were an engineer. You came here on a ship with warp drive, is that not so?"

"That's so, but—"

"Can't—or won't, Tucker? Which is it?" Kairn took a step closer and looked Trip straight in the eye.

"Won't," he said. "I won't help you."

The tension in the room, already high, ratcheted up several notches.

"A decision of that magnitude—it's out of my hands," Trip continued. "Only the captain can make that kind of call."

"But your captain's not here now, is he? He may not even be alive, for all you know."

Trip nodded. "You might be right. But until I know that for sure . . ."

Kairn was shaking his head. "I don't understand you, Tucker. Sadir has attacked your vessel. Captured your crew—most likely, killed some of them. And yet you won't help us fight him?"

"I won't supply you with warp technology." Trip shook his head. "It would significantly alter the balance of power between you and this Sadir. My captain wouldn't allow that to happen."

And Trip wouldn't allow himself to make the same mistake twice. To jump into the middle of a cultural dispute he didn't understand. He'd done that with the Vissians, and his interference—well-meaning as it had been—had cost the cogenitor's life.

"Balance of power." Kairn shook his head again, and then was silent a moment.

"Like I said, there are things I can help you with," Trip said. "Your reactor, for one thing. Looked to me like it was running pretty inefficiently. I might be able to do something about that."

"As I said—I'm not interested in your repair skills."

"You ought to be," Trip said. "You get the reactor running more efficiently, you'll use a lot less fuel."

"Fuel is the least of our concerns."

"Marshal, you ought to know that an inefficient reactor does a lot more than just waste fuel. You could actually damage—"

"Don't lecture me, Tucker." Kairn glared. "I know my ship."

Trip opened his mouth to reply in kind—

And felt a hand on his shoulder.

"Commander."

It was Hoshi.

He waited for her to say something else, but she simply stood there.

Which was when Trip realized she'd only spoken to calm him down. A good move. Whatever he'd been about to say (and the anger that had been fueling his responses was suddenly gone) would not have been productive.

He took a deep breath, then turned back to Kairn.

He was still angry. Furious, in fact, glaring at Trip, waiting for his next words so he could respond.

And all at once, he sensed something else behind Kairn's anger. Something he should have seen earlier, something evident in the hollowed-out circles beneath the marshal's eyes, and those of the other Denari he'd met. How thin they all were, the ragged clothes they wore, the disrepair of their ship. Evident, too, in Kairn's rush to escape Sadir's patrols, his single-minded focus on the warp drive, the way he'd reacted to Trip's talk of a "balance of power."

Desperation.

He could think of only one reason for that desperation.

The Guild had to be losing this war, he realized. And losing badly.

"I'm sorry," Trip began. "When it comes to reactors, and engines, and engineering—that's exactly what I tend to do. Lecture. Everybody on *Enterprise* tells me that."

Kairn's glare softened—ever so slightly.

"You rescued us," Trip said. "I guess I was just looking for a chance to return the favor."

Eclipse's commander remained silent still, for several long seconds.

"I am on edge as well," he finally admitted. "I should apologize, too."

"Not necessary," Trip said. "But—appreciated."

Kairn was silent a moment.

"Thank your lucky stars we were the ones who found you, Tucker," Kairn said. "Sadir would have no qualms about doing whatever it took to get you to surrender the secrets of your technology."

"I understand."

Trip kept his face level, but inside he heaved a huge sigh of relief. He had been afraid—just for a second there—that Kairn would do just that. Torture them—torture Hoshi, actually—to get Trip to give up the secrets he wanted.

"You say you are willing to help with our reactor."

"That's right."

"I would appreciate that." Kairn allowed a

small trace of a smile to creep across his face. "We are having problems with it, as you guessed. With our entire power distribution network, in fact, which leaves us with—"

"A very cold ship," Trip guessed.

Kairn's smile broadened. "Yes. A problem my engineering staff has fixed on more than one occasion." He shook his head. "But that is of minimal significance. What is important is that we've been unable to maintain our engine speed. Which puts our arrival at a very important rendezvous in jeopardy."

"I'd be happy to take a look," Trip said.

"Thank you. And in exchange, we will help seal the hull breach on your ship. A fair trade?"

"More than fair," Trip said.

"Very well then. Ferik?"

The man stepped forward.

"You'll escort Commander Tucker to engineering?"

"Yes, Marshal."

"Good." He turned back to Trip. "I'll check in with you shortly, Commander. Doctor," he said, nodding to Trant.

And with that, Kairn and the two men he'd entered with were gone.

"It's a long trip down to the engineering chamber," Trant said, turning to Hoshi. "Considering your ankle, Ensign, you should probably remain here."

Trip and Hoshi exchanged a glance. He nodded. Trant was right.

"Not much I can do in engineering anyway," Hoshi said. "But if you wouldn't mind answering a few more questions about this war between you and Sadir . . . ?"

"I'll do better than that," Trant said. "Some of our workstations are hooked up to a central database—which should provide you with more than enough background on the war. We'll get you settled in with one of those."

"Sounds like a plan," Trip agreed.

A quick rush of goodbyes then, and they all went their separate ways.

Trip—wondering what sort of situation he and Hoshi had landed in the middle of—followed Ferik down through the bowels of *Eclipse*.

Followed as best he could, that is, having to take two steps to the bigger man's every one just to keep up. Ferik took no notice. Trip felt like a little kid trying to tag along with the grown-ups.

It wasn't just Ferik that made him feel like a child. After they'd gone down one level, in a lift that creaked every inch of the way, they'd emerged into a corridor easily twice as tall and wide as those aboard *Enterprise*. Trip wondered why the size differential. He would have asked Ferik, but the man seemed preoccupied, and the last thing Trip wanted to do was disturb him. His arm was still sore where Ferik had gripped it before. Sore—heck, the bone felt bruised. He rubbed where it hurt.

When he looked up, Ferik was looking down at him.

"Okay?"

"It's all right."

"Good." The man offered an awkward smile. Trip returned it.

Ferik slowed his pace. "Sorry. I thought you—" He frowned. "You were going to hurt Trant."

"No. Just trying to help her." Which he was still trying to do—when they left the medical ward, Trip had left her with the sensor from the medkit. Trant hoped to find information in the device that might explain why he and Hoshi had been affected by the supposedly harmless decontamination ray.

"Help. Trant helps me. Help is good," Ferik said, nodding to himself, talking like a child who had just discovered what the word meant.

Trip still couldn't get a handle on the man. Was he as simple as he sounded? Then why had Kairn trusted him to escort Trip to engineering? Or to work the airlock? And Trant—she clearly trusted Ferik as well. Again, Trip wondered why.

But in the next instant, he told himself not to wonder too hard. He needed to focus on the job that lay ahead of him, in engineering.

And yet . . .

"Trant helps you?" Trip asked hesitantly. "How?"

"Sometimes I don't think right. She..." Ferik frowned. He reached into a pocket of his uniform, and pulled out a large blue pill. "She gives me these. They help me concentrate. Help me remember."

Trip's eyes went unconsciously to the scars on the back of Ferik's head. Not just his speech centers, then, but his memory had been affected as well.

Again, Ferik saw where he was looking, and nodded.

"What happened?" Trip asked gently.

"Sadir," Ferik responded almost instantly, his face twisted up in anger. "But I don't..."

He shook his head, and all at once the anger was gone, leaving only a plaintive, sad expression. "I don't remember that, either."

There was a desolation in his voice that made Trip wish he'd never brought the subject up at all.

"It's all right," he said hurriedly. And then, to change the subject, he asked:

"Why are the corridors so wide on this deck?"

"On all the cargo decks," Ferik said quickly. "To help transport the ore. Carts."

Trip nodded. Of course—he should have seen it himself. It would have made sense to have some sort of processing equipment aboard the ship, to minimize the amount of raw ore they needed to transport.

"But the ship doesn't do anymore mining?"

"No more." Ferik shook his head. "We..."

Trip nodded. Sadir again.

And again, Trip thanked his stars he and Hoshi hadn't wandered into the general's clutches.

They walked the rest of the way to the engineering deck in silence.

Ferik left him there, in the care of *Eclipse*'s engineer, a woman named Ornell.

It took Trip less than ten minutes to find why the fusion reactor was operating so inefficiently.

It took him that long again to explain the problem.

Because to explain what was wrong with the reactor (magnetic containment field down to eighty-five percent of nominal), he had to first go into some detail about the concept of nuclear fusion, how the reactive materials (the Denari used slush deuterium and tritium—same as *Enterprise* did for the reactor that ran its impulse engines) had to be superheated into plasma, which called for a temperature of about a hundred million degrees Kelvin, which required a lot of energy to reach, and still more to maintain. He had to explain why at eighty-five percent strength, the magnetic fields—which were designed to contain the energy from the fusion reaction—were in fact almost useless, because the amount of energy leaking out was almost equal to the amount they had to feed back in to keep the reaction going.

"So what we need to do," he finished, "is to get those magnetic fields back up to nominal. On *En-*

terprise—my ship—it's usually just a software routine."

Ornell's eyes, which had glazed over scant minutes into his explanation (a few minutes of conversation with her was all it took to learn that she had only just been appointed as ship's engineer, largely because she was the only one aboard *Eclipse* who could fix things as they broke) suddenly brightened again.

"Our main workstation is over here," she said.

Trip followed her to the computer. She brought up the code he was looking for on the display . . .

Whereupon Trip realized he was looking at a much longer job than he'd anticipated.

First, because he needed the written code translated as he worked.

Second, because based on a sample Ornell deciphered for him, the routines themselves were so poorly written, so sloppy and unnecessarily complex, that it was going to take him forever to identify the parameters he needed to change.

With a sigh, he got to work.

The process was very stop-and-go—Ornell would translate a routine and hand him a printout, he would scan it for the parameters he sought, and handwrite in the changes he wanted made—so while he waited patiently in front of the console for each new print-out, his mind wandered elsewhere.

Back to *Enterprise*, specifically.

He kept flashing on the image of the armory as he'd seen it from the Suliban ship, with a hole blown clean through—on the note of panic in Mayweather's voice as Sadir's ships had first attacked—on the captain's confusion as they'd identified the Denari . . .

He wondered where they were now—Archer, and Travis, and all the others. Where they were, and what was happening to them. What had happened when the ship was boarded—he couldn't picture Malcolm surrendering without a fight, it just wasn't in his nature, though he had to think the captain would have seen how senseless any kind of resistance would have been at that point, and stopped Malcolm from doing anything stupid or suicidal. . . .

For some reason, then, he thought of the captain's dog.

Porthos—had the beagle attacked the Denari when they boarded the ship? Archer had a struggle getting Porthos to listen to him sometimes. The dog might have just kept barking and growling at the intruders—an image that made Trip smile for a moment.

Until he pictured an annoyed Denari soldier drawing his weapon and aiming it at the dog, and the captain shouting at the soldier, and—

Trip shut his eyes and banished that image.

He focused on the Denari code for a while.

Thoughts of *Enterprise* wouldn't leave him, though. He wondered if anyone knew that he and

Hoshi had escaped. Maybe they were waiting for the two of them to come charging to the rescue in the cell-ship—as he and T'Pol had that time when the captain and Malcolm were on the verge of being hanged. That world—the name escaped Trip at the moment—they had been more primitive than the Denari. More brutal.

Well . . . almost certainly more brutal.

The image of Ferik's scars flashed before his eyes. Sadir had caused them, the man had said. In an attack? Deliberate torture? Was that what was happening to the crew of the *Enterprise* now?

Focus, Tucker, Trip told himself. *Focus.*

He bent back to the code, redoubling his efforts.

Some time later, he finished. Ornell took the last page of code from him and went to input it. While she worked, he ate—a ration pack he'd grabbed out of the medkit on his way out of the medical ward. He gobbled it down in less than a minute. It revitalized him somewhat—though what he really needed, Trip realized, was coffee. A big, steaming mug of it. Just the way chef brewed it, back on *Enterprise*. Coffee, a piece of cherry pie, a good night's sleep on his bunk, in his quarters, back on his ship . . .

A nearby speaker crackled.

"Engineering, this is Kairn. How are you progressing?"

Ornell, who sat at another workstation, next to the reactor chamber itself, pressed a switch and spoke.

"Marshal. I've just finished inputting the code. We're about to reset the containment fields."

"Good. I'll stay on this channel."

Ornell stood and walked to the wall nearest the reactor, the entire surface of which was a ten-foot-square series of panels—LCD displays, and various other controls.

She brought up the core-field monitor—a three-dimensional display of the magnetic fields within the chamber itself. They writhed and twisted on the screen before him, like an army of snakes wrapping themselves around an oversized basket-ball. A status bar next to the visual indicated the field strength as a percentage of nominal.

"Resetting the fields—now." Ornell pressed a button at her workstation.

The status bar responded almost instantaneously.

"We're up six percent already," she said. "Field strength at . . . ninety-one percent, and rising."

Trip walked over next to her. They stood together, watching the numbers climb.

Ninety-five percent. Ninety-seven. Ninety-nine.

"Field strength at one hundred percent," Ornell announced.

"Excellent." Kairn's voice came over the loud-speaker again. "Commander Tucker?"

"Right here."

"Thank you."

"You're welcome. But let's not count our eggs until they're hatched."

Silence. Trip suddenly realized why.

"Another Earth saying," he explained. "Just means let's make sure this adjustment did the trick—I mean, did what we wanted it to."

He could almost hear the laugh in Kairn's voice. "Well then, Ornell—let's push the engines a little, shall we?"

"Yes, sir."

Eclipse's engineer crossed to another panel on the control wall and began manipulating controls. A mind-boggling amount of levers and switches and buttons seemed to be involved in what she was doing—mind-boggling to Trip, at least. *If I had a week in here,* he thought, *I'd have all that controlled by a single software program.*

He turned his attention to a schematic a few panels down—a visual representation of the energy flow throughout the ship—pulsing lines of power superimposed on a two-dimensional model of *Eclipse*. There was something odd about it, he thought. A second later, he realized what.

Eclipse's silhouette as pictured on the screen before him was different than the vessel as he'd recalled seeing it from the cell-ship.

The weapons he'd noticed on the underside of

Eclipse—they weren't there. Or rather, there were no lines on the schematic indicating power flowing to those weapons.

Those weapons had obviously been retrofitted to the ship—was it possible the software hadn't been updated to reflect those changes? Was the schematic before him outdated?

No. It couldn't be. If that was the case, then the system would be continually malfunctioning. The computer delivered power across the ship according to the schematic—if the schematic was wrong, the entire power grid would be . . .

Trip's train of thought rolled slowly to a stop.

The entire power grid would be unreliable. Just as Kairn had said it was.

No wonder the environmental systems wouldn't stay fixed. No wonder they couldn't maintain a constant speed.

But that wasn't the problem right now, Trip realized.

The problem right now was that he had just boosted the total amount of available power by a fairly significant amount, which would add another level of stress to the system. Which might result in . . .

The display next to him chimed.

The power flow schematic suddenly started flashing—more precisely, the blinking lines leading from engineering to the bridge, which changed from green to a furious, insistent bright red.

"Kairn to engineering. Ornell, we're getting warning lights up here. What's going on?"

Ornell turned to Trip. "Tucker? What's going on?"

Trip opened his mouth to respond—but before he could say a word, the schematic suddenly stopped flashing altogether.

Over the com, on the channel Kairn had opened, Trip could hear a noise he recognized all too well. The unwelcome sound of power conduits giving out, one by one.

"What's going on?" He sighed heavily. "Overload."

Eight

"How bad is it?" Kairn asked.

Trip shook his head and looked around the
bridge—or to use Denari terminology, the command deck, which proved to be as cramped as the
engine room had been spacious. Trip was surprised at first, given the size of the ship.

After spending the last few minutes tracing
conduits around the room, though, he understood why. Like the weapons systems, most of the
stations here—communications, sensors, a sec-
ondary engineering monitor—had been retrofit,
built right on top of the preexisting shell. Which
only made sense—*Eclipse* had been designed as a
mining ship, not a fighting vessel.

The retrofit, however, had obviously been done
in haste. Not only did power conduits, data lines,
optic signal flow structures, and wires and pipes
of almost every conceivable sort crisscross underneath the hull plating without any regard for in-

terference considerations—but more important, the power conduits themselves were barely adequate to deliver the current the command deck systems required.

When Trip had amped up the system, they'd fried.

"Well?" Kairn prompted again.

He sat in the center of the command deck, which rather than the horseshoe-shape of *Enterprise*'s bridge, was built more like a triangle. His chair was parked next to a half-sized console that—judging from the number and variety of conduits and wires that ran to it—functioned just like Archer's command chair aboard *Enterprise*.

"Half your conduits are shot," Trip said.

"Can you fix them?"

"Anyone can fix them. It'll just happen again, though." He explained why.

Kairn shook his head. "What do you recommend we do?"

"You should put in for a month or so in a spacedock, rip everything out, and rewire it the right way."

"Not possible."

Trip suggested some quick hardware and software modifications instead.

"How long will it take to implement those?"

"A couple days, give or take," he said.

"During which time we'll have to stay right where we are, I assume?"

"Not a good idea to go whizzing through an asteroid belt with sensors down."

Kairn shook his head. "The rendezvous I told you about—our presence there is critical."

"You'd better have a damn good pilot, then."

"I am a damn good pilot, as you put it. But I need sensors as well."

"Then I need a day."

"Five hours."

Trip had to smile.

Kairn was beginning to remind him of the captain.

"What?"

"Nothing." He crawled back underneath the nearest workstation, dragging a set of tools with him. "I'll get to work."

A few hours into the job he began getting careless. Dropping a line of code here, crossing a wire there. Exhaustion, or hunger, Trip couldn't tell which. Probably a combination of the two, he decided.

He pulled himself out from underneath the console and stood.

Kairn had left the command deck. Royce was in the marshal's chair.

"I need coffee," Trip announced.

"Coffee?"

"It's a stimulant. Caffeine. You have anything like that?"

Royce looked at him strangely.

"You want drugs?"

"Yes. No. It's something we drink—it is a drug, but—"

Royce held up a hand. "I'll call the doctor."

Five minutes later Trant was on the command deck. She instantly grasped what Trip was after, and left again, only to return quickly with two thermoses.

She squatted down on the deck next to him.

"*Seela,*" she said, pointing to the one on her left. "*Fossum.*" She pointed to the one on her right. "Either of these should have the effect you're looking for."

"And they're safe to drink?"

"They should be, yes. I've been analyzing the results of those tests we took and haven't detected any systemic predilections that would indicate otherwise."

Trip smiled again and shook his head.

Now Trant was reminding him of T'Pol.

"I guess that means it's safe, then."

"As I said."

Trip unscrewed the lid of the first thermos and almost gagged.

It was that same metallic smell from before, the one he couldn't quite place, only magnified a hundredfold.

Trant caught the look on his face.

"Not the *seela*, then." She took that thermos from him. He opened the other.

It smelled like tea—very strong tea.

He poured a cup and raised it to his lips.

"Here goes nothing," he said, and took a sip, preparing himself for the worst.

"Nothing?" Trant frowned, and Trip realized he was going to have to take it easy on the colloquialisms, or spend as much time explaining himself as conversing.

He realized something else, too.

This *fossum*, whatever it was, wasn't bad at all.

It tasted like it smelled—like very strong tea, black tea actually, with a hint of something sweet.

"Thank you," he said to Trant, and took another sip.

She nodded to the mass of wires and conduit behind Trip. "How's it going?"

Trip shook his head. "It's going. Another few hours and you should have sensors back."

"A few hours." She frowned. "The stimulants will definitely wear off in that span of time. You should have something to eat to maintain your strength."

Trip shook his head. He was hungry, true enough, but if he put food in his system right now, he'd fall fast asleep.

"No, thanks. I'll stick to this," he said, lifting his cup.

"As you wish," Trant said. "I'll have a fresh thermos sent up later as well."

"That would be great."

She poured herself a cup of the *seela*, then, and sat. "Do you mind?"

"No. Not at all. Please."

He could use a break, not just from the work but thinking about the work. He'd gotten the entire command-deck crew involved in repairing the conduits, so that was all anyone was thinking about—and talking about—in his presence.

"I've been studying the readings I took earlier—of you, and Ensign Hoshi."

"And?"

She shook her head. "I still can find no reason why the decontamination rays should have affected you that way. It is possible your systems are more sensitive to ultraviolet radiation than ours."

"Well. I wouldn't know."

"I'm still looking for that information—in the diagnostic sensor you lent me. It's a remarkable piece of equipment." She shook her head. "I would like to have technology like that at my disposal."

Technology. That was one direction Trip did not want to take the conversation in.

He tried to steer it away.

"Well, technology is all well and good," he said. "But our doctor—on *Enterprise*. He doesn't always go the high-tech route."

Trip explained then about Phlox's tendency to use naturally occurring biological cures—alien insects, animals, plants, and so on—to treat the crew.

Trant frowned. "But he must use technology to make the proper diagnoses."

Trip granted her that.

"Still," she continued. "It would be interesting to see your doctor at work."

"Someday. Maybe," Trip said, realizing that he'd taken the conversation in another unwelcome direction, one that brought to mind something he'd almost forgotten in the last few hours.

Enterprise and her crew.

"You're doing what you can, Commander," Trant said.

He looked up at her. "Excuse me?"

"You're worried about your ship, obviously. I'm just saying you're doing what you can to rescue her. Which right now involves helping us, so that we'll help you. There's little else in your power to be done at the moment."

"Thanks," he said. "I appreciate that."

"You're welcome."

She smiled. Trip smiled back.

Midnight black. Her hair. And longer than he thought at first—it was braided and piled high on her head. Her eyes were aqua.

Stop it, Tucker, he told himself.

You don't need this right now. Interspecies romance had its definite attractions—and he'd been down that road more than once over the last few years, with the engineer from the Xyrillian ship,

with the princess, and that shore-leave planet—
but right now he had to stay focused on the task
at hand. The tasks at hand.

Fixing *Eclipse*, and then the cell-ship. Rescuing
Enterprise.

"Better get back to work," he said abruptly, and
got to his feet.

"Of course," Trant said, rising as well. "I don't
want to keep you."

Was there a spot of color in her cheeks, or was
he just imagining it?

She turned and left the command deck before
he could tell for sure.

Three hours (and that promised second thermos of *fossum*) later he stood next to Kairn as
systems began to come on-line again.

"Communications reestablished."

"Weapons back on-line."

"Defensive systems operative."

"Sensors . . ."

Kairn frowned. He and Trip turned as one to
the sensor station, directly to the left of his command chair.

"Royce? Is there a problem?"

Royce, at sensors, had a frown on his face as
well. "Picking up a lot of background noise, Marshal. Hard to separate it out from the incoming
telemetry."

"My fault," Trip said. "I tweaked the hardware."

Tweaked it, in fact, to be more accurate. In repairing the conduit, he'd noticed some redundant circuits—probably a result of the haphazard nature of the retrofit—which he'd simply eliminated. Incoming telemetry was probably considerably more accurate, which was throwing Royce off. What he was seeing as background noise was likely just low-level radiation from Denari's sun, or possibly the anomaly.

The sensors just needed to be recalibrated to eliminate it, that was all.

"Here," Trip said, leaning over the man's shoulder. "Let me—"

He stopped. Royce was right. There was indeed a broad band of energy coming in—not noise, though. He studied the U-V spectrum, and frowned.

"Can you map this radiation to specific coordinates?" he asked Royce.

The man nodded and brought up a map of the space surrounding *Eclipse*.

A trail of white dots led from the lower left-hand corner of the display to the upper right, growing denser as it went.

The trail, he noted, paralleled *Eclipse*'s course.

"Marshal." He motioned Kairn forward. "I think you should see this."

"What am I looking at?"

"A stream of energized particles."

"All right. What does that mean?"

"In my experience..." He shook his head. "Only one thing."

"Don't keep us in suspense, Tucker."

"This is an engine trail—exhaust from a ship's reactor."

"Engine exhaust? Are you sure?" Kairn looked skeptical. "We're the only Guild ship in this part of the Belt right now...."

And then his eyes widened.

"Sadir," he said, and almost immediately shook his head. "This far in? No. It can't be."

"It's somebody," Trip said.

"Another Guild vessel, then. *Shadow*, perhaps." He turned away from the display then, and looked up at Trip. "Can we trace the trail backward? Find its source?"

Trip shook his head.

"No. A particle stream like this one degrades very quickly."

And suddenly Trip realized something else.

These streams tended to degrade so quickly, in fact, that for *Eclipse* to be even picking up a trail...

"Shut it down," he said quietly. And then louder, "Shut it all back down!"

Kairn frowned. "What?"

Trip slapped open a circuit to engineering.

"Ornell, shut down bridge power. Right now!"

The lights on the bridge dimmed again.

The workstations all went dark.

Kairn was suddenly standing right in front of him.

The marshal was as thin as everyone else aboard *Eclipse*—but on him, the leanness suggested power. Taut, condensed, compacted energy.

Right now all that energy—in the form of anger—was focused on Trip.

"You have a reason for this?"

"You bet. If we're picking up this particle trail . . . the ship that made it has to be very close. Within sensor range, is my guess."

Kairn frowned. "Then why didn't they . . ."

His voice trailed off, as understanding dawned in his eyes.

Trip nodded. "We were powered down. That's the only reason they didn't pick us up. I hope they didn't just notice that power surge."

"How close do you think they are?"

"Let's find out. Ornell?"

The engineer's voice came over the comlink.

"Here."

"Can you restore power to station . . ." Trip walked over to Royce's workstation and looked under the console. "Twelve–A–seven?"

"I could. Marshal?"

"Do as Tucker says."

"Aye, sir."

Seconds later Royce's station lit up again.

"All right." Trip leaned over him. "Can you do a long-range scan? A passive scan?"

The man nodded, and a second later the display in front of him came to life.

At the very edge of the screen, the trail resolved into a number of distinct images, moving slowly but steadily away from them.

"Bingo," Trip said softly.

"A dozen ships," Royce confirmed. "Moving directly across our course."

Kairn cursed under his breath.

"I gather they're not Guild ships," Trip said.

"We barely have twelve ships left in the fleet. No, they have to be Sadir's." The Marshal shook his head. "How long till they clear our path?"

"Twenty minutes," Royce said. "Half an hour, to be safe."

"Enough time." Kairn nodded. "We should alert *Night* and *Shadow*. The presence of Sadir's ships this far into the Belt—he must be planning a major—"

"Marshal," Royce interrupted, not looking up from the display. "One of the ships is breaking formation. Headed in our direction."

Trip leaned over his shoulder and saw the man was right.

A white dot, against the black screen, moving straight for them.

"They spotted us." Kairn punched open a channel to engineering. "Ornell, full power to—"

"No," Trip said quickly. "Marshal, they—"

"Tucker, I am tired of you countermanding my orders on my ship."

"I'm sorry—but listen to me. If you—"

"Vonn. Stannis." Kairn motioned to two of his officers, who rose from their stations. "If Commander Tucker says another word, remove him from the command deck."

"No. Will you listen to me, please?" Trip said quickly. "They haven't spotted you, or they would have sent all their ships. They spotted the power surge, that's all."

The two men each grabbed an arm.

Trip shrugged free.

"Marshal . . ."

"Your point is academic, Tucker. That ship will be on us in—how long, Royce?"

"A minute. Maybe less."

"A minute," Kairn continued. "Best to prepare to fight."

"Prepare to die, you mean?" Trip shook his head. "There are twelve ships out there."

"If you're suggesting we surrender, think again. Sadir does not accept surrender from Guild ships."

The men grabbed him again.

"Hold on, damn it!" Trip shrugged himself free a second time. "I'm not suggesting that. If you give me a damn second here. I'm suggesting we do something else."

"What did you have in mind?"

"I don't know," Trip heard the frustration in his

voice and tried to damp it down. This was not a time for panic, this was a time to think things through logically. "They saw a brief power surge, that's all. They're not sure what it was. They're not expecting to find you here, anymore than you were expecting to find them."

"So?"

"Give them something else to find," Trip said, thinking out loud. "Something else that could have caused that surge."

"What?"

"I don't know."

"Another ship."

That was Royce who had spoken.

"Marshal, the diggers. We could jettison one from the launch bay—"

Trip turned on him. "Diggers. What are they?"

"One-person mining ships."

"Fusion reactors?"

"No."

"No good. It has to have a fusion reactor."

Silence.

Kairn broke it by slamming his fist down on the chair.

"*Strand,*" he said.

Royce got to his feet and turned to Kairn.

"Sir?"

"We jettison *Strand.*"

"No, Marshal. You can't do that. Without *Strand*—"

"We have to do it. It gives us a chance, at least."

"And the mission?"

Kairn shook his head. "We worry about that later."

Trip had no idea what they were talking about. But from the ashen look on Royce's face, Kairn's decision to use *Strand* to throw off Sadir's ship was a momentous one.

Trip couldn't help but wonder why.

The marshal punched open a com channel. "Kairn to launch control. Open Bay One doors."

There was a pause. "Sir?"

"Open Bay One doors," Kairn said slowly and distinctly. "We're jettisoning *Strand.*"

"Sir. I can't do that. We have crewmen working on the ship."

Trip looked down at Royce's console.

Sadir's ship was getting awfully close.

"Evacuate them. Now! And open those doors."

"Sir—"

"Do it."

"Marshal." Royce pointed to his display. "No time."

Kairn nodded, grim-faced.

"Launch control, this is a direct order. Open Bay One doors. Now."

A split second later a red light began flashing on Kairn's chair.

On Royce's console a second, smaller white dot suddenly appeared, moving erratically.

"*Strand* is away," Royce said quietly.

Kairn rose from his seat and stood next to Trip. They both watched the sensor display.

"I assume it has a fusion reactor," Trip said.

Kairn nodded. "It's an old government courier ship we salvaged some time ago. We've spent the last few months repairing it, putting it back in working order. No small task, I assure you."

"All in vain, now," Royce said bitterly.

"Not necessarily." Kairn, to Trip's surprise, didn't rebuke his subordinate. Instead, the marshal simply continued to watch the display.

Sadir's ship slowed and came to a halt.

Then it altered its course and turned after *Strand*.

Trip let out a breath he didn't even know he'd been holding.

Kairn smiled.

"Sadir's ship is activating weapons," Royce announced. "Targeting *Strand*. Firing."

Trip looked down.

Where there had been two white dots on the screen, there was now only one.

"*Strand* is destroyed, sir," Royce said. "Sadir's ship, returning to formation."

Kairn nodded and walked slowly back over to his chair. He sat and sighed heavily.

"Not in vain, Royce. Our work on *Strand*. Not what we had hoped for, but not in vain."

"Yes, sir," the man said, clearly not convinced.

"Half an hour till they clear our course, you said?"

"Yes, sir. To be safe."

"Half an hour it is, then." Kairn swiveled in his chair and fixed his gaze on Trip.

"Thank you, Commander."

"You're welcome."

Kairn shook his head. "You're a strange man, Tucker. First you won't help us, and now you won't stop helping."

Trip smiled and tried to formulate an appropriate response.

The com on Kairn's chair beeped.

He punched open the channel.

"Command deck. This is Kairn."

"Launch control, sir."

The instant he heard control's tone of voice, Trip's heart sank.

"Go ahead," Kairn said, the smile on his face gone as well.

"Lieutenant N'Rol was unable to evacuate in time. He was inside *Strand* when the bay doors opened."

The man needed to say no more. Everyone on the command deck knew instantly what he meant. This Lieutenant N'Rol was dead.

He'd either died instantly, if *Strand* hadn't been pressurized, or a few minutes afterward, if he'd been in the ship when Sadir's vessel destroyed it.

Not that it made one bit of difference.

"I see." Kairn closed his eyes. "Thank you, control. Kairn out."

No one spoke for a long moment.

"That's a helluva bad break," Trip said. "I'm sorry."

"Fortunes of war, Tucker," Kairn said, and stood. "You have the command chair, Royce. I'll be in launch control."

The marshal was going to talk to the crew down there personally, Trip knew at once. To explain what he'd done, and why.

Again, Trip was reminded of the captain. Kairn was doing exactly what Archer would, under the circumstances.

It wasn't Starfleet's war, as he'd told Kairn.

And yet at that moment, for Trip, it was hard not to feel part of it.

He slept the sleep of the dead.

When he woke, he had no idea how much time had passed. It could have been ten hours, it could have been ten days. However long it had been, it wasn't long enough. Trip felt as if he'd been hit by a truck—the same kind of feeling he got, he realized, when he was about to get sick. An ache in his bones, a heaviness in his eyes . . . he wanted nothing more than to go back to sleep. But his stomach was growling. And he had things to do.

Miles to go before I sleep, he thought, swinging his legs to the floor. *Millions of them, probably.*

His quarters were spartan, to say the least—the bunk he'd slept on the only piece of actual furniture in them. He guessed that they'd once served as a storage room of some kind—they clearly weren't meant as sleeping cabins. Oh, well. He could rough it as well as the next guy.

He made his way down the hall to a washroom, and then Hoshi's quarters, both of which the crewman who'd escorted him to his bunk had pointed out last night.

"Anybody home?" he called out, rapping on her door.

A muffled voice answered.

Trip pushed the door open, stepped inside . . .

And stopped in his tracks.

"Hey," he said, frowning. "I thought rank was supposed to have its privileges."

Hoshi, sitting in front of a workstation, spun in her chair and smiled.

"First come, first served," she said.

Her quarters were twice the size of Trip's. In addition to the workstation, there was an actual bed, and a sink, and what looked like . . .

"Tell me that's not a shower."

"Doesn't work," she said. "Believe me, that was the first thing I checked."

Trip saw something else then as well.

A stack of ration packs on a table by the workstation.

"Help yourself," Hoshi said, following his gaze.

Trip did. They talked while he ate. He told her everything that happened yesterday—the overload, Sadir's ships, the lieutenant's death . . .

"Sounds like it hit you pretty hard," she said.

"How could it not? I was part of that decision."

"No." Hoshi shook her head. "You weren't. As I'm sure Kairn would be happy to remind you."

Trip had to smile. She was right about that.

"You helped save this ship, Commander. And everyone aboard it," she reassured him. "Trip, you have nothing to feel guilty about."

"Yeah." But he did anyway.

"Sir, now that you've lived up to your half of the bargain—fixing the engines—it's their turn. They have to help us fix the hull breach."

Trip nodded. Talking to Kairn about that was on his mental to-do list. That, and a working shower.

He finished eating and turned to Hoshi.

"So fill me in on what you've been doing?"

"Finding out a little more about this mess we've landed in the middle of," she said, tapping on the workstation. He saw she'd tied the UT into the Denari system. "Like Trant said—this hooks up to an entire library of articles. Not much from the last decade or so—General Sadir seems to have pretty well muzzled the news organizations. But I did find some interesting material from before that time—political history, technological papers, a lot on the conflict between the miners and the planetary authorities, even before Sadir seized power—"

"So this war predates Sadir?"

"It wasn't a war then. But there is a history of conflict between the two sides. I found a piece that gave a lot of background—ah. Here. Take a look."

She let Trip have the chair. He sat down in front of the screen and began to read.

NEW AGREEMENT EASES DECADES OF TENSION

With a handful of senior officials from both the Denari government and the Miners Guild looking on, Councilor Dower Sang and First Guildsman Lind Usdan signed a historic treaty this afternoon at Vox Prime, in the very heart of the Asteroid Belt. This pact grants the Miners Guild limited political autonomy within the Belt in exchange for an acknowledgment of Denari ownership rights to the vast mineral resources the asteroids contain.

The signing of the agreement, which must still be ratified by both the Presidium and the Guild, takes place almost exactly four years after the historic battle of Vox Prime, during which a handful of outnumbered Guild vessels managed to defeat a vastly superior battalion of the First Denari Expeditionary Force. It was only fitting, then, that both Guildsman Lind and Colonel Sadir Lyatt, opposing command-

ers in that conflict, were present at yesterday's signing. Sadir's appearance at the
ceremony was particularly critical, coming at a time of increasing political tension
between conservative and liberal forces
battling for influence within the Presidium.
In a step aimed at reducing that tension,
the Presidium had only recently announced the formation of a special
peace commision, whose members were
appointed specifically to bring about
such steps as Sadir's appearance.

The article continued, to a second, and a third
screen of text. More about the disagreements between the Guild and the Denari government—the
Presidium. More about the history of each, and
the gradual rise of tensions between them.

There were pictures, too. Of the base at Vox
Prime, and of Councilor Dower, and Guildsman
Lind. And then-Colonel Sadir, a man of medium
height and almost nondescript appearance, so in-
nocuous-looking that Trip had trouble squaring
him with the monster that Kairn and Royce had
described. The colonel stood in the back row of
officials at the signing ceremony, wearing a broad
smile that looked entirely genuine.

The man next to him caught Trip's eye.

A tall, thin, dark-haired man dressed in a simple
coverall. Something about him looked familiar.

Trip scanned the caption, found the man's name, and almost fell out of the chair.

"Hoshi, did you see this?" he asked without turning around.

"Sadir? I know."

"Not Sadir. This man. Here." He pointed to the screen. "Do you know who he is?"

"I saw the picture, but—"

"No, Hoshi. Look."

She did.

Her mouth dropped open as well.

"My God," she said.

"I know." Trip shook his head. "It's Ferik."

Nine

SPECIAL PRESIDIUM ENVOY FERIK REEVE, according to the caption. And now that Trip knew who the man in the picture was, the resemblance was easy to see. There were differences though. The Ferik in the picture, thin as he was, had a good thirty pounds on the Ferik of now. Not to mention a full head of hair.

But the biggest difference was in the eyes.

The Ferik of then radiated confidence. Intelligence. Trip understood now why Trant and Kairn found things for him to do, why they were trying to make him feel a part of things.

He also understood the desolation he'd seen in the man's eyes.

And he wondered how much—if anything— Ferik remembered of his former life.

"I can't believe it," Hoshi said. "What do you think—"

Trip nodded.

"What do you think—"

The door, which Trip had left partly ajar, swung all the way open.

Trant, carrying a tray with two metal containers on it, stepped through.

"Good morning," she said. "I'm glad to see the two of you together. I thought, Commander, since our experiment with *fossum* was so successful yesterday, you might like to try a little Denari food for . . ."

Her voice trailed off as she saw the picture on the workstation screen.

"Ah," she said, the lilt completely gone from her voice.

She carried the tray over to the table without another word and set it down.

"You have been busy," she said to Hoshi, without turning.

"I'm sorry," Hoshi said, clearing the screen. "We just wanted to know more about the war."

"It started the day after that picture was taken, actually." She moved the containers from the tray to the table, then lifted the lids. "Although I'm not surprised you haven't found the reference—the database hasn't been maintained for quite some time now. Not a priority, as you might imagine."

Steam rose from the dishes. Hot food.

Despite the fact that he'd just eaten, Trip's stomach rumbled. It had been a long couple of days.

"The day after the picture?" Hoshi prompted.

"Yes. The entire conference was a sham, actually. A way for Sadir to lure a number of important officials into the same place. Make it easier for him to kill them all at once."

"This attack," Trip said. "Was that when Ferik was injured?"

Trant shook her head. "No. His injuries took place later. But this is hardly breakfast-table conversation. Come sit. Try this."

She attempted a smile. It fell flat.

"Sure," Trip said, sensing her desire to change the subject. Being reminded of what had happened to Ferik was probably not high on Trant's list of favorite things.

He and Hoshi exchanged a quick glance and sat down at the table.

Trant had put a plateful of what looked like scrambled eggs—a little darker in color, perhaps—in front of each of them.

"It's called *pisarko*," Trant said. "A fairly bland mixture of starches and sugars."

Trip shook his head. "You make it sound incredibly delicious."

Trant caught the sarcasm in his voice and smiled. "It's filling. And nutritious. And since you may be with us awhile, you should have something to eat besides those ration packs."

Trip couldn't argue with that.

He picked up a forkful and took a taste.

And frowned.

"What is it?" Trant asked.

Trip shook his head but didn't respond. Couldn't respond—he didn't know exactly what to say. It was just that the *pisarko*, whatever it was, tasted . . . strange.

Starches and sugars. He'd been expecting something like oatmeal, or grits even, but this was . . .

"I don't know," he said. "It's weird."

Hoshi had taken a taste as well. She had the same look on her face.

"Give me some help," Trant said. "I'm not a cook, but is it too sweet? Too bland?"

"No." Trip shook his head again and tried to think.

The word *alien* suddenly popped into his head. Which he was sure would be even less helpful to Trant than *weird*. Of course the Denari food was alien—they themselves were alien. But Trip had had alien food before—some of it was delicious, some of it inedible, but none of it had hit him quite the way this *pisarko* had.

Weird, he thought again, and set his fork down.

"I give up," he said. "It's just not my cup of tea."

"Mine, either," Hoshi said. She set her fork down as well.

Trant was frowning. "Cup of tea?"

"Not to our taste," Hoshi explained.

"All right," Trant nodded thoughtfully. "Clearly, there are differences between our two species."

"Thanks anyway," Trip said.

"Of course," she said, standing. "The thing to do is probably to have you come down to the mess now, if you're amenable. We can gauge at least your visceral reactions to some of our foods then. Put the ones you favor under a microscope."

"If we find some," Trip said.

"Oh, we have a fairly limited menu, it's true, but—"

A com sounded.

"Commander Tucker."

That was Kairn's voice.

Trip stood and looked around the room.

"Over here," Trant said, and walked to a panel Trip hadn't noticed by the wall. She waved him over and pressed a button on it for him.

"This is Tucker. Go ahead."

"Good morning, Commander. I'm sorry to bother you, but I need a few minutes of your time."

"Sure. Whenever you'd like."

"Now," Kairn said. "It's rather urgent, I'm afraid."

Trip frowned.

"Something to do with the engines?" he asked.

"No. Nothing to with the engines." Kairn hesitated. "I'd rather explain to you in person."

"Fair enough," Trip said. "Where should I meet you?"

"We're in the main briefing room. I'll send an escort—"

Trant stepped in front of him. "Not necessary, sir. I'll show Commander Tucker the way."

"Very well, Doctor. Five minutes. Kairn out."

The channel closed.

Trip looked at Hoshi. Main briefing room? Urgent?

What did Kairn want now?

Trant led him two decks up, to a section of the ship Trip had never seen before. This part of the ship had been designed for crew, not cargo—the corridors were scaled down in height and width, the hatchways and conduits on a different, more human scale.

There were more people here, too—dozens of them, of all ages. Several said hello to Trant as they walked by.

All of them stared at Trip.

Alien on board—no doubt the first one they had ever seen. Trip supposed he would have stared, too. All the attention made him a bit uncomfortable.

He wondered, suddenly, if Phlox or T'Pol ever felt this way.

Trant caught the stares as well.

"You'll have to forgive them, Commander.

You're the first new thing most of them have seen onboard *Eclipse* in quite some time."

"The first alien thing, too, I imagine."

She smiled. "That's right—though anything much beyond these corridors is alien to most of the people up here."

"What do you mean?"

"The people up here are passengers—family. Not crew. They're basically confined to this part of the ship."

"Family?" Trip shook his head. "You mean, like children?"

"Some. Not as many as we'd like."

"But . . ." He frowned. "Isn't this ship a little dangerous for families. I mean, you're—"

"At war?" She nodded. "It's dangerous. But safer than any other place we could put them. At least here, on board *Eclipse*, we can protect them."

"All those asteroids out there, though. Couldn't you—"

"We know the Belt inside and out—that's what's enabled us to hide from Sadir so long. But to set up any kind of permanent outpost . . ." She shook her head. "The general's forces would find it within weeks."

Gypsies, Trip thought. They were like the old gypsies that used to travel across Europe in wagons, with no permanent home.

No. That wasn't quite right.

They were more like the Native Americans,

driven from their homes by the U.S. Army, forced to live on the run for a few years until they were caught, and exterminated.

Morbid thoughts. He banished them from his mind.

They walked on in silence a moment.

"How about you?" Trip asked. "You have family on board?"

She hesitated before answering. "My parents are on Denari. A sister as well. I haven't spoken to them in . . . ten years now, I think. Since the last of the Presidium outposts on the planet fell."

"That must be hard."

Trant nodded. "Occasionally we have defections. From Sadir's side to ours. We learn things about life on Denari. From what I've heard, the city they live in has been fairly untouched by the war. So I'm hopeful." She smiled. "Besides, all of us on *Eclipse*—we've been together so long, we're practically family."

"I noticed."

"Part of the reason everyone was staring at you, I suspect."

Trip frowned. "Excuse me?"

"News travels fast on this ship, Commander. Everyone here"—she nodded to the cabins on either side of the corridor—"knows what you did last night."

She stopped walking then and turned to face him.

"You saved *Eclipse*. And everyone aboard it. We all owe you a debt of thanks."

She smiled.

"In a way, that makes you part of the family as well."

Warning bells went off in Trip's head again.

Not Starfleet's war.

No interspecies romance.

He kept the smile he was feeling inside off his face, and shifted gears.

"Well, you're welcome, of course." He started walking again. "Just keeping up my end of the bargain, I guess. I fix your engines, you fix my ship."

He sensed, rather than saw, the smile slip off Trant's face.

"Of course," she said, a noticeable chill in her voice.

They walked on in silence a moment.

"Commander," Trant said suddenly. "May I be blunt?"

She didn't wait for an answer.

"Effusive gratitude is not normally part of my personality. But you should know that what I said earlier—about saving everyone's life aboard this ship? It was no exaggeration. Sadir does not take prisoners from Guild vessels."

"Marshal Kairn said that. I didn't mean—"

But Trant hadn't finished.

"Do you know what Sadir does to those Guild ships he does capture? To every man, woman, and child aboard? He kills them—those whom he's not interested in. And they're the lucky ones, I can tell you." Her voice was clipped, and cold as ice. "So the thanks I offered you on their behalf is genuine. For you to belittle that gratitude is highly offensive."

Trip felt a flush creep over his face.

"You're right," he began. "I'm sorry if—"

But she still wasn't done.

"Everyone on board *Eclipse* has lost a loved one to this war. So please, if others do offer their thanks, try to think of what they might be feeling before you answer."

"I understand. And again—I'm sorry."

She took a deep breath, and nodded.

They walked on, in silence.

Trip struggled to think of something to say, unsure whether or not he should try and explore the subject—obviously a very sensitive one—further.

While he struggled, Trant spoke.

"I'm sorry, too," she said, shaking her head. "A quick temper is also not normally part of my personality, Commander."

"It's all right." He smiled. "And the name is Trip, by the way."

"Trip?"

He explained.

"Charles Tucker the third," she said. "It sounds like a heavy burden to bear, being the third."

"You have no idea." He smiled. "What about you? Is Trant your first name, or—"

"Neesa," she said quickly. "No one's called me that for years, though. On *Eclipse*, I'm Doctor Trant. Or just Trant."

"Same for me. On *Enterprise*. It's just Commander. Or Commander Tucker."

"No close friends on your ship?" she asked.

"No, that's not it." He thought a moment. "The captain calls me Trip sometimes, I guess."

"You're close to him."

"As close as anyone can get to a commanding officer, I suppose. There has to be a bit of distance."

She nodded.

"How about Marshall Kairn? Are the two of you close?"

"As you said—there is a certain distance. But we are—friendly, if not friends."

Trip nodded.

"Do you have any idea what this is about—why he wants to see me now?"

She hesitated a second before replying.

"I'm not privy to the marshal's inner councils, I'm afraid."

Trip noticed the hesitation. And the fact that she hadn't really answered his question.

He let it slide—Trant knew something, obviously, something she didn't want to tell him. Which was all right. Trip suddenly realized he knew something, too.

This was just about the time that *Eclipse* had

been scheduled to make her rendezvous—the one that Kairn had been so insistent they not miss.

File that away under not likely to be a coincidence, he thought.

At that moment, Trant pointed to a door straight ahead of them.

"The briefing room," she said. "We're here."

Kairn wasn't the only one waiting for him. There were at least a dozen others as well—crowded around a long, low table with an opaque black surface, talking to each other.

The talking stopped when Trip entered.

Kairn stood. "Commander Tucker. Thank you for coming. Please. Have a seat."

Trip took the nearest empty chair. Kairn sat almost directly opposite him, flanked on one side by a middle-aged woman with steel-gray hair in a uniform identical to the marshal's, and on the other by a much older man, hair gone white, dressed in a simple blue robe.

The older man, who all at once looked familiar to Trip, cleared his throat.

"Marshal—if I may?"

"Of course, Guildsman."

"On behalf of the Guild, Commander Tucker, I would like to thank you for meeting with us on such short notice. Introducing so many people is impractical, Commander, but you should know that gathered around you in this room are the command staff of three Guild warships—*Eclipse, Night,* and *Shadow.*"

Trip was only half-listening. The second Kairn had called the older man Guildsman, it had triggered a memory in his mind. And now, looking at the man closely, it came to him whole.

"Guildsman Lind," he said.

The old man raised an eyebrow.

"Yes." He frowned. "How do you know my name?"

Trip explained about the photo Hoshi had found.

"That was a long time ago. When the Guild was a government, not the army it is now." Lind shook his head. "I'm here now in my role as commander of the warship *Night.* You should also know Vice-Marshal Ella'jaren"—he nodded at the woman on the far side of Kairn—"who commands *Shadow.*"

The two of them—the vice-marshal and Trip—exchanged nods of greeting.

Lind continued speaking.

"We've asked you here, Commander Tucker, because we have a problem. One we hope you can help us with."

"I'm happy to do what I can." Accent on the *can,* Trip felt like adding, hoping that he was not going to have to remind Kairn yet again about the limits on his ability to provide assistance. No warp drive, he felt like saying, but held his tongue. "Go on."

"Our three ships have made this rendezvous today—which I believe Kairn has told you about—"

Trip nodded.

"—as the final stage in a mission we have spent literally years preparing. A mission we feel will enable us to turn the tide in the war." He turned to Kairn. "Marshal?"

Kairn touched a button on a panel next to him, and all at once the dark surface of the table lit up from underneath and became a starchart. Trip recognized the area it displayed immediately.

The Denari star system.

Kairn leaned forward, and picked up where Lind had left off.

"Over the years, as he has tightened his hold on power, General Sadir has ruthlessly eliminated those who stood in his way—those who he felt posed even a potential threat to him. Included among those are virtually the entire staff of his base in the Kota system."

"Kota system." Trip shook his head. "I'm not familiar with it. Where—"

Kairn anticipated his question and pressed a second button on the panel. The map on the screen zoomed out, so that Trip was looking at a much wider view of this sector of space.

He was looking, he realized, at the K'Pellis Cluster.

"This is Kota," Kairn said, pointing to a binary star system directly next to Denari's.

All at once Trip flashed back to that moment in the shuttlebay, when Travis's voice had crackled over the com, telling them *Enterprise* was under attack.

"Mayweather here Commander sorry can't talk right now we've got two dozen hostiles approaching at warp two from the next system over."

Kota. That was the next system over.

"Commander?"

Kairn was looking at him. Trip realized he'd drifted away for a second.

"Sorry. The staff at Kota Base, you were saying . . ."

The marshal nodded. "Yes. The scientists and engineers there—they were the ones who developed warp drive for the general, gave Sadir the weapons he needed to overthrow the Presidium. Apparently, Sadir grew concerned they might share those secrets with others. So he had them . . . detained."

Kairn brought up the map of the Denari system again and pointed to the Belt. More specifically, to a large asteroid at one edge of it. "Two years ago we received intelligence that they were being held here—Vox 4. In a prison on the far side of the asteroid. Our mission is to break into that prison and rescue them."

"We have little doubt," Ella'jaren added, speaking for the first time, "that they will be eager to repay Sadir for the treatment they received at his hands."

Trip nodded. "True. But I'd think Sadir would keep a pretty close eye on these people."

"He did initially," Kairn said. "But as I said—it's been two years. The prison is no longer as well-manned as it once was. We think it vulnerable. Our plan is to land ships here"—he pointed to the near side of the asteroid—"and break in from below."

Trip frowned. "You mean go through the asteroid?"

"Exactly."

Trip took a closer look at the chart. "That's a lot of digging."

"Ten miles' worth," Kairn said.

"I don't want to burst your bubble," Trip said, "but that's going to take quite a while. Not to mention make an awful lot of noise."

"The digging's already been done." The marshal smiled. "Half a century ago Vox four was an important source of both iron and other heavy metals. Its interior is honeycombed with mining tunnels."

He pushed another button on the panel next to him.

The starchart on the table disappeared.

Its place was taken by a maze—thousands of squiggly lines that looked like nothing so much as children's doodlings.

"Here, Commander." He stabbed the table with his index finger. "We come up beneath the prison here—undetected—and complete our rescue."

"Sadir doesn't know about these tunnels?"

"No. We're fairly certain of that."

"Fairly?"

Kairn nodded. "The probability is high enough to risk this mission."

"Which, frankly," Lind said, "is our last hope."

Silence fell around the room.

"Supplies, personnel, ships, morale . . . we're low on all these things, Tucker. Critically low." Lind looked across the table at him. "I know Kairn has hinted at the problem, but let me be blunt. Sometime in the next few months, unless the situation changes dramatically, we'll be forced to surrender. Sadir will win."

I thought Sadir didn't accept surrender from Guild ships, Trip was about to say. Then he caught the looks around the table that followed Lind's announcement and realized that—of course—everyone already knew that.

There would be no surrender.

"The mission is critically important," Kairn said. "We cannot afford to fail."

"Okay." Trip looked from Lind to the Marshal, and then Ella'jaren. "I get all that. But why did you want me here?"

Lind sighed. "As I said, we have a problem."

"Which you need my help with."

He nodded. "That's right. Our plan requires three ships, of a very specific profile, to successfully complete the mission. The ships must be powerful enough to make precise course adjustments, large enough to help ferry the escaped prisoners, and yet small enough to enter Vox four's orbit without being detected by the prison's defense systems."

Trip looked up and met Kairn's eyes.

"*Strand*," Trip said. "One of those ships was supposed to be *Strand*."

"That's right."

Now Trip understood why Royce had made such a fuss about the decision to jettison it.

The Guildsman spoke again.

"*Strand, Irgun, Lessander*. Three courier ships, once used by the Presidium, which we stole over a year ago from one of Sadir's bases on Denari. We've spent that time modifying those vessels for this mission. Now, as you say, *Strand* is gone. *Irgun* and *Lessander* have been ferried aboard *Eclipse*, are now down in the launch bay as we make final mission preparations. But the third ship . . ." Lind shook his head. "We have none. No vessel which fulfills the mission requirements."

The Guildsman met Trip's eyes—at once, Trip saw where this was going. "Except yours."

"The cell-ship."

"Exactly." Kairn leaned across the table. "We need your ship, Tucker. And we need you to pilot it."

Trip had thought himself the center of attention before, while Trant was escorting him through the passenger cabins.

But it was nothing compared to the intense scrutiny he felt right now.

Every pair of eyes in the room was focused on him.

"We are natural allies in this, Commander," Lind said quietly. "Kairn tells me Sadir has already attacked your main vessel—*Enterprise*. Captured your shipmates, as well. This is a chance for you to strike back at him."

"You've helped us already." Kairn spoke now. "You fixed our engines. Found Sadir's fleet, and helped us escape them. Done good things, for a good cause. Help us do this now."

Trip's mind raced.

Not Starfleet's war. Not his either. And yet . . .

Somewhere in the middle of initializing the magnetic fields, tweaking the sensors past their original design specs, advising Kairn on military strategy, and not least of all, talking to Trant . . .

He'd trespassed into some very murky territory.

He was, Trip realized, beginning to feel a part of *Eclipse*. A part of this fight.

But actually flying a combat mission for them—which was what this prison rescue amounted to, call it what you like . . .

That, as his momma used to say, was a whole 'nother kettle of fish.

He shook his head.

"You're asking an awful lot."

"We realize that."

Trip suddenly realized something as well.

149

"There's no sense in me flying the cell-ship and not being part of the mission."

Lind and Kairn exchanged a quick glance.

"We hadn't intended on asking you to participate in that way," the Guildsman replied. "Still . . . there's no denying. Space is tight about your ship. If you do decide to help us . . . we will be going with one fewer person on the mission than originally planned."

Trip had been on enough covert and semicovert operations himself to know what that meant. Fewer mission personnel, the less likely a successful mission would be.

If he did this, there was absolutely no sense in not doing it all the way.

"I need some time to think," he said.

Actually, what he needed to do was talk to Hoshi. In lieu of Captain Archer—and even more, perhaps, in lieu of T'Pol—the voice of noninterference—he badly needed another perspective on the whole situation.

"Time is something we have very little of," Lind said gently.

"I understand. Give me an hour."

The three commanders looked back and forth at one another.

Kairn spoke for them, finally.

"One hour," he said, nodding. "No more."

Kairn insisted on escorting Trip back to quarters himself.

They walked in silence most of the way, Trip preoccupied with the thoughts racing through his head. On those few occasions he did look over at Kairn, the marshal seemed preoccupied as well. Trip thought he knew why—Kairn had obviously asked to escort him in order to say a few last words. Something to influence his decision? That seemed the most likely reason, but it didn't quite jibe with what Trip was coming to know of the man's character.

It was only as they approached Hoshi's quarters that Kairn finally did speak.

"I want you to know one thing, Commander," the Marshal said, the words coming all in a rush. "Whatever you decide to do, I plan to honor our agreement. To repair your hull breach—see you safely on your way."

"I appreciate that," Trip said. He was going to say more but drew a blank.

He simply had no idea what he was going to do.

The door to Hoshi's quarters burst open, and she staggered out into the corridor.

She slumped against the wall and looked up at Trip.

Her face was pale, her brow covered with sweat, her eyes wide in panic.

"Help me," she gasped. "I can't breathe."

Ten

TRIP RAN TO HER SIDE. Kairn ran ten feet down the hall, and slapped open a channel.

"Medical Emergency. Corridor B, Section Seventeen. One of the humans."

Trip took Hoshi's hands in his.

Her skin was hot to the touch. She was burning up.

"Easy," he said. "Don't panic."

Hoshi nodded, her eyes still wide. Trip noticed small bumps running down the side of her face. She continued to breathe—short, shallow gasps for air. Trip gripped her hand tighter.

"Hang in there, Hoshi," he said. "Trant's on her way."

"It started right after you left," she said between breaths. "I thought there was something wrong with the environmental systems again. I got hot. And then—"

"Easy."

"—I couldn't breathe."

"It's all right."

A hand touched his shoulder.

"Let me."

Trant. She knelt down next to him, holding out the sensor he'd lent her.

"Vascular dilation, respiratory contraction, the urticaria here . . ." Trant looked down at the sensor, and then back at Trip. "If she were Denari, I'd say we're looking at some kind of allergic reaction."

"That food she ate."

"The *pisarko*." Trant nodded. "Most likely . . ."

Hoshi was still gasping for breath. Trip leaned down next to her, stroked her forehead, tried to help her stay calm.

He glanced over at Trant, silently urging her to hurry. She was still looking at the sensor.

"Something called epinephrine—that's what she needs, according to this device. I should be able to find a molecular analogue for it—ah. Dicodnine."

Trant reached into the medical bag she'd brought, pulled out a small ampule and a hypo, and injected Hoshi.

"A minute before it takes effect," Trant said.

They waited.

Trant watched Hoshi.

Trip watched the doctor and Kairn as they leaned over Hoshi, concern written all over their faces.

Not Starfleet's war, he thought.

By that way of thinking, Hoshi was no concern of theirs either.

"Oh." Hoshi swallowed and shook her head. "I thought I was going to pass out there. Or worse."

"You had a severe allergic reaction," Trant said. "You're lucky Tucker came back when he did."

"Doubly lucky the marshal was with me," Trip added. "I wouldn't have known how to get you down here, Doctor."

"Has anything like this ever happened to you before?" Trant asked Hoshi.

"Never."

"No food allergies of any kind? Or reactions to other substances or chemicals?"

"Nothing."

Trant handed him back the sensor. "We'll have to do a thorough analysis of that *pisarko*—see what it is that set off your system. We'll table our culinary experiments—and in the meantime, you and Commander Tucker should stick solely to the food that you brought."

Hoshi nodded weakly.

"I'd like to bring you down to the ward as well," Trant said. "Keep an eye on you."

"I'll come, too," Trip said.

"I was going to ask you to do just that. We need to make sure that you're not suffering any adverse reactions, either."

"I think I would have felt something."

"Most likely. Just the same . . ."

Trip nodded. "Give me a minute, Doctor."

He turned to Kairn. The marshal spoke before he could.

"No need to ask, Tucker. We can stretch that hour a little."

Trip shook his head. "That wasn't what I was going to say."

Kairn frowned. "What then?"

"I've decided," Trip said. "I'll fly the cell-ship."

He let Trant examine him. He made sure Hoshi was settled in the medical ward. He told her what he planned to do, and why, and gave her a direct order: If he didn't come back, she was to do whatever she had to in order to reach Starfleet, to make sure that Captain Archer and everyone else aboard *Enterprise* did not spend the rest of their lives as Sadir's prisoners.

Then he left her in Trant's care, and followed Kairn's escort to the launch bay, where the mission would depart from.

The room was cavernous—the size of both bays aboard *Enterprise* put together and then some. The cell-ship was there. So were two other vessels, each roughly the size and shape of one of *Enterprise*'s shuttlepods. The courier ships, *Irgun* and *Lessander*.

The escort led him around the ships to a staging area.

A row of metal chairs faced an LED display the size and shape of *Enterprise*'s viewscreen. Kairn stood in front of it. He saw Tucker and smiled.

"Commander Tucker. Join us, please."

Half a dozen people occupied those metal chairs—all turned at Trip's approach. He recognized Royce and his silent partner from the airlock tunnel. The other four he didn't know. All men, all wearing the same kind of uniform, all with an upright, military bearing. Soldiers.

Trip took an empty chair, next to Royce.

"We've been reviewing the mission profile," Kairn said. "To recap, for Commander Tucker's benefit—"

He pointed to the LCD screen, which displayed a starchart of the Denari system.

"Vox four."

He pointed to a spot two inches to the left of the asteroid.

"Our current position—just outside the range of the prison's sensor systems. About two hours' travel time for the courier vessels—excuse me, the courier vessels and the cell-ship. Here"—he pointed again—"is the debris field we'll use as cover for our approach."

Trip felt compelled to interrupt. "Cover? How? If their sensors are any good at all, they'll pick us up anyway. Even if we shut down all systems, the hull alloys alone would still be enough to set off alarms."

Kairn smiled. "As I told you, we've been planning this a long time. Six months ago one of our operatives snuck aboard a prison supply transport. As it drew within range"—he pointed to the asteroid—"she set off an explosive device that blew the transport to pieces. The wreckage scattered everywhere—across a ten-mile-wide radius of space. Your ships, in the middle of that wreckage, should manage to remain undetected."

"Should manage?" Trip asked.

"The mission is not without risks, Commander." Kairn touched the edge of the LCD screen, and the starchart disappeared. The tunnel network filled the screen.

"Once you land, you'll proceed until this point—here—where you'll split into two teams. Alpha team"—he looked up and nodded at the four soldiers—"proceeds to this spot, directly underneath the prison's central defense systems. They take those systems off-line.

"At the same time Beta team—that's you, Commander Tucker—Royce and Vonn are with you—proceeds along this tunnel and enters the prison here. You'll free the Kota base prisoners, and—"

Trip's hand shot up. "Another question."

"Go ahead."

"How do we find the Kota Base prisoners? I mean, this is a pretty big facility, isn't it?"

"Two hundred twenty eight inmates." One of the soldiers—a man with close-cropped blond hair—answered. "Twelve wings, A through L. Kota prisoners are in L wing, block nineteen."

"Which is right here." Kairn pointed at a spot on the chart.

"If they've moved . . ."

Kairn shook his head. "We have intelligence—a source within the prison—that says they haven't."

"Recent intelligence?"

"Six months old," Kairn admitted. "But still—worth taking a chance on."

He straightened and returned to the briefing. "Once you've freed the prisoners, you return through the tunnel network to your vessels, and from there, back to *Eclipse*. We'll be well out of sensor range before their defenses come back on-line." He looked up at Trip. "Any questions?"

Yeah, he felt like saying. About a million.

For one thing, he had trouble believing an operation like this could go unnoticed, security systems or not, for longer than five seconds. And just because those security systems were automated didn't mean there weren't plenty of people around the prison, too—good old, unpredictable people, who were likely to investigate anything that looked or sounded every remotely suspicious. And if they were planning on the prisoners filing out of the jail in nice, neat, orderly rows . . .

A debris field as cover.

Six-month-old intelligence.

A last-second change of mission equipment and personnel.

All at once Trip had a bad feeling about the entire plan.

But at this late stage of the game, it was pointless for him to pull apart the plan, piece by piece. It was either going to work, or it wasn't.

They'd know—he'd know—very shortly.

"No. No questions."

Kairn nodded. "Good enough. If you have any before you launch, see me. Afterward . . . Royce will be with you. He knows the mission as well as any of us."

Kairn touched the LCD again, and the screen cleared. "All crews, preflight check. Commander Tucker . . . we'll need to see to that hull breach on your ship."

Trip stood. "Funny. I was just gonna say that."

"Talk to Ornell. She'll supply what you need. And Commander—one more thing."

The marshall smiled then, the first full-out smile he'd seen from the man.

"Welcome to the team."

Trip borrowed a portable sensing device to analyze the breach. What he had originally thought a pinprick-sized hole was actually a microscopic crack in the ship's hull, where the hatch joined the main frame. *Eclipse*'s engineer supplied the materials he needed to fix it, and Trip got to work.

Twenty minutes on, he had sealed the breach from the interior side. He stood, hopped down to the deck, turned to work on the frame from the hull side . . .

And started.

Trant was standing next to the cell-ship, watching him.

"Sorry," she said. "I didn't want to disturb you while you were working."

"It's all right," he said. "What's up?"

"You're flying the mission?"

"I am. Once I get this breach fixed."

Trant frowned. "I'll be out of your way in a moment."

"No, no. That's not what I meant. I can work while we talk." He found sealant in the kit Ornell had given him, and started to apply it. "So how's Hoshi?"

"Fine. Resting comfortably. All her symptoms have vanished." Trant hesitated. "I am going to need to do a much more extensive round of tests on her—you, as well, once you get back."

"All right." Trip continued working, waiting for her to continue. She didn't.

He looked up then, and saw Trant was standing in exactly the same position as before. Hadn't moved a muscle.

From the glazed expression on her face, her thoughts were a million miles away.

"Trant? What is it?"

She shook her head, and her gaze cleared.

"Sorry. Just thinking." She focused on Trip then. "Commander. I didn't come up here to tell you about Hoshi."

"I didn't think so."

"Kairn asked me to talk to you. About the mission."

He wasn't sure exactly what he'd expected her to say, but that wasn't it.

"I'm all ears," he said—and then, a split second later—"Another human expression. Means I'm listening."

"I think I could have puzzled that one out, Commander."

"I suppose you could have at that."

Trip crouched down then, working at the bottom edge of the breach.

"You're aware of how important this mission is," she said. "That if we don't succeed, we may as well surrender."

"I heard."

"It's true. But at the same time . . . we have to be pragmatic. The rescue attempt might fail."

"Well." Trip looked up and regarded her a moment. "I'd like to say it's good to hear someone being realistic about this little adventure, but honestly, it doesn't make me happy to hear those words."

"I wouldn't expect that it would." She sighed. "Commander Tucker—I have every confidence in your abilities, and those of everyone on the mission. But as I said, there is a chance you'll fail. A chance that you may be taken captive. And if that happens . . . you should know that Sadir has no compunctions about using torture to extract information from his captives."

Trip sighed and set down his tools.

That, he was even less happy to hear. Not out of concern for himself so much, as for his shipmates.

Who had been in the general's custody for close to three days now.

"Why are you telling me this?" he asked. "To cheer me up?"

"No." She reached into a pocket then, and pulled something out. Something shaped like a thimble, and about a quarter as big. "In the event that you are caught—"

"You made me a poison pill."

She didn't need his help in deciphering that expression.

"That's right. The other members of the team all have them. Kairn thought you should as well. Though, of course, you're under no compunction to use it." She held the pill out. "It fits over your tooth. If you—"

"I know how it works. Thanks, but no, thanks." Trip certainly didn't want to think about the possibility of being captured, but even if that happened, killing himself was not an option. Not now. Not with Archer and everyone else already in Sadir's custody, and even though he himself had every confidence in Hoshi's ability should anything happen to him . . .

No. Suicide, even to avoid being tortured, was not in the cards.

He turned back to the breach.

"Commander." Trant knelt down next to him. "You have no idea what Sadir is capable of."

Trip set down his tools. "I appreciate your concern, but I can't. It'd be selfish. My shipmates—"

"Please." She held out the pill again.

Trip shook his head.

"It would—" she began, and then her voice caught, and she closed her eyes, trying to compose herself.

When she opened them again, they glistened.

Which was when Trip realized he wasn't the only one who'd been thinking about interspecies romance.

"It would kill me," she said softly, "to know that you had been caught, and that there was nothing to be done about it."

"From what you're saying," he said, smiling gently, "it would come close to killing me, too."

"IT'S NOT A JOKE!" she shouted.

Trip blinked.

Trant exhaled, then shook her head.

"I'm sorry."

"It's all right." He moved to brush the tears from her eyes. She pushed his hand away.

"Don't," she said softly.

It was his turn to apologize. Trant nodded acceptance.

"Commander—"

"Trip."

163

"All right. Trip."

She hesitated. Clearly, there was something she wanted to say to him. Just as clearly, she was having trouble finding the words.

Just as Trip was about to help her out, she spoke.

"You saw that picture," she said. "Do you want to know what happened?"

"Picture?" Trip had no idea what she was talking about.

And then all at once, he did.

"Ferik."

"That's right. Ferik. If you knew him—if you'd met him then, before that conference—before the attack. Before Sadir captured him and did . . . what he did . . ."

She didn't need to finish the thought. Trip had the whole picture now.

Sadir had tortured Ferik. Hence the scars—the damage to his mind. His memory.

Trant held the pill out again, gesturing for him to take it.

And again, Trip shook his head.

"You're being an idiot, Commander," she said.

"Trip, remember?"

She didn't smile. But there was something in her eyes—a twinkle of amusement . . .

"You're being an idiot, Trip."

"Well." Trip met her gaze. "I've done my share of idiotic things, that's true."

Her eyes sparkled again. A smile tugged at the corners of her mouth.

Her face was inches away from his.

Trip leaned over to kiss her.

Trant's eyes widened, and she stood up.

Trip was barely able to stop himself from falling over.

The doctor spoke. Not to him, however.

"Ferik?"

Trip turned.

The man stood at the far edge of the cell-ship hull, just visible from where he and Trant were.

Trip had the feeling he'd been standing there awhile.

"Hoshi tests," he said. "Centerfuge finished."

"Centrifuge," Trant corrected. Her face was bright red.

She was embarrassed—at Ferik finding them. At what they'd been about to do.

Why?

Trant turned back to Trip.

"I'll let you get back to work, Commander," she said. She held out the pill a second, then pocketed it. "But if you change your mind . . ."

"I won't," Trip said.

"If you do, you know where to find me."

Then she and Ferik were gone.

Trip stared after them, wondering what—exactly—had just happened, and why.

Eleven

A SYSTEMS CHECK. A quick tutorial for Royce and his silent partner—Vonn—in the Suliban sensor displays. A quick tutorial for him as well—mission details once they were inside the prison.

And all at once their hour of prep time was up. They launched.

Royce had the seat to his left, where Hoshi had been. Vonn was off to his right, and slightly behind him. He reminded Trip of Mayweather. Absolutely unflappable. His expression never changed, like no matter what happened next it would be nothing he hadn't seen before. He radiated a sense of calm.

Trip tried to draw on it as he followed *Irgun* and *Lessander* through the Belt, and the asteroids that whizzed by them with alarming regularity.

"Shouldn't we take this at about half-speed?"

"Easy, Tucker." Royce had figured out the Suliban sensor display—he had a rough grid of the space surrounding them up on screen. "We've been running simulations through this part of the Belt for months now. Just stay close, and you'll be fine."

A rock twice the cell-ship's size suddenly whizzed by a hundred meters to starboard.

Irgun and *Lessander* stayed on course. Trip resisted the temptation to pull hard aft, and stayed with them.

Which he was glad of a second later, when an even bigger asteroid shot past on their right.

He was sweating already. It wasn't just nerves, either. They were all in containment suits—virtually identical to *Enterprise*'s EVA suits, except the air circulation in these was beyond lousy. Trip was dreading having to put the helmet on—it would probably feel like a sauna.

Redesign, he thought. *The second we get back to* Eclipse.

We, he realized. He was thinking of himself as part of the Guild—part of their war.

He was also thinking about Trant. Doctor Trant. Neesa.

"Tucker."

That was Royce who'd spoken.

"Yeah?"

"You with us?"

"I'm here."

"You didn't look it just then."

"Thinking, that's all."

"Stay sharp. This is the hard part right here. The Ribbon."

Trip was about to ask him what The Ribbon was, when all at once *Irgun,* and then *Lessander,* dived, at an almost ninety-degree angle.

Trip's stomach went out from under him as he banked the cell-ship to follow.

The next five minutes were among the most nauseating of his life.

A series of sharp turns, dips, and dives that reminded Trip of nothing so much as a roller-coaster ride—more specifically, the Twister, an old wooden roller coaster in Walters County he used to go on, over and over again, until they closed the fair for the night.

Back then, of course, his stomach was a lot stronger.

"The Ribbon," he said, when they'd finally stopped all the perambulations.

"The Ribbon." Royce nodded. "That's the densest part of the entire Belt back there—the hardest part to navigate without getting slammed into the next system. Big reason why Sadir put the prison on Vox 4. Not many people can get through that." He turned sideways and smiled. "Not without getting sick, anyway. Congratulations."

Trip nodded.

"Although I haven't seen anyone turn quite that shade of green before."

Vonn laughed. The first sound Trip had ever heard him make.

"I'm glad you found that funny," Trip told him.

Royce turned back to Vonn and smiled.

Then both men laughed.

"We have a simulator program on *Enterprise* I'd like to introduce you to," Trip said. "Devil's Peak. We'll see who's green then."

"You have to get your ship back first," Royce said.

"Yeah. I know that. How about you, Vonn?" he asked, keeping his eyes glued to *Lessander* in front of him lest they run into some other obstacle that required a quick hand on the throttle. "You up for a little time in the simulator?"

Vonn smiled and gave him a thumbs-up.

"Your friend is not much of a conversationalist," Trip told Royce.

"Not his fault," Royce said, and all at once the smile was gone from his face. "You can thank the good general for that. Show him, Vonn."

The other man leaned forward then, and opened his mouth.

No tongue. Trip looked quickly away.

"Part of the reason why he volunteered for the mission, I think. Am I right, Vonn? Get a chance at some of those guards?"

Vonn smiled and gave another thumbs-up.

"You got your happy pill, right?" Royce asked.

"Happy pill?" Trip asked, and a split second later realized what he was talking about. The pill Trant had tried to give him.

"No." He shook his head. "I don't."

Royce frowned. "The doctor was supposed to—"

"She tried. I wouldn't take it."

He told them why.

"That's a mistake," Royce said. "You—"

"Whoa," Trip said, cutting power to forward thrusters, bringing them to a dead halt.

Ahead of them, *Irgun* and *Lessander* had done the same.

And right in front of them was the reason why.

A trail of wreckage—metal, plastic, and glass—stretching as far as the eye could see. The remnants of the transport Lind had referred to in the mission briefing.

The two courier ships eased into the line of debris, between two hull fragments that were each easily the size of *Enterprise*'s main deck. Trip maneuvered into position a few hundred behind them.

"*Irgun* to cell-ship. Power down all systems. Over."

"Roger that," Trip called back. "Over and out."

He checked their speed and angle of drift relative to the wreckage, made a last-minute course adjustment, and shut down. As far as any passing ships were concerned, they were now all just part of the wreckage. Which they would be for another ninety minutes or so, according to the chronometer Kairn had supplied.

At which point it was on to Phase Two—the landing.

Trip sat back in his chair.

"If we're caught," Royce continued, picking the conversation right up where they'd left off, "you do not want to let Sadir's people get ahold of you."

Trip shook his head. He was all for being pragmatic, but this was ridiculous.

"You people have got to have a more positive attitude about this mission," he said.

Vonn chuckled.

Trip nodded. "That's what I'm talking about."

Royce was not smiling.

"Have it your way, Tucker. Don't say I didn't warn you."

"You and Trant both."

"Well . . ." Royce shrugged. "Put yourself in her shoes. After what happened to Ferik."

Trip nodded. "I guess you're right. They are close."

"Close?" Royce was looking at him strangely. "You mean you don't know?"

Trip frowned. "Know what?"

"About Ferik? And Trant?"

Trip shook his head.

Royce smiled, and turned around to look at Vonn, who had a big grin on his face.

"What?" Trip asked. "What about Ferik and Trant?"

Royce continued to smile. "You like her, don't you, Tucker? Can't say as I blame you. Good-looking woman, our doctor."

Dave Stern

Vonn leaned forward, between the two of them, and nodded agreement.

Trip was getting a little tired of this.

"What, Royce? What don't I know?"

The two Denari exchanged a smile. Vonn laughed. Royce looked Trip dead in the eye.

"They're married, Tucker. Doctor Trant and Ferik."

"Married?"

Trip blinked.

"Married?"

"Married," Royce repeated. "Sorry to be the bearer of bad news."

He looked anything but, though.

Trip didn't know what to say.

Royce settled back in his seat. "We better get some rest. All of us. It may be the last chance we get for a while."

Vonn eased back into his own chair. Royce turned to Trip.

"Sweet dreams, Tucker," he said, and smiled.

Vonn grunted out a laugh. Both men closed their eyes.

Trip looked out the viewscreen, at the debris field before them, and thought:

Trant and Ferik? Married?

He couldn't stop thinking about it.

A lot of things made sense now. His concern for her safety, when Trip had pulled out the sensor.

Her expression when she saw the photograph of the peace conference. Her reaction in the launch-bay when Ferik had suddenly appeared.

Fourteen years ago. He wondered how long they'd been together at that point. Not long, he decided. She was still young. She was—

He pictured Trant then—sitting with him on *Eclipse*'s command deck. Watching over Hoshi, in the medical ward. Arguing with him in the launch bay. Him, leaning forward to kiss her . . .

Married.

Behind him, Vonn started to gently snore.

In a way this was good, Trip told himself. Take your mind off the mission, take your mind off *Enterprise*, concentrate on something totally unrelated.

Trip put himself in her shoes, just as Royce had suggested.

Fourteen years with Ferik. All the time remembering who he had been, and contrasting that with who he was now.

No wonder she'd wanted Trip to have that pill with him. To have the choice to . . .

Did she wish Ferik was dead? Had died fourteen years ago?

His head was swimming.

He sighed and closed his eyes. Maybe rest was a better idea.

Right then the console beeped softly.

Trip looked up.

A red rock filled the sky in front of him.

"Vox Four." Next to him, Royce sat up. "We're here."

The side of the asteroid facing them was bare ground. No signs of habitation anywhere. Rock, sand, and more rock. A miner's paradise. Trip was reminded of Mars's smaller moon, Deimos.

Lessander's engines suddenly flared to life for a split second, and then the courier vessel fell away from the debris field, heading to the asteroid below.

Irgun's thrusters followed next—again, for just a split second. This was the most dangerous part of the mission, as far as Trip was concerned. They were right in the sights of Vox 4's defenses—on radio silence. The engine burns to take them out of orbit, though, were necessary. For the split second that they fired, the three ships were vulnerable.

It could all end right here.

Trip powered on, checked their course, and fired his thrusters, too.

And just as quickly shut down.

They coasted through the atmosphere.

"We're in," Royce announced, looking down at the sensor display. "Underneath the prison's radar system."

Trip smiled.

He fired thrusters again and set them down on the asteroid, fifty feet away from *Irgun* and *Lessander*. They donned helmets and exited their craft.

Alpha team was waiting, in formation and ready to go. Each of them carried backpacks—filled with weapons and explosives. Vonn, alone out of Beta team, was similarly outfitted—they needed far less gear for their part of the mission.

One of the soldiers stepped forward.

"We're on schedule. Let's synchronize chronometers, everyone."

He held up one arm of his suit, to which a small chronometer—black faceplate, with blinking red display—was attached.

They all had them—Alpha and Beta teams. The mission had been timed down to the exact second—these chronometers would enable the teams, even separated, to work in perfect synchronization.

"On my mark," the Alpha leader said. "Three—two—one—initiate mission countdown."

Trip pressed a button on his chronometer.

The display flashed. Four blinking red LED's against a black background.

9999. 9998. 9997 . . .

"Ten minutes marching time to the tunnel entrance. There," the Alpha leader said, turning and pointing toward a rock formation in the distance.

And without another word, they set off.

9441.

Right on schedule. Even a little ahead. They were at the rock formation, proceeding along its face, past jutting shards of rock and fallen boulders, some as large as the courier ship.

The leader waved them to a stop. He reached up and switched on a headlamp. His men did the same, then branched out and disappeared from sight.

Trip, Royce, and Vonn—Beta team—waited.

One of Alpha team stepped back into view and motioned them forward. Not five seconds later the other members of Alpha team reappeared.

They followed the first man down a steep ravine, then up to a sheer cliff wall.

A second later he disappeared into it.

One by one the others followed. Alpha team, then Royce, Vonn, and at last, Trip. Only then did he see the opening in the rock wall—a notch, the size of a half-open door, barely wide enough for them to squeeze through, completely invisible unless you were looking for it.

He stepped through, and the notch widened. Light from his helmet and those of the others splashed all around, revealing a passage perhaps half a foot shorter and significantly narrower than one of *Enterprise*'s corridors.

Trip held up his chronometer.

9367.

They were now half a minute behind schedule.

The passageway sloped steeply down. They followed it.

Before long, though, Trip lost all sense of up and down. He was moving forward—not exactly walking, the gravity wasn't strong enough for his forward motion to qualify as walking exactly, more like bounding, or hopping. It was fun for a while.

And then it wasn't.

He continued on.

6110.

The halfway mark, going by the clock, at least. There was no way to tell how far along they actually were.

Trip was drenched in sweat already.

The Denari environmental suit was not as stuffy as he'd feared, but going five miles—whether you did it naked or in a parka, or in near-weightless conditions as they currently enjoyed—was hard work. Thirsty work. The suit was equipped with a water pack, and a straw he could reach by turning his head, but Trip sipped sparingly. He concentrated on Royce, ahead of him, and putting one foot in front of the other.

Time passed.

He tried to focus on the mission. These prisoners, from—where was it?—Kota base. Sadir's weapons team.

He wondered what kind of shape they'd be in after so long in one of the general's prisons. From what everyone on *Eclipse* was saying, not good.

And that brought him round to Ferik again. And Neesa.

No. Best not to think of her that way. She was Trant. Doctor Trant.

Trip looked down at his chronometer again.

2910.

He activated the com unit in his suit.

"Royce."

"Tucker." The man sounded as fresh as when they'd started out.

"Shouldn't we be there by now?"

"The map's not a hundred percent accurate. We anticipated the actual distance to the prison superstructure might be slightly longer. Or shorter."

Trip frowned. Not a hundred percent accurate.

Somebody might have told him that earlier.

His water pack ran dry.

He used the catheter.

He wondered, exactly, how much oxygen they had. How long could they go before having to turn back, before they wouldn't have enough air for a round trip?

No. He checked that thought. There were environmental suits scattered throughout the prison, according to their source. In case of a catastrophic air loss. That was how they intended to get the Kota prisoners safely back through the tunnels. There were probably more than enough for them as well, if it came to that. If they—"

"Stop." The Alpha leader's voice, after so long a span of silence, startled him. "We're here."

Trip looked ahead. The passage dead-ended in a wall of grey metal, curving outward towards them.

The prison.

Six meters down that grey metal wall, they found an airlock. Maintenance access. A minute later—2380—they were inside. A service tunnel, much larger than it looked from the outside. A grooved track ran down the center—power for a vehicle of some type. Conduit—communications and power, judging from the two different gauges he saw—ran along the walls at shoulder height. Ventilation shafts above, water pipes below, and pressure gauges staggered along both sides of the wall.

The tunnel was pressurized. They peeled off their suits, refastened the chronometers around their wrists. The Alpha team leader walked to a panel on the inside wall. Now he read the writing he found on it.

"F-twenty-one." He pointed to his left. "Alpha team in that direction. Beta"—he pointed right—"down there."

The two teams separated.

"Twenty-two ten," he said, reading his chronometer. "We will take security systems off-line at exactly nineteen hundred. Five minutes from now. We will keep them off-line until . . ." He paused. "Until one triple zero. One thousand. By that point we have to be back in the tunnels, with the Kota prisoners, with that airlock"—he nodded toward their entry point—"resealed. Questions?"

There were none.

There were no further words, either.

The two teams split and set about their separate missions.

Royce led the way, hugging the interior tunnel wall. Their source had warned them that the tunnels were patrolled—on rare occasions.

All of them had hand weapons drawn, just in case.

2106.

Royce stopped next to a wall panel.

"L-ten," he said, reading off it. "Not long now."

He slowed his pace, counting the panels, and finally stopped again.

"This is it," he said, and pointed up, toward the ventilation shaft above.

An access ladder along the wall led up to it. Royce began to climb it. Vonn, then Trip, followed.

Royce reached the top of the ladder. Trip saw an access hatch on the shaft to his immediate right. A small light above it blinked green.

The shaft was alarmed—part of the security system. They couldn't touch it without sending the prison guards down on them.

Once Alpha team disarmed the system, though,

they could enter it with impunity. And the shaft would lead them directly into block L-19.

Trip looked down at his chronometer.

1941. Not long now.

"Tucker."

Trip, hanging on the ladder below both Royce and Vonn, looked up. "Yeah?"

"Stay back when we enter. At least at first," Royce said. "No disrespect intended, but Vonn and I have trained together. We know what to expect."

"Your ball game," Trip said. "You make the rules."

Royce looked down at him and frowned.

"Ball game?" he asked.

Trip opened his mouth to explain.

Vonn held up his arm and tapped the chronometer on it.

1909.

Trip and Royce both nodded and fell silent.

1903.

1858.

1850.

Royce cursed under his breath.

"Give it a minute," Trip said.

They did just that.

1758.

Royce cursed again, louder this time.

"Something's gone wrong," he said. "Something's happened to them. Alpha team."

Trip frowned. "We don't know that for sure. How long do we have before—"

The green light next to the hatch started flashing red.

At the same instant, Klaxons—alarm Klaxons twice as loud—shrieked through the tunnel. The sound was deafening.

Something had most definitely gone wrong.

Twelve

"LET'S MOVE," ROYCE SAID. "Back down the ladder, both of you. Back to the tunnels. Quickly."

Trip could hear a tinge of panic in his voice.

For a split second he almost wished he'd taken that pill from Trant.

"Tucker!" Royce shouted. "Let's go. Hurry!"

Trip stepped down one rung . . .

And paused.

"Hold on a second," he said.

"What?"

"Wait." He looked up at the access hatch. The red light—security breach—was still flashing. Something had happened—was happening—to Alpha team. No doubt about that. But did they have to abandon the mission?

"They'll fight—won't they? Alpha team?"

"As long as they can. To give us time to escape. Time that we're wasting right now, Tucker."

"Don't use it to escape," Trip said. "Use it to complete the mission."

Royce looked at him as if he'd grown two heads.

"Are you out of your mind?"

"No. Hear me out." He glanced down at the chronometer. 1710. "The guards won't expect a second team."

"Of course they will," Royce shot back. "That's the first thing they'll check for."

"Not if Alpha keeps them busy enough. Not right away, at least."

"They'll keep them busy, all right," Royce said.

But he was frowning. Considering what Trip was saying to him.

"Royce—think about it. How long have you planned this mission? How many years? Do you think you'll ever get another chance?"

"No, but—"

"That woman—the one who blew up the prison transport. Lieutenant N'Rol. They sacrificed themselves to give us the chance to do this. Don't—"

"There were others who sacrificed themselves, too. But their sacrifices meant something. This"—he nodded upward, in the direction of the access hatch—"this would be a waste of life, not a sacrifice."

"I say we go."

"Last time I checked, you didn't have a say, Tucker. You're not one of us."

"Check again." Trip glared at him. "I'm right here

with you, aren't I? It's my neck on the line, too."

Royce shook his head.

"You have a death wish? Is that it?"

"On the contrary. I didn't take that pill, you'll recall."

"All the more reason not to put yourself in Sadir's hands."

Trip smiled. "Like I said—you have got to have a more positive attitude about this mission."

All at once Vonn, who'd been hanging on the ladder between them the whole time, listening, let out a short laugh.

He looked at Royce, and then pointed up to the shaft.

"Seems like you're outvoted," Trip said.

Royce didn't say anything. Trip looked in his eyes—he saw the man considering his options.

"Even if they think there's a second team, they won't know where we're going," Trip prompted.

"All right," Royce said. "We go."

He took two quick steps up the ladder then, and swung the access hatch open.

1644.

They'd crawled seven meters down the shaft. The Klaxons were still sounding. Trip was pretty sure that was a good thing. He took it to mean the prison staff was occupied with the threat at hand—Alpha team—and would not have time to collect their thoughts and search for other possible threats.

Of course, he could be wrong.

Ahead of him, Royce and Vonn suddenly stopped moving. Trip looked up and saw why.

There was a grate off to their right. An entrance to the prison itself.

Royce peered through it.

"A hallway," he announced. "No guards that I can see."

"Let's not wait for any to show up."

Royce nodded. He pressed his fingertips up against the grate and gently pushed.

It swung to one side, and out of the way.

Royce peered out, then brought his head back inside.

"Give me ten seconds before you follow," he said, and then turned himself around in the tunnel.

He slid out the grate, feet first, and dropped to the ground.

Trip heard the sound of his boots hitting the floor, and then footsteps.

He and Vonn waited.

1610.

Vonn took a quick look out of the grate, and then slid out.

Trip was right behind him.

No waiting ten seconds. No peering out first to check the lay of the land. Time was short. Besides, he reasoned—if there was a problem, he would have heard something.

He fell, feet first, and landed on a gray concrete floor.

He looked up. The walls were gray concrete too. Featureless—no doors. No markings. Nothing. They ran for twenty meters in each direction before intersecting another corridor at right angles.

Vonn and Royce were huddled together by the intersection to his right, where the wall ended. Peering around a corner.

Quietly as he could, Trip jogged over to join them.

"Guard," Royce whispered.

Trip leaned around him to see.

He was looking down another corridor. This one had cells on either side of it—steel doors set into the concrete walls, every ten feet apart. Directly ahead—ten, maybe twelve meters from where they crouched—was a guard post, which sat at the middle of yet another intersection of corridors. A long, low, semicircle of gleaming metal. The open end faced them. Video screens ran around the inside of the security station—an LCD, same size as the one Kairn had used for the mission briefing—hung down over it. Writing filled the screen. Trip couldn't read it from where he was, and then remembered that didn't matter. It was in Denari, anyway.

A single guard sat at the post, his back to them. Though the Klaxons were still ringing—at the same deafening volume—the guard looked, from what Trip could tell, completely uninterested. As Trip watched, he swiveled in his chair and punched in a series of commands on the console.

The video screens all changed.

The guard sat back in his chair and started to swivel in Trip's direction.

He ducked back around the corner.

To find Vonn holding out a mask to him. He and Royce were wearing them already.

"Why is he just sitting there? Why isn't he more worried about the Klaxons?" Trip whispered, taking the mask.

"Don't ask me. Don't ask me why the other four guards that are supposed to be at that post aren't there either. It's not our concern," Royce said. "Quickly, Tucker. Put it on."

Royce held a small glass ball in his hand. A green gas floated inside it.

Trip put on his mask and pulled it tight.

Royce stood then, stepped out into the corridor, and hurled the ball. Trip heard glass shatter, and a second later the sound of a body, hitting the floor.

The three of them ran to the guardpost.

Royce stopped before the hanging LCD screen.

"Prisoner manifest," he said. "It'll tell us which cells are occupied."

"How do we know who the Kota prisoners are?"

"If they're in this ward, they're from Kota base." He ran a finger down one side of the screen, and frowned. "No. This can't be right."

"Problem?" Trip stepped over the guard's unconscious body and up next to Royce.

He was still shaking his head. "No," he said again.

"What is it?"

"The cells. They're all empty."

He pointed to the screen. There were two columns of text. The right-hand one was identical all the way down. Royce was running his finger down the one on the left.

"Nineteen A. Nineteen B. Nineteen C . . ." He got to the bottom of the list, and then looked up at Trip. "Empty. Empty, empty, empty. They must have moved them."

"No," Trip said. "That can't be."

But it was true. It was the only explanation that fit. The reason why only one guard had been left on duty, and why he'd acted as if he had nothing to protect.

The Kota base prisoners were gone.

"It was all for nothing," Royce said, his voice numb with shock. "The entire mission. All of it."

Trip felt numb inside.

He looked down at his chronometer: 1440. Almost eight minutes since the Klaxons had started going off. Alpha team was good—he didn't doubt Royce's assertion for a second—but no matter how good they were, four men were not going to be able to hold off an entire prison full of guards for much longer.

It was time—past time—for them to get out of here.

Trip turned to go . . .

And something flashing at the bottom right-hand corner of the LCD screen caught his eye. An arrow, pointing to the right.

"Royce," Trip said. "What's that?"

Royce leaned closer. "The manifest continues on another screen."

"There are more cells?"

"Apparently so."

Trip felt a spark of excitement. It must have shown on his face.

Royce moved between him and the screen. "I know what you're thinking. I admire your persistence. But they've moved the prisoners, Tucker. We—"

"We don't know that for sure. Let's see that next screen."

Royce smiled.

"It's just like the marshal said. First you won't help, and now you won't stop helping."

Before Trip could respond, Royce raised his finger to the panel.

And hesitated.

"I'm not sure," he said, "that pressing buttons at random is such a good idea."

"We'll check the cells then," Trip said. "The ones that aren't listed on the first screen."

Royce frowned.

"We came all this way," Trip reminded him. "Let's not go home empty-handed unless we have to."

Royce looked down at his chronometer. Trip did the same.

1406.

"We take a minute," he said. "And a minute only. Till thirteen fifty. Then we meet back here. Agreed?"

Trip nodded. "Agreed."

Royce pointed to his right. "I'll go that way. Tucker, you down there." He pointed straight ahead. "Vonn, to the right. The manifest stops at cell Nineteen G. Check any numbers beyond that. Understood?"

Trip nodded. He turned to go—

And the Klaxons stopped.

Royce looked up at Trip.

"Thirty seconds," he said. "Thirteen seventy. Then we go."

"That's barely enough time to—"

"With or without you, Tucker," Royce said.

And he ran.

Trip shut his mouth and did the same.

The second he reached the first cell, Trip realized the flaw in Royce's plan.

He couldn't read Denari. The markings on the cells made no sense to him.

He stopped dead in his tracks, then, and started to laugh. It was either that or break down in tears.

Or keep going. He didn't need to read Denari to see if a cell was occupied, after all.

He ran, his head swiveling from right to left,

scanning cells on both sides of the corridor as he went.

The corridor ended in a T. Trip looked down at his chronometer.

1378.

Trip went left.

And stopped, almost immediately. In the cell to his immediate right, there was a man.

He cowered in the corner of the cell, mumbling to himself.

"Kota?" Trip shouted through the bars. "Are you from Kota?"

"Kota." The man wobbled to his feet. He was old—Lind's age, at least, white-haired, with a beard that stretched to his chest. Santa Claus, Trip thought at first.

Then the man stepped forward, into the light, and any resemblance to Santa was gone.

There were bruises on his arms and legs. His nose was bent to one side, in a way that suggested it had been broken, and the beard was dirty, and flecked with bits of food, or phlegm, or vomit. Or all three.

And his eyes . . .

They were vacant and completely devoid of intelligence.

No Santa Claus. Just another one of Sadir's victims.

But still—there was a chance . . .

"Are you from Kota?" Trip asked again. "Kota Base?"

The man blinked and looked up at Trip.

All at once his eyes widened.

"Lieutenant?" he said. "Lieutenant, my God, is that you?"

The man took a step toward him, and stumbled.

Trip reached through the bars and stopped his fall before he slammed into them.

"Easy," he told the old man. The red LEDs on the chronometer caught his attention.

1360.

He had to go. Now.

"I'm not your lieutenant," Trip said softly. "He'll be along in a minute. In the meantime—"

"I know who you are," the old man said. His grip on Trip's arm tightened. "Don't you know me? Don't you remember me, Trip?"

Trip. The man knew his name. How?

He stared at him.

All at once, something about the man was familiar.

The eyes, the face, the way he stood . . .

But the beard was wrong. Trip peeled it away, in his mind.

And almost staggered from the shock of recognition.

"Professor?" Trip's voice came out like a croak, but it was all that he could manage.

The old man was Victor Brodesser.

Thirteen

AT LONG LAST it was warm aboard *Eclipse*.

At least, it felt warm to Trip. Maybe it was just the *fossum* he'd been drinking—the second, already half-empty mug of which sat at his right hand, on the table before him. He could already tell he would need a third—whatever the stimulant in this drink was, it was nowhere near as strong as caffeine. And he was not going to be able to stay awake through this without chemical assistance.

It had been, in every way imaginable, a long and trying day.

Vonn and Royce, who had struggled through it with him, along with Marshals Kairn and Ella'jaren, and Guildsman Lind—as well as their command crews—had assembled in *Eclipse*'s briefing room to review the events of the last twenty-odd hours. A review of the mission that had quickly degenerated into an argument over what had gone wrong—and why.

"Our intelligence is no longer completely reliable," Kairn was saying. "Our sources are too far removed from the center of power, our knowledge of Sadir's organization and operations too imprecise. The lesson is clear. We must—"

"We're not certain this intelligence was faulty," Lind replied. "For all we know, the prisoners may have been moved only a day or two ago."

"Granted," Kairn replied. "But the conclusion we should draw is still the same."

"And that conclusion is . . . ?"

"We've been conducting our fight against Sadir like a war. Striking at his bases, harassing his ships where we can, seeking to defeat him militarily. But such a defeat of the enemy—to engage him on the field of battle, like an opposing army—it's no longer possible. It hasn't been possible, Guildsman, from the moment Sadir took power. His technological advantage is simply too great," Kairn said.

"Which—if you'll remember—is why we devised this plan," Lind began. "To reduce that technological disparity—"

"No, sir. Forgive the interruption, but we need to be realistic. There simply isn't time to overcome that technological advantage—even if the operation had been completely successful, and we'd succeeded in bringing Sadir's entire brain trust with us back to *Eclipse*—how long would it take to build even a half dozen ships? A year? Two? You've said it yourself, sir, on many occasions. We are months—weeks, perhaps—from being forced to surrender. Unless we change our strategy. Unless we acknowledge that we cannot gain ground against Sadir by striking conventional targets, with conventional weapons."

"What are you saying, Kairn?"

"I think you know, Guildsman."

"We will not resort to attacking civilian targets," Lind said, his face grim. "Or taking innocent lives."

"This is war," Kairn said. "People are going to die. The question is, will all of them be on our side, or are we going to make Sadir's people suffer as well?"

"We are all Denari, Kairn—something I would urge you never to forget," Lind said.

"I haven't forgotten it. Nor have I forgotten Alpha team—or the others who sacrificed their lives for this mission."

There was silence around the table.

"Kairn may be right, sir," Ella'jaren said hesitantly. "The weaponry we have may not be sufficient to confront the general's ships directly, but if we use alternate delivery mechanisms, pick locations where minimal force will achieve maximum psychological effect, we can still fight effectively—quite effectively, I would think—for some length of time."

"New Irla." Royce spoke for the first time now. "An explosion, there, in the heart of Sadir's compound—"

"New Irla is too well-guarded," Kairn said.

"One of the administrative centers on Burkhelt—Sadir's support there is weak, at best."

"The administrative centers are staffed by Burkhelters, Marshal," Lind said. "You expect to kill them and gain their support?"

Trip didn't recognize the names they were bandying about—places, most likely, from the context—and he certainly didn't want to get drawn into the middle of the conversation on how the Guild should conduct its war—but he did have something he wanted to say.

"Excuse me. I'm not sure it's my place to say something here—"

"You've earned your place at this table, Commander," Lind said. "Go ahead."

Trip nodded. "Thank you. I just wanted to point out one thing it seems everyone's overlooking."

Lind raised an eyebrow. "Which is?"

"We don't know yet how successful—or unsuccessful—the mission was."

"Ah." The Guildsman nodded. "Your Professor Brodesser?"

"Exactly."

He had filled in Lind and the others on the professor's history—who he was, the relationship between the two of them, the Daedalus Project, and the explosion that Trip had thought resulted in Brodesser's death, and that vessel's destruction.

Obviously he'd been wrong—Brodesser's presence in the cell was proof of that. Somehow, the professor had survived.

Brodesser's presence in the cell—indeed, in that wing of the prison—was most likely proof of something else as well.

That he had worked at Kota base. Had helped Sadir develop the weapons that had enabled him to overthrow the Presidium and seize power.

The question, obviously, was why.

There had been no time for that question, or any other, down in the prison, down on Vox 4. There had barely been time to shout for Royce and Vonn (who hadn't left without him, after all, despite what the chronometer had said), to get their help freeing Brodesser from his cell, and make the long journey back to *Eclipse.* A journey through mile after mile of tunnel, Trip bringing up the rear again, all the time looking back and expecting to see, at any moment, a troop of prison guards chasing after them.

But no one came. They made it safely to the cell-ship, and then on out to the debris field and open space—all of it a blur, a necessary blur, a rush to make their launch window and return safely to *Eclipse.* Brodesser had barely enough strength left to settle into his seat, whereupon he'd promptly collapsed. And once in the launch bay Trant had immediately taken the professor— suffering from exhaustion and malnutrition at the least, possibly the aftereffects of mental and physical torture as well—into her care and rushed him into the medical ward, where she was currently tending to him.

Despite pressure from both Trip and Lind, she had been unable to say exactly when he would be conscious and able to talk.

Of course, there had been other things Trip wanted to say to Trant—about the two of them, about Ferik—but they'd faded in importance, at least for that moment.

"Commander Tucker." Kairn shook his head. "Even if Brodesser were willing and able to do what you have not been—help us obtain a warp engine— the same argument I made applies. There simply isn't time to use that technology against Sadir."

"I think you're probably right about that," Trip said. "But think about this—if Brodesser did help Sadir for any length of time at all, he's going to know a lot of things about his ships. Their weaponry, defense systems, any possible weak points . . ."

He met Lind's eyes on the last phrase, and the Guildsman nodded thoughtfully. "Valuable information, I agree. We'll have to wait and see what the professor has to say."

"We can't wait forever," Kairn said. "Brodesser's escape has to have been discovered by now. They'll move quickly to close off any weaknesses in their defenses he might be privy to."

"True enough," Lind said. "But I suspect we have more time than you may think. Sadir obviously did not trust his prison staff with knowledge of who the prisoners were. The information will have to work its way up a long chain of command before it reaches someone who fully understands its implications."

Maybe, Trip thought. But even if Lind was right about no one at the facility knowing exactly who Brodesser was, he would bet that jailbreaks were not an everyday occurrence under Sadir's rule.

The sooner they talked to Brodesser, the better.

"What else can you tell us about the professor, Tucker?" Kairn asked. "Why would he help someone like Sadir?"

"I can't think it was voluntary," Trip said, remembering what Brodesser had looked like those first few seconds after Trip had found him. A shell of his former self. An unrecognizable shell.

There was little doubt in Trip's mind that he'd been tortured.

A loud buzz sounded. The com.

Kairn pressed a button on the panel next to him. "Briefing room. This is Marshall Kairn."

"Trant here, sir. Professor Brodesser is awake and ready to speak with you."

"Very well. We'll be down shortly."

Kairn closed the channel, then stood.

"We'll continue the debriefing tomorrow. Same time. For the moment . . ."

He turned to Trip.

"Commander Tucker. Guildsman Lind. If you'd care to accompany me . . ."

"Wild horses," Trip began, getting to his feet as well.

But he stopped short of completing the thought.

He was too tired to explain colloquialisms right now.

He settled for a "lead the way" and followed Kairn out the door.

Brodesser was the only patient in the ward.

He lay on a cot halfway down the right-hand side of the wall.

Trant sat at his bedside, holding his wrist in one hand, looking at a sensor in her other.

She avoided looking up at Trip. Was she still embarrassed about what had—or rather, hadn't—happened in the cargo bay earlier? Just as well, he decided. He had a lot to say to her, and now didn't seem like the time—or the place—to start that conversation.

The professor caught sight of Trip and smiled. "Tucker."

There was color in his cheeks now. A trace, at least, of that familiar sparkle in his eye. The transformation, in such a short span of time, was incredible.

"Professor." Trip smiled as well. "You look a million times better."

"Thank the miracle worker here," Brodesser said, nodding at Trant.

"You have a very healthy constitution, Professor," she replied. "Despite what you've been through."

From the grim expression that flitted across her face then, Brodesser had obviously shared some of those unpleasant details with her. Trip wondered exactly what sort of hell Sadir had put the professor through.

"Guildsman Lind," Brodesser said, peering around Trip. "I recognize you—though of course we've never met."

The two shook hands.

"This is Marshall Kairn," Lind said, nodding in the officer's direction. "He commands this vessel—and devised the rescue mission that freed you as well."

"Marshall," Brodesser said. "You have my eternal thanks for getting me out of that hellhole."

"You're welcome, of course. But you should be thanking Tucker here—and the two men who were with him."

"I feel gratitude enough to circle round the entire ship, sir. Have no fear."

"I hate to bother you so short a time after your ordeal, but I'm afraid I have no choice," Kairn said. "This is the first time we've ever had a chance to talk to someone who has been so heavily involved with Sadir's weapons program, and—"

"Excuse me." Brodesser held up a hand. "I wonder if—before we begin our conversation—I could have a word alone with Commander Tucker?"

Lind and Kairn exchanged a look.

"Professor," Lind began. "I understand your desire to talk to Tucker, of course. But time is of the essence here. Some of the information you have—it's entirely possible that—"

"Five minutes is all I'm asking, Guildsman. At which point I will be happy to answer as many questions as you have, and to share with you everything I know about the general and his organization. Even if I need to take stimulants from Doctor Trant here to stay awake long enough to do so."

Everyone laughed. Even Lind.

The Guildsman stepped forward.

"Five minutes, Professor. We'll hold you to it. Marshal?"

Lind touched Kairn's arm then, and turned the obviously reluctant man toward the door.

Trant rose. "I'll leave you alone as well. But first . . ."

She walked to the far end of the room and came back with a thermos. She set it down in front of Brodesser.

Trip could smell it even before she lifted the cover. *Seela*. The drink she had tried to give him the other night.

The one that had almost made him sick.

"Drink as much as you can," Trant told Brodesser. "We'll see about some food later."

"Thank you, Doctor."

Trant nodded, and then turned to face Trip.

He met her gaze head on. Married.

"Commander," she said. "Try not to tax his strength."

"I won't."

"Good." She looked as if she had more to say. Trip supposed that she did.

"Commander," she began hesitantly.

"We'll talk later," Trip told her.

She nodded, and left the room.

Trip turned back to Brodesser, who was focused on the *seela* he'd been given. He was drinking it down like he'd never tasted liquid in his life.

The metallic smell was so strong Trip almost gagged.

"God that's good," Brodesser said when he finally came up for air. Another thing Trip suddenly remembered about him—the professor had an appetite to beat the band. On more than one occasion, Trip had watched him polish off two two-centimeters-thick steaks and go back for seconds.

At last, Brodesser pushed the cup to one side and turned to Trip.

"So," he said. "Commander, is it?"

"That's right. Chief engineer aboard *Enterprise*—she's the first ship warp fire to come out of the NX program."

"Henry Archer's engine?"

"Yes, sir. His son—Jonathan—is the captain."

Brodesser shook his head. "Archer's son. I don't think I ever met him, but God knows Henry talked about him enough. . . ." His eyes glazed over for a second, as if he were looking into that past, then quickly cleared. "But what's going on, Trip? Why are you here, with the Guild? Where is your ship?"

Trip had to laugh. "I was going to ask you the same questions, sir."

"You can stop with the *sirs*, Trip. *Daedalus* was a long, long time ago."

"True enough." Trip hesitated. "Sure. Professor."

"Professor? Not Victor?" It was Brodesser's turn to smile. "I'm that imposing a figure, am I?"

"No. Victor, then."

The whole situation suddenly struck Trip as completely unreal. He was talking with a man he'd thought dead for close to fifteen years, and all they could find to talk about was what they should call each other.

He quickly filled in Brodesser on what had happened to *Enterprise*—why he was here.

And then it was his turn to ask questions.

"What happened, sir?" He leaned forward. "Where is *Daedalus*? The crew—Captain Duvall, Chief Cooney—where are they? How can you be alive? That explosion—"

"The explosion." Brodesser sighed. "The best

place to start, I suppose. Since we had you to thank for it."

"Me?"

"You." Brodesser offered a thin smile. "Not to imply that you were the cause of it. On the contrary—you were the reason we survived. None of us would have lived through that moment if not for you."

"I still don't understand."

"The cascade reaction." Brodesser's eyes caught his and held them. "You were right. We should have held the streams longer."

Trip suddenly felt nauseated.

"Oh, God." He shut his eyes, and it all came rushing back to him again. The night before the launch, being summoned to Brodesser's quarters, the professor informing him of their decision to slow the reaction down, his own hesitancy about whether or not they'd slowed it enough.

Five percent more, he recalled. That was the proper safety margin, he'd calculated. He hadn't fought for it. All these years he'd wondered if that had anything to do with what had happened.

And now here it was, proof that it had.

"What's wrong?" Brodesser asked.

Trip told him.

"If I'd hadn't held my tongue that night," he began, "if I had spoken my mind—"

"It wouldn't have made a difference," the professor interrupted. "Cooney was furious at me for damping down the reaction at all—said you were a wet-behind-the-ears, arrogant little snit who had absolutely zero deep-space experience and we had no reason at all to listen to your opinion about such a critical decision."

"Cooney said that, huh?"

"And a little more."

It wasn't hard to believe. Cooney had never been shy about expressing his opinions. *Daedalus*'s chief engineer was a big man, imposing in every sense of the word. Trip had less to do with him than many of the other engineering staff, but back then, the thought of a confrontation with the man—which was what every encounter with Cooney seemed to turn into, the man simply didn't know the meaning of the word *conversation*—had been enough, more than once, to stop him from making the walk from the ops center to *Daedalus* itself and composing an e-mail message instead.

"You weren't responsible for the explosion, Trip," Brodesser said quietly. "The fault lies with me. As does the responsibility for everything that happened afterward."

The professor took a breath before continuing.

"We knew something was wrong as soon as the initiation sequence began, Cooney and I. Duvall did, too, I think." Duvall being Monique Duvall, *Daedalus*'s captain, older sister of the Duvall who had ended up being the first to crack the warp three barrier, several years later, in the NX program.

Dave Stern

Duvall being, as well, a very close friend of Jonathan Archer's.

"The ship felt wrong, she said. We were at T minus fifteen seconds, and she started to make noises about calling off the launch. I wouldn't hear of it, of course. My big moment in the sun."

All at once, Trip frowned. He had a vivid picture in his mind of the scene on *Daedalus*'s bridge those last few seconds before launch, before everything went to hell. As far as he could recall, Duvall had seemed not the slightest bit concerned.

But Brodesser had been there, on the bridge next to her. Trip hadn't.

"And then we launched," Brodesser said.

"Tried to launch, you mean. That's when the drive exploded."

"No." Brodesser shook his head. "The drive worked, exactly as it was supposed to. We warped space. But the cascade reaction was too powerful. Out of control. At T plus ten seconds the warp field destabilized—violently."

Brodesser shuddered with the remembered memory.

"We lost the impulse deck, Trip. Gone, in a flash. Acker, Jerrod, Yermish—all of them vanished in an instant. Twenty-five crewmen, in all."

Brodesser was silent a moment.

"They didn't even have time to scream. Nothing. Later—when we'd managed to shut down the engine—we realized we couldn't even be sure

208

when the deck had ripped free. I hoped"—he looked up at Trip—"I hoped it might have happened in those initial few seconds. That you'd managed to recover the wreckage somehow—give those families some closure." He managed a small smile. "I can see from your eyes, though—you didn't."

"No, sir." Trip shook his head. They hadn't managed to recover anything from *Daedalus*—the explosion had atomized the entire ship and every member of the crew. At least, that's what the prevailing wisdom had been—at the time.

The prevailing wisdom obviously was wrong.

"The field destabilized, and you shut down the engine. And then . . ." Trip prompted.

"We set about making repairs. Lost two more crewmen doing that—Cox and Brigida. An EVA accident. I had argued against them going EVA, though at that point in the mission, as you can probably guess, my voice carried very little weight."

Trip sighed. "I'm sorry, sir."

"So was I. But I have to say—in a way, I was a little relieved to have Duvall and the others making all the decisions. It gave me a chance to relax. To clear my mind. It wasn't the end of the world—at least, I didn't think so at the time. My mind was occupied elsewhere, obviously."

"Trying to figure out what went wrong."

"That, of course. And to figure out if there was a way back through the anomaly."

The anomaly.

Trip saw it in an instant.

"You caused it," he said. "*Daedalus* going to warp—you somehow caused it."

"Yes. When the warp field destabilized—it ripped a hole in space, Trip. And I thought—not that we could go back through, obviously, the ship was too badly damaged to manage that—but I thought we might manage to get a message through, use the subspace node we'd created to send for help."

Trip saw something else then, as well.

Just as he'd reminded Captain Archer, K'Pellis had been in *Daedalus*'s initial destination matrix. That was why they'd ended up here.

"But you weren't able to do it," he said. "To send that message."

"No. We never got the chance."

"What happened?"

"What happened?" Brodesser looked genuinely surprised to hear the question. "Can't you guess?"

And all at once then, Trip could. "Sadir," he said.

Brodesser nodded. "Sadir. And Duvall."

Trip frowned. "Duvall? What does she have to with it?"

"Everything." The professor shifted in his cot, propped up the pillows behind him. "But I think our five minutes are up. We should call in Lind, and the marshal. They'll want to hear this as well."

Fourteen

RATHER THAN TRYING to conduct a conversation in the cramped medical ward, Brodesser suggested the four of them go for a walk.

"After so long, being locked up in that little cell—it would do me some good to stretch. Take a short stroll through your ship."

"Make sure that it is short," Trant—who'd been waiting outside with Lind and Kairn—told the professor. "Your strength—your stamina—is nowhere near where it should be. If you feel even the slightest bit weak, come back immediately."

"It will be short, Doctor. I can assure you of that," Kairn said. "Time is of the essence." From the look on his face, he would just as soon start firing off questions at Brodesser from where he stood.

Trip helped the professor stand then, and walk to the door of the ward. There, he pried Trip's arm loose.

"I'm not ready for a wheelchair yet, Commander," he said, and stepped out into the corridor, where Lind and Kairn were already waiting.

Trip was about to join them when Trant stepped in front of him, blocking his way.

"Commander Tucker," she said. "Could I have a moment?"

"Now is not exactly the best time for—"

"It will be quick. I promise you."

Trip was about to tell her it would have to wait when Brodesser spoke up.

"Go ahead, Trip. I can use the time to fill them in—" he gestured to Lind and Kairn "—on what we've talked about so far."

He looked at Brodesser then, and suddenly wondered how much of the subtext of his previous conversation with Trant the professor had picked up. Probably all of it, Trip decided. Brodesser was as perceptive as he was brilliant.

"All right," Trip said. "I'll catch up."

Trant stepped past him and into the ward. She closed the door to the corridor.

"Doctor," Trip said, "what's on your mind?"

"A lot of things." She met his gaze head-on. "First of all . . ."

I should have told you I was married, he filled in, silently prompting her.

"I'm still working on what happened to Hoshi."

Trip tried not to look surprised. "Hoshi?"

She nodded. "Hoshi. What specific compound

in the *pisarko* could have caused the allergic reaction. You've had no symptoms?"

"Not unless you count exhaustion."

"No. At least not in your case. Considering." She frowned. "I will want to run those additional tests we discussed—a more thorough blood-chemistry workup. That may point me in the right direction."

"Hoshi's all right, though?"

"Resting comfortably." Trant nodded toward a closed door at the other end of the medical ward. "I gave her a mild sedative. She should sleep until morning."

"Good."

"Second," she began, "is the fact that . . ."

I'm married, Trip supplied again.

And again, found that he'd guessed wrong.

"Professor Brodesser has been subject to a lot during these last few years. While he was in captivity."

She walked back to the bunk Brodesser had been lying on, and picked up a folder. His medical chart.

She turned to Trip and began reading from it.

"First of all, he's severely undernourished. I found evidence of scurvy—"

"Scurvy?" Trip shook his head. Scurvy? In the twenty-second century? Scurvy?

"Scurvy," Trant repeated, and kept reading, "as well as scarring on one arm that suggests the sereus manta virus."

Trip frowned. "Sereus manta? I don't—"

"The closest analogue to a human disease—according to your diagnostic sensor—is smallpox." She hesitated. "Judging from the unnaturally localized nature of the scarring, I have to conclude the virus was deliberately transmitted."

"Biological experiments."

She nodded. "Multiple lesions on his chest, trace evidence of second- and third-degree burns—"

"He was tortured."

"Repeatedly. Over a number of years."

Trip shook his head. "I think I've heard enough."

"Not yet." She took a breath and continued. "There's one other thing you need to know about. Evidence I found of a very specific kind of torture."

Trant set down the folder then and walked across the ward to a workstation. She sat down and powered it up.

"Sadir's doctors," she said, keying in a series of instructions, "have—"

She stopped and shook her head. "No. Not doctors. I won't dignify them with that title. Sadir's scientists," she resumed, keying in her instructions, "have developed a very effective technique for extracting information from . . . reluctant prisoners. It involves direct electrical stimulation of the cortex—the triggering of specific memories—in combination with a series of drug treatments. Powerful hallucinogens. Depressants. The subject, in effect, relives the past, and in doing so, provides the scientists with the information they seek."

Trip shuddered.

Trant keyed in a final set of instructions, and the workstation display filled with an image. A negative—like an X ray—of a human skull.

She manipulated the controls and spun the skull on the screen, till it faced away from them.

A dark line, a break in the bone, ran from the top of the cranium to just above the base of his skull. There was a second, smaller break in the bone, just beneath it. The dot, under the exclamation point.

Trip recognized it immediately.

"Ferik has this same scar," he said.

"That's right."

"This technique—they used it on him?"

She nodded.

"On Ferik. And on the Professor," she said. "The long-term effects of this interrogation method are—disabling. Degenerative. The patient's thought processes become disorganized. Their memories—unreliable. And they are—occasionally—subject to violent mood swings. Any information you and the Guildsman, and Marshal Kairn, receive from Brodesser—you have to evaluate it in that light. You understand?"

Trip nodded. He understood that. He understood something else too. It was time for him to talk.

And again, there was no sense in beating around the bush.

"You should have let me know you were married."

Trant's gaze darted to him, and just as quickly, away. He saw surprise and shame in her eyes.

"Royce told me."

"Noble of him."

"You should have."

"You're right." She threw up her hands. "I should have."

"Why didn't you?"

The second the words were out of his mouth, Trip wanted them back. He knew why she hadn't. Because he would have left her alone.

She looked up and met his eyes.

"He's been like that for fourteen years," she said. "The walking dead. What am I supposed to do?"

"It's not his fault."

"No. It's not mine either." She sighed. "I sound like a monster, don't I?" She shook her head helplessly.

Trip wanted to go to her. No, he wanted to say, You're not a monster.

But he held his tongue. He stood motionless.

"I'm sorry," he finally said.

"So am I." Trant nodded to the door. "That minute is long past. You should go."

Trip nodded. "Maybe we can talk later."

"About what?"

Trip couldn't think of an answer to that.

So he left the room.

Brodesser was standing in the middle of the passageway, his head cocked to one side, listening to something. Lind and Kairn flanking him, looking puzzled.

"Professor?" Trip asked.

Brodesser shook his head and held a finger to his lips—*shhh*.

He stood without moving another few seconds before straightening.

"Just listening to the engines," he explained. "Cooney used to say that he could tell the difference between engines by the way they sounded. I'm trying to determine if he was right." He looked up at Kairn. "Fusion reactor?"

"That's right."

"Sounds in good working order."

"We have Commander Tucker to thank for that," Kairn explained.

"Glad to see you haven't lost your touch, Commander. I'm not sure I could do the same anymore. It's been a long while since I worked on any sort of engine. In my cell, to pass the time, I used to take apart an imaginary drive assembly—put it back together. Cid, mostly, of course. Think about how I might approach it differently, next time. If there is a next time."

Brodesser looked up then, and smiled. "Shall we?" he asked.

The four of them started off down the corridor together. Trip in front, taking Brodesser's arm despite the older man's protests, Kairn and Lind a step behind.

"*Daedalus*," Trip said. "We were talking about *Daedalus*."

Brodesser nodded. While Trip had been talking to the doctor, he'd brought Lind and Kairn up to speed on the story. To the point where they were preparing to send a message to Starfleet.

"Which is when the general showed up," the Guildsman supplied.

"General Sadir. We all thought he was the answer to our prayers. A gift from heaven."

"He was friendly, I take it?"

"He was the picture of welcome." Brodesser clasped his hands behind his back and quickened his pace. It was as if, all at once, the rest of them weren't there. Eyes glued to the floor, he seemed suddenly to be charging headlong into the memories he was recounting.

Or trying his best to run away from them.

"He gave a long speech about the honor he'd been given, to be the first Denari to receive extraterrestrial visitors. The importance of interspecies cultural exchange, and intragalactic commerce, how much they desired to help us in what was clearly an hour of great need. Lies, all of it—and we bought in just the same. All of us, except Cooney, that is. He didn't like Sadir—or trust him—from the very beginning." The professor shook his head. "If only we'd listened to him—blasted those ships out of the sky. Everything would have been different."

"I don't think that response was in the mission profile, if I remember right," Trip said.

Brodesser smiled. "No. I suppose not. Though the first contact guidelines we were given were a bit—hazy, at best."

Still are, Trip almost said, but held his tongue.

"We spent two solid days exchanging messages before we were able to understand each other. I don't think Sadir could have slept more than two hours through that entire time—he was always there, on the viewscreen, or the comlink—always watching us. Filtering what we learned about your planet—about the Guild, and the Presidium, his exact role in the government." Brodesser shook his head. "My God. What fools we were."

Lind spoke up. "No more fools than we, Professor. I sat with the man—at a peace conference, for God's sake—the day before he mutinied. The day before!" The Guildsman shook his head. "And I knew nothing of what was about to happen. I'm lucky to be alive."

"I suppose I should consider myself lucky as well, then," Brodesser said, sounding as if he felt anything but.

"That third day," he continued, "Sadir sent over a courier ship supposedly loaded with food and medical supplies. We opened the launch bay, and got two dozen soldiers instead. And after that . . . there was nothing any of us could do."

"You fought him?" Kairn asked.

"We tried. But we were scientists—explorers. Sadir and his men were trained soldiers. It was no contest." Brodesser shook his head. "He put us all into the cargo bay for the night—the forty-three of us left, after the accident, and the explosion. We all agreed—no help for Sadir, no matter what. The next morning he killed five people. Pulled them out at random, murdered them right in front of us. And then he did it again—the next morning. And the next, and the next. And then . . ."

"Why?" Lind asked.

Trip knew the answer before Brodesser opened his mouth. He suspected the Guildsman—and Kairn—knew as well.

"The warp drive," Brodesser said. "He wanted warp drive."

"You gave it to him," Kairn said. There was no pity in his eyes. "God forgive you, you gave it to him."

Brodesser nodded. "We did. And you're right. God forgive us."

All four men were silent a moment.

Trip had known that admission was coming, had known it from the moment that he'd absorbed the full impact of finding Brodesser in the prison back on Vox 4. Yet to hear those words from his lips . . .

This changed everything, he realized. All his

concerns about technological contamination, all T'Pol's lectures about noninterference went out the window. They were irrelevant now—completely beside the point. This wasn't just the Guild's war, or even his. It was Starfleet's—if Brodesser hadn't given Sadir warp technology, there would be no battle. The Presidium would still be in power.

Trip suddenly realized something else.

"Sadir's ships, Professor," he said. "That's not an ion drive they use?"

"No. Of course not. Standard matter-antimatter engine. The *Daedalus* technology is unstable. I know that now."

Trip frowned again. "But, sir—if you'd given them *Daedalus*'s drive instead, they might never have developed a working warp vessel. This whole war might never have happened."

"No. I'm sorry." Brodesser shook his head. "I'm not making myself clear. I didn't give Sadir his warp engine."

"I don't understand. How could he have built one without you?"

"A matter-antimatter drive? All the information he needed was in *Daedalus*'s library, Trip. There for the taking."

Trip shook his head. "It was there, but he wouldn't have known what to look for, or how to access it, if you hadn't helped him."

"He didn't need me," Brodesser said, suddenly

sounding both impatient and tired. "He had the captain to help him. He had Duvall."

"Had Duvall?" Trip was confused. "What do you mean? Are you telling me Duvall surrendered?"

"No. Not surrendered." Brodesser shook his head, with a resigned smile. "After Sadir's attack—after that first day of executions—she asked to meet with him. We didn't see her again after that—not for a long time. I thought she was dead."

"He took her prisoner."

"No. We saw her again—after Sadir took us to Kota."

"I don't understand."

"We were in our cells one night," Brodesser continued. "Doing I don't know what. Reading. Relaxing. All of a sudden—there were soldiers everywhere. Pushing us to our feet. Standing us at attention. Like an inspection. Which they used to run every few months. Just to keep us on our toes. Just to make sure we weren't planning anything, I think.

"Except this time, instead of the base commander, Sadir strolled in with her."

Trip was frowning. No. He couldn't believe it.

"It's true," Brodesser said. "It was Captain Duvall. Dressed up like a queen. I didn't even recognize her. Not until she spoke."

"You're not serious," Trip said. "You can't be serious."

Brodesser nodded. "They were together, Trip. Like a couple."

"No." He looked up at Lind first, and then Kairn, both of whom wore the exact same shocked expression that Trip was sure was on his face as well. "What did she say to you?"

"Nothing." Brodesser smiled one last time. "She didn't talk to any of us. She just wanted to point us out . . . to their son."

Trip's mouth dropped open. "Their son? Her and Sadir?"

Brodesser nodded.

There was nothing Trip could think of to say.

The professor grew tired.

Kairn suggested they grab something to eat in the mess and continue their talk there. All agreed—save Trip, who simply followed, still in somewhat of a daze.

Duvall? And Sadir? He would want independent confirmation—it was just too much to swallow. He hadn't spent much time with her while working on *Daedalus*—command crew and engineering did not interact all that frequently on the project, especially during the last few weeks—but on the few occasions when they had worked together, she'd struck him as remarkably competent. Remarkably professional—the prototypical Starfleet captain. In a way, of course, she had been—*Daedalus* had launched more than a decade before *Enterprise*.

Trip felt he knew her best, though, by reputation—by what Archer had told him, over the years, about her. A. G. Robinson times two. An amazing pilot. An inspiring commander. The way the captain sometimes talked about her, Trip wondered why Archer didn't put up a shrine to her in his ready room.

He could not believe the Monique Duvall whom Archer had lionized was capable of doing what Brodesser had accused her of.

There had to be something else going on, Trip decided. Some plan she had in mind—though if that were the case, she was certainly taking an awful long time to implement it.

He wanted more details from Brodesser—about everything. Not just what Duvall had said, and done, but about Kota. What technology they had given Sadir there, what weaknesses it might have. . . . There were other questions, as well, that needed answering. What had happened to the rest of *Daedalus*'s crew, and the ship itself? El Cid?

From the determined looks on both Kairn and Lind's faces, they wanted answers as well.

The mess was up two decks, just past the passenger quarters.

As they approached the door—hard to miss, as people were walking in and out of the room constantly—Trip wrinkled his nose.

That metallic smell was back.

Or perhaps it had never truly gone away. It was

certainly true that on almost every occasion when he had a moment of peace, a moment to himself, he noticed the odor. He should let Trant know—perhaps there was something in the atmosphere inside *Eclipse* that was hitting him the wrong way.

Inside, the mess was huge—the size of one of the launch bays aboard *Enterprise*, and then some. Ceilings not as tall, but that in no way made the room feel crowded.

There were tables—most of them empty—along the far wall, near what Trip assumed was the kitchen, judging by the constant foot traffic coming in and out of it, and a long, low row of portholes—observation windows, though not much bigger than a seat cushion—along the near one.

Kairn led them toward the far wall. The tables, and the kitchen.

The metallic smell grew stronger the closer they got. It was overpowering.

Trip took a breath and wobbled on his feet.

Kairn grabbed his arm, righted him.

"Commander?"

"Give me a minute," Trip said

They were all—even Brodesser—looking at him with concern.

"Are you all right, Trip?"

He pinched the bridge of his nose and took a deep breath. Through his mouth, not his nose. That was better—the smell noticeably less present.

"I think so," he said. "Sorry. Just the smell in here. Hitting me the wrong way."

"Smell?" The three men looked at each other, and all made the same face. A confused face.

Kairn smiled then. "You have a sensitive nose, Tucker."

"I suppose."

"We can find someplace else to talk."

"No, that's all right." Trip shook his head. "I'm fine now."

Not looking entirely convinced, Kairn led them to a corner table.

They sat.

The marshal started in at once on Brodesser—asking him questions about Sadir's ships and weaponry. From the frustrated look on his face, he wasn't getting the answers he hoped for.

Trip tried to listen but had a hard time paying attention. He felt very strange indeed.

Light-headed. And hot. Not exactly feverish, but . . .

He wondered if he should go to Trant. Or call for her.

No. He hadn't slept for close to twenty hours. Or eaten anything substantial in that span of time, either.

The ration packs. He should get in the habit of carrying one with him at all times, he realized.

He was starting to feel dizzy again. A little delirious, even.

He tried to focus in on the conversation going on around him.

"You have to understand," Brodesser was saying. "Kota was years and years ago. They've been at war. Few of the exact systems we designed will still be in use."

"Nothing about the ships themselves?" Kairn asked. "Any blind spots in sensor coverage—weak points in their shields? Anything?"

Brodesser shook his head. "I'm sorry. I wish I could help."

"Leave aside the ships a moment, Marshal," Lind said. "Talk to us about the ground-based weaponry, Professor. The Kresh's defensive systems, for example. How do—"

"I had little to do with those, I'm afraid." Brodesser sighed. "I know it may sound . . . disingenuous of me, but I tried not to work on weapons systems. Even defensive ones. My work there, as on a number of other networks, involved interface design. . . ."

His voice trailed off.

His eyes widened.

"My God," he said. "I don't know why I didn't think of that before."

Kairn and Lind looked at each other.

"Sir?" Trip asked.

"Communications," Brodesser said. "I wrote the coding algorithms for Sadir's entire communications network."

227

Lind shook his head. "I don't understand."

Brodesser started to explain it to him. But Trip didn't need to listen.

The professor's realization boiled down to this:

Brodesser had written the codes Sadir's transmitters used to scramble their messages. The Guild could now unscramble those communiqués, listen in on every single one of Sadir's transmissions, and the general would never know it.

Trip smiled. His stomach rolled over.

"If you all will excuse me," he said, getting to his feet, "I'm going to—"

Go back to my quarters, he was about to say.

But instead, he stumbled and almost fell.

"Commander." Kairn was up in a second and had his arm. "We'd better get you down to Doctor Trant, I think."

He was right, Trip realized.

The dizzy feeling was back. He felt feverish again.

"Sure," Trip said. "Let's go."

He took a step forward, Kairn holding tight to his elbow, and swayed on his feet.

Then he collapsed, and everything went black.

Fifteen

TRIP DREAMT of *Daedalus*.

It was the morning of the launch. Duvall and Brodesser were together, on the bridge. Laughing. Not at all nervous about the test to come. Nor was anyone else, apparently. Cooney was holding forth on the pros and cons of the ion drive to a group of eager young engineers, and Doctor D'Lay—my God, he'd forgotten all about D'Lay for fourteen years; the old man had the misfortune to come out of retirement just in time to get blown to pieces—D'Lay was walking around the bridge with a bag full of ration packs, handing them out to everyone, whether or not they wanted them.

"*Seela* or *fossum*," the old man called out. "*Seela* or *fossum*."

Brodesser walked past him, then, and down onto the main deck. He strode over to the helm officer—who for some reason was Travis, and not Westerberg, who had piloted *Daedalus* in real life.

Dave Stern

"Warp eight, Mister Mayweather," Brodesser said. "Let her rip."

Duvall walked up next to him.

"You heard him, Travis. Let her rip."

Mayweather smiled. "Aye, Captain. Aye, Professor."

He punched in a command on the console, and the engines began to whine.

The lift door burst open, and Trip walked out.

"The cascade protocol," he said. "We've got to slow it down!"

No one paid any attention to him.

"The protocol," Trip said again, louder this time, because he had to compete with the whine of the engines, which were also growing louder.

And still no one listened. He spun around the bridge in frustration.

Suddenly he—the Trip watching—became the Trip in the dream. The frustration he felt trebled.

He ran straight to Brodesser.

"Professor," he said. "You've got to listen! The cascade reaction—"

Brodesser shook his head. "Later, Trip. It can wait. Right now I've got a flight to catch."

The lift doors opened, revealing the cell-ship, which had been somehow squeezed inside.

Someone had written in big letters across the viewscreen:

230

KOTA BASE OR BUST

"See you in fourteen years, Trip!" Brodesser yelled, and hopped in the cell-ship, which promptly cloaked and vanished from sight.

"Captain," Trip said, turning to Duvall. "You've got to listen, at least. Help me—"

She had changed clothes, somehow.

Instead of a Starfleet uniform, Duvall was wearing an evening dress. A long, red velvet gown. She had a crown on her head.

"Is this about the menu?" she asked. "If I told you once, I told you a thousand times. Let them eat cake."

"No." Trip shook his head. "This is not about the menu, this is about the ion drive. Captain, you've got to . . ."

"Captain?" She shook her head. "I'm not the captain anymore. He's the captain."

She pointed behind Trip, toward the center of the bridge.

He turned and saw General Sadir sitting in the command chair, a frown on his face.

"Tucker." Sadir got to his feet. "You shouldn't be here—didn't we talk about this already? Non-interference?"

The general, Trip noticed, had pointed ears.

"Don't tell me we need to jog your memory again, Trip."

Sadir pulled a hypo out of a medkit that looked remarkably like *Enterprise*'s. Then he smiled, showing a mouthful of sharp white teeth, and advanced.

Trip stepped backward, trying to get away.

But his feet got tangled up with each other and he fell.

When he looked up, Sadir was looming over him. "Relax," he said. "Think happy-pill thoughts."

The hypo came down.

Trip shut his eyes.

And when he opened them again, he was in *Eclipse*'s medical ward, lying on a cot. The lights were dimmed—ship's night.

Trant stood two bunks down, her back to him, leaning over an empty cot—the one Brodesser had been in, Trip realized. She looked back and forth from the display next to the cot to a chart she had in her hand, frowning.

He blinked away the last remnants of his very strange dream and dragged himself into a sitting position. His arm muscles were like jelly. He felt wrung out, dehydrated. Like a dishrag.

He was wearing a hospital nightgown.

He couldn't help but wonder who'd changed him into it.

Trant turned, saw he was awake, and smiled. "Commander Tucker."

She crossed to his bedside. "Feeling better?"

"Better. Not a hundred percent yet, but better. What happened to me?"

"The same thing that happened to Hoshi, I'm afraid."

"An allergic reaction?"

"I believe so." She held up the chart in her hand. "I've been doing a detailed workup on Ensign Hoshi's immune system. She has sensitivities to a number of fairly common substances—allergies, for lack of a better word. It seems you may share those sensitivities."

"No." Trip shook his head. "Not possible. I've never been allergic to anything in my entire life."

"In your world." She smiled. "This, unfortunately, is not your world, Commander."

True enough. Trip sighed. "How long was I asleep?"

"The better part of a day." She glanced at a display behind him. "Almost nineteen hours."

"Nineteen hours?" He shook his head. "I should feel better if I've been asleep for nineteen hours."

"Your system is still out of balance. You'll need to take it easy for some time yet."

The way he felt, that was not going to be a problem.

"Thirsty?"

He nodded.

"I would imagine so."

She went away, then, and came back with a glass of water. He drank it down, greedily.

Trant pulled up a chair and sat down next to the bunk.

"If you have the strength . . . I'd like to ask you a few questions about what happened."

"Go right ahead. It's not my voice that's tired."

So she did—asked him to describe for her, in as much detail as he could remember, what he was feeling before he collapsed. She listened intently. When he got to the part about the metallic smell, she stopped him.

"And you've noticed this smell before?"

"Several times."

"When, exactly?"

He told her.

"The *seela*," she said, nodding when he'd finished. "That makes sense."

"What makes sense?"

"*Seela* is brewed from a plant of the same name—one which is also a fairly common food ingredient. That's why you smelled it so strongly up in the mess. But a metallic smell?" She shook her head. "That seems strange. Can you describe it in a little more detail?"

"I don't know—it smells like metal. When you're trimming a conduit, or a relay to size, and—"

Trant was smiling.

"I don't suppose you do a lot of that."

"No," she said. "But I get the idea."

She was a silent a moment, thinking.

"What?"

"Just trying to remember a few things from my studies. Chemistry." She frowned, and stood.

"I took the liberty of drawing blood while you were asleep, Commander. I'll do the same sort of workup on your immune system as on Hoshi's. I've also scheduled some time on the ship's electron microscope—I think that may give us a few more clues about what exactly is going on here. In the meantime, I would stay completely away from our foods. And the mess, obviously."

"All right. When can I get out of here?"

"Whenever you feel strong enough."

They looked at each other a moment.

For the first time since he'd woken in the ward, Trip was suddenly all too aware of Trant—not as a doctor, but as a woman.

A married woman, he reminded himself.

"I need my uniform," he said brusquely.

"I'll get it for you. In a minute. But there's something else I need to talk to you about first."

She nodded to the closed door at the end of the ward.

Trip's heart thudded in his chest.

Hoshi.

She was sleeping peacefully. At least that's what it looked like to Trip.

If he discounted the sensors and tubes attached to her.

"It's a low-grade coma—by that I mean there's a chance she could come out of it at any time."

"I don't understand. She was fine, you said."

Trant nodded. "I don't understand it entirely, either. But as I said—there are a number of fairly common substances she seems to be allergic to. Her system has—for lack of a better word—shut down to concentrate on fighting against them."

"Well—" He shook his head. "What do we do?"

"The first thing we do is find exactly what is triggering this response—which specific chemical compounds are provoking her system to react. Once I know that, I'll know better how to fight it. That's why the electron microscope is necessary—it will enable me to review these reactions at the molecular level."

"And you're doing this when?"

"In a few hours."

"Why not sooner?"

She sighed. "The microscope has to be sterilized and recalibrated for medical work. Trust me, this is a priority."

"All right." Trip looked down at Hoshi. "Just keep me posted."

"I will. And I want you to check in here every four hours, at least. I'll want to make sure there's no reaction building in your system, either."

He nodded.

There was a knock on the door.

Trip turned, just in time to see Victor Brodesser enter the room.

The professor had shaved off the beard. Cleaned himself up. He was wearing a simple one-piece coverall that reminded Trip of the old work uniforms they used on the Daedalus Project.

He looked almost exactly as he had, in fact, fourteen years ago—a little thinner, for sure, a few more wrinkles in the face, but that same spark in his eyes, smile on his face . . .

A very broad smile on his face, in fact.

"Commander. Good to see you up and about." He looked past Trip to Trant. "Doctor. How is Hoshi?"

"Unchanged."

Brodesser nodded and turned back to Trip. "And you?"

"Ninety-five percent, I'd say," Trip said. "I was just coming to find you, sir."

"And I you. I've got news I'm sure you'll want to hear."

"Sir?"

"It's your ship, Commander. *Enterprise.*" Brodesser's smile grew even broader. "We've found it."

Sixteen

BRODESSER LED HIM DOWN to the launch bay, an area of which had been sectioned off and converted into a war room for the use of the assembled commanders and their top officers.

While Trip slept, the professor explained, he'd given the coding algorithms to Kairn, who'd had them programmed into *Eclipse*'s computers—giving the Guild, in effect, a decoding machine. One that they were now using to decrypt every message sent by Sadir and his forces over the last several weeks. The result: They had a complete picture of the general's battle strategy, ship movements, and Sadir's own schedule—normally a very close secret.

"We're now altering our ship movements and mission planning to incorporate this new information." Kairn stood at the far end of a massive row of computing stations, all now involved in the decoding operation. "Needless to say, it gives us an entirely new outlook on the war."

Trip nodded. He was pleased to hear it. But the war was not what he was interested in at the moment.

"The professor said *Enterprise* was mentioned in the transmissions?"

"Yes." Kairn straightened. "It's not entirely good news, I'm afraid, Commander."

"I wasn't expecting it to be."

"Your ship is being taken to the construction docks above New Irla. The crew has already been removed to an unspecified detention facility."

"I see," Trip said, his voice sounding surprisingly small and thin to his own ears.

The news was not unexpected—as he'd told the marshal. He'd seen *Enterprise* being boarded with his own eyes, seen the damage the ship had sustained, the size of the attacking force, and knew there was no way in hell Archer and crew were getting out of the situation.

Still—the captain had performed near-miracles on so many other occasions. . . .

Trip supposed he'd been hoping for another.

"I'm sorry," Kairn said.

Trip nodded. "I appreciate that."

He was about to ask if there were any mentions of casualties or damage to the ship, when he noticed that the marshal was looking at him expectantly.

"What?" Trip asked.

"There's more," Kairn said. "These intercepts—

they include portions of your own ship's transmissions."

"Excuse me?"

"For some reason—Sadir's ships beamed *Enterprise*'s last few communications to their base at New Irla."

Trip shook his head. "What—why would they do that?"

"We have no idea."

Neither did he.

"Can I hear them?" Trip asked.

"If you want to." The marshal looked at him with concern on his face. "If you're up to it."

"Hell, yes, I'm up to it," said Trip, suddenly impatient. "Play them."

"Of course." Kairn walked him and the professor over to one of the stations, where a young woman sat with a stack of what looked to be old-style memory chips in front of her. "This is Lieutenant Fane. *Shadow*'s communications officer. She discovered the messages."

"Lieutenant," Trip said. "What do you have?"

She spoke without looking up from her station.

"Our computers hold all incoming communications traffic in a memory buffer—it's cleared every seventy-two hours." She held up one of the chips. "These are messages intercepted the day before yesterday—late morning. Traffic between Sadir's ships and his command post at New Irla."

She slid the chip into a square metal tray, about the size of one of their communicators, and then inserted that tray into a slot in the workstation.

There was a burst of static.

And then Captain Archer's voice filled the room.

"Approaching vessels, this is Captain Jonathan Archer of the *Enterprise*. We represent Starfleet and the planet Earth, and are on a peaceful mission of exploration. You have nothing to fear from us. We're reading your weapons systems as charged, and your vector as an attack approach. We ask you to stand down and remain at hailing distance. Please respond."

A welcome, and a subtle warning. Just what Trip would have done.

Archer's voice came on again.

"Denari vessels, this is *Enterprise*. Stand down weapons, and break off your current approach vector—this is our second warning. I can only assume the first did not reach you."

A curter tone, a more explicit warning, wiggle room for the opponent to back away without losing face. The captain was putting on a brave front.

"*Enterprise* to any vessel within range. We are under attack by hostile ships in the Cole One-twenty-eight sector of space. Our coordinates are—"

There was a sudden, loud series of explosions in the background.

Someone screamed. A man.

Archer turned away from the com then and shouted something unintelligible. Trip heard another voice—Malcolm's, he thought—shout back.

An instant later a second, louder series of explosions came over the channel.

And then there was nothing but static.

The lieutenant popped the tray back out and removed the chip.

"We're still decoding the visual component of the message," she said.

Trip nodded blankly.

He didn't want to see the images—hearing what had happened to the ship—*Enterprise* being captured—was bad enough. Worse in some ways, than he could have imagined.

Brodesser must have seen the look on his face.

The professor put a hand on his shoulder. "I know how you feel, Trip. Believe me."

He nodded. If anyone could know how he felt—it would be Victor.

"We were hoping," Kairn said, "that you might be able to tell us why Sadir's troops would send those on to New Irla."

Trip shook his head. "I don't have a clue."

The lieutenant—Fane—spun around in her chair. "Nothing unusual about the content? Mode of transmission?"

"The captain's last message," Trip realized. "The distress signal—it's possible he sent it wideband. In which case we might get a response in a few weeks. Which Sadir would want to be prepared for."

"There's something else you should be prepared for, Commander," Kairn said. "Sooner rather than later, I suspect."

"Excuse me?"

"Your ship. *Enterprise.*" The marshal's eyes found his. "There can be only one reason why Sadir is moving it to New Irla. He intends to repair it and put it in service as part of his own fleet."

Trip nodded. The marshal was right, of course.

Right then he had a sudden, horrifying vision of *Enterprise*'s phase cannons blasting *Eclipse* out of the sky.

He couldn't allow that to happen—Sadir to use *Enterprise* against the Guild. Starfleet technology had done enough damage here already. He had to get that ship back.

And suddenly he knew exactly how to do it.

"Marshal," Trip said. "You've got to show me where this New Irla is. And then I'm going to need four of your best men."

"What did you have in mind?"

"Another rescue mission," he said. "Only this time we bring back a starship."

Silence greeted his pronouncement.

"Your starship? *Enterprise?*" Kairn shook his head. "I admire your nerve, Commander—steal the prize back out from under Sadir—but it simply can't be done. New Irla is the center of Sadir's power—his headquarters, his palaces, his government are all there, guarded by the most impregnable air defenses on the planet. There is no way for a ship to get within five hundred thousand ~~kilometers of~~ the city without being identified, tagged, and shot down. It simply can't be done."

Trip smiled. "Oh, yes, it can," he said.

And then he told them about the cloaking device.

"And you didn't see fit to mention this before because . . ."

"Guildsman, before I thought this battle between you and General Sadir was an internal affair." After a brief demonstration of the cloak at work, Trip and Kairn had come straight to *Eclipse*'s command deck, where they were now talking to the image of Guildsman Lind, and Vice-Marshal Ella'jaren, speaking from their respective vessels.

"Now that I realize it's a war of our making—that our technology is responsible for Sadir coming to power in the first place—well—I've got to do whatever I can to fix that."

"Which includes using this cloak," Ella'jaren added.

"That's right."

"Five will be enough for your plan?" Lind asked.

"It'll have to be." Trip smiled. "That's as many as we can squeeze in."

A very well-trained five, he added silently. He was going to have to spend quite a lot of time over the next few days briefing those five, whoever they were, on *Enterprise's* systems. He was also going to have spend a lot of time figuring out exactly how to take over—and run—the starship with so few people. He already knew one thing—he was going to have to fly the vessel. He doubted very much that there would be anyone from the Guild even remotely qualified to do that. He was hoping that between *Night* and *Shadow,* there was an engineer better-qualified than Ornell, to maintain the systems from the engineering deck. Then they would need someone on weapons, and probably someone on sensors as well, and the fifth person—probably in the armory. Taking over *Enterprise* was only going to be half the fight—from what Kairn had said before, they were going to have to blast their way clear of New Irla as well.

And even before then, they were also going to need to monitor Sadir's com traffic very closely, to keep an eye on the status of *Enterprise's* repairs. No sense in mounting a rescue mission to take over a ship that couldn't fly.

A lot of work over the next few days.

"Commander."

Ella'jaren's voice broke his train of thought.

"I want to make sure we understand each other. If we give you the men you need to undertake this mission—and it is successful—you will be willing to place yourself and your ship—under our command? To fight this war at our direction?"

Trip whistled softly.

That was a tough question.

But there was really one answer.

"Yes," he said. "If"—he looked at Kairn, and then at the other commanders—"if I have a say in how that war is fought."

"Which means what?"

"Guildsman," he said to Lind. "You said before—I earned a place at your table. I guess that's what I'd ask for, then. To take it."

The three were silent.

"An equal place?" Lind asked.

"Well . . ." Trip thought about that. "I'm not sure, to tell you the truth. I'd certainly want to be part of any major decisions involving the use of *Enterprise.* You were talking before about changing strategy—bombing civilian targets. I couldn't allow that."

Lind nodded. "We'll have to decide this among ourselves, of course, but it doesn't seem . . . unreasonable to me, on the face of it."

Ella'jaren nodded as well.

"I can agree with that," Kairn said.

Trip suddenly thought of something else.

"I have to add one other thing. I'm going to want to find the crew—and rescue them—as soon as we can."

"Of course," Kairn said.

"And once that happens—assuming the captain is with them and that he's"—Trip hesitated, because he was thinking and trying not to think all

at the same time of what had been done to
Ferik—"that he's fine, everything we've agreed to
will have to be talked about all over again.
Though I can bet you he's gonna feel pretty much
the same way I do about what's happened—about
Sadir using fleet technology."

"Understood," Lind said. "Again, we will consider what you've said."

"Commander." That was Kairn, who turned to
face him now. "I'm afraid we must also consider
the possibility that your mission to rescue *Enterprise* will fail, and that you—and this cloak—will
be captured. Under those circumstances—"

"It won't happen," Trip said.

"But if it does," Kairn continued, and Trip knew
where he was going with this, straight to the
happy pill again, which he was still not going to
agree to take, "then Sadir will not only have your
ship, but he will have the cloaking device."

The reply that Trip had been preparing died in
his throat.

"It won't matter."

Trip turned.

Victor Brodesser had just entered the command deck.

"Professor?" Kairn frowned. "What do you
mean by that?"

Brodesser smiled and stepped up next to them.

Once Trip had demonstrated the cloak,
Brodesser had insisted on an explanation of the

fundamentals behind the device's function, which Trip had provided to the best of his ability (the professor's instantaneous, innate grasp of those fundamentals made Trip feel like a first-year engineering student again, looking at his first warp function—completely, hopelessly, totally inadequate). Brodesser had stayed behind then, to explore the cloak further, while Trip and Kairn proceeded to the command deck.

"What I mean by that," Brodesser said, "is that while the cloaking device is a remarkable piece of technology—the manner in which it performs its function almost immediately suggests a method by which the device's effect can be neutralized."

Lind smiled. "Why is that scientists seem unable to use everyday language?"

Brodesser smiled back. "It gives us the appearance of knowledge, sir—though in this case, it's not just the appearance. All I mean is this—it will be easy to build a device to see through the cloak. A week or so, for a working prototype."

Trip stared at the man.

And felt, once again, hopelessly inadequate.

"I've been thinking, though," the professor continued. "About the mission you've proposed, Trip. I'm not so sure that's the best use of a cloaked ship."

Trip turned to Brodesser. "Sir?"

"In fact, I believe that—"

"Professor," Trip interrupted. "Can you imagine

what would happen to these ships if Sadir had *Enterprise?*"

"Yes, I can imagine. But—"

"Sir, with all due respect, I'm not sure that's true. *Enterprise* has phase cannons, which are" —he shook his head—"they're quite a powerful weapon. Much more so than anything Starfleet had in your day."

He struggled for a way to impress upon everyone just how powerful. His eyes fell on one of the workstation displays, which had a starchart of the Belt up on it.

"Vox Four—the asteroid the prison was on." He made eye contact with the two commanders on the viewscreen, then Kairn and Brodesser. "During our initial test of the phase cannon—before the last upgrade we had—we fired a phase cannon at an asteroid roughly that size. We split it in half."

There was silence around the command deck, as everyone digested Trip's news.

"*Enterprise* is a powerful weapon, Commander. But—think about chess."

"Chess?"

"Yes. Chess. You play it?"

"Not in a long time." Trip didn't understand where this was going.

"Professor." That was Lind. "I don't wish to interrupt, but—"

"Bear with me a moment, sir. I want to make a point to Commander Tucker." He smiled and raised his index finger. "Now, Trip—if you please. What is the object in the game of chess?"

Trip sighed.

In his mind—his memory—Victor Brodesser had taken on near godlike stature. The omnipotent, all-wise elder. A father figure, in a lot of ways. Sometimes—especially later, when he'd worked in the Warp Five program—he'd run across people whose own feelings about Brodesser were far more critical. About his theories, of course, but about the man as well. Trip had written those feelings off as jealousy, in large part. Now that he was with the professor, again, though . . .

He could see why some people found him annoying.

"Chess," Trip said. "You have to capture your opponent's king."

"Exactly. Capture the king. And as in chess—so in this war we fight."

He paused then, and looked around the command deck, and up at the screen.

"I propose a different use entirely for the cloaked vessel," Brodesser continued. "Which is not to say we abandon your plan, Trip. We can mount that rescue later. But consider—capture *Enterprise* and we capture a powerful weapon. Capture Sadir"—he smiled—"and the game is over."

"Capture?" Kairn said. "You mean take him hostage?"

"No." Brodesser shook his head. "I'm speaking metaphorically, of course."

The smile disappeared from his face then, and all of a sudden Trip was seeing a Victor Brodesser completely unfamiliar to him. The light coming from his eyes was not the familiar twinkle Trip knew so well, but a glint that hinted of darker, more powerful desires.

"I mean kill him," Brodesser said, looking around the room. "Kill General Sadir."

Seventeen

KAIRN WAS THE FIRST to break the silence that followed.

"You're wrong, Professor," the marshal said. "Killing Sadir will not end this particular game. Even with him gone, the war will continue. His command staff will fight on. His ships, his soldiers—Kota base—other significant, very strategic assets . . ." Kairn shook his head. "None of those will surrender to us simply because Sadir is dead."

"Marshal?" That was Ella'jaren. "Think it through, though. Yes, the council will fight on, but Sadir is the glue that holds all of them—Makandros, Dirsch, Elson—in line. With him gone, they would be at one another's throats in an instant. Their troops—their ships—as concerned with defeating each other as fighting us. More concerned, in fact."

Kairn nodded. Brodesser smiled.

Trip didn't know what to say.

He was surprised, that was for sure. Not so much at the plan, but the fact that the professor was the one who came up with it. The Victor Brodesser he remembered could never have contemplated murder. But then, the Victor Brodesser he remembered had never spent seven years in a jail cell.

All at once, Trant's words—her warning—about how the torture Sadir had inflicted on Brodesser, how it could affect the man—came rushing back into his head.

The patient's thought processes become disorganized. Their memories—unreliable. And they are—occasionally—subject to violent mood swings.

It didn't seem like that was happening to the professor. Still . . . Trip should talk to Kairn and Lind. Fill them in on what Trant had said.

"No."

That was Lind.

"I will not be party to any assassination."

"Guildsman," Kairn began. "May I remind you of how many innocents Sadir has deliberately—"

"Remind me?" The man's face was bright red. Trip had never seen him so angry. "I know what this man has done. I know better than anyone. But who will suffer the most in the chaos that will follow an assassination? Not those generals you mention—not their soldiers. The Denari people will be the ultimate victims in any sort of civil war. No. Assassination is not an option. I will not hear of it."

"Sir," Kairn began. "With all due respect—"

"I sense no respect here, Marshal. I am the guildsman, and I have made my decision."

The two glared at each other across the command deck.

This was a repeat of the argument between the two men that had followed the botched mission to Vox 4, Trip realized. And now it came to him that both arguments were about something even bigger—a divide in the Guild, between Lind, who seemed to Trip to represent its conscience, for lack of a better word, and Kairn (and probably the vice-marshal as well), who were clearly soldiers, first and foremost. A struggle that, he suspected, played out time and time again, in a million different ways, some subtle, some not so, as the Guild fought for survival.

The longer he stayed and worked with the Guild, he suspected, the more he was going to see of it.

"I ask you to hear me out, sir," Kairn said, and went on so quickly that Trip doubted Lind could have interrupted him if he'd tried. "People may die—I grant you, will die—if there is a struggle for power. But we can be part of that struggle— especially now, with Commander Tucker, and the professor here—with them helping us."

"Part of the struggle." Lind shook his head, and all of a sudden his anger was gone, depleted entirely. The Guildsman looked—and sounded— every one of his considerable years. "Struggle for what? What are we fighting for? What do we stand for? If we kill Sadir, and somehow manage to restore the Presidium, what's to stop anyone from doing the same to our new leaders? To one of us?"

"Guildsman," Ella'jaren said. "I must point out—as you well know, Sadir has sanctioned multiple attempts on your life."

Lind just shook his head.

"Excuse me," Trip said. "Can I say something?"

Kairn nodded. "Of course."

"Off the subject a little—or maybe not . . . what about Captain Duvall? Where does she fit into all this? Is she part of this council of Sadir's?"

"We don't know," Lind said. "We knew of Sadir's son, of course, and that the general had a wife, but other than that . . . any speculation about her role would be just that. Speculation."

"Why do you ask, Commander?" Ella'jaren said.

"Because if she is part of this council, even informally . . ." He looked around at the three commanders. "I wouldn't underestimate her ability to hold those men you talked about"—he tried to remember their names—"Makender, Dirsch—"

"Makandros. Dirsch. Elson," Kairn supplied. "They're the three most powerful members of the council."

Trip nodded. "I wouldn't underestimate her ability to keep them in line. In fact," he continued, thinking out loud, "my guess is that even if she isn't part of this council, she'll do everything in her power to keep Sadir's government together. It's the only way she can hold on to her own position."

"That time I saw her," Brodesser said, stepping forward again. "At Kota base. The guards—they jumped as high for her as they did for Sadir."

"Because of Sadir, I'll warrant," Ella'jaren said. "She has no official role."

"I wonder," Kairn said. "If"—he looked up at Lind—"if we all agreed on assassination, could she hold the government together?"

"No," Ella'jaren said quickly. "She is not Denari. Neither the council or the soldiers would follow her. But"—the vice-marshal smiled—"But. There is the son."

Kairn nodded. "The son. Now that is a possibility."

He looked up at Lind again. "Guildsman?"

Lind was frowning.

"He's young."

"Agreed."

"And we know very little about how the council would respond to him. Still . . ." He stroked his beard. "It bears further consideration."

Score one for the soldiers, Trip thought.

Kairn turned to him. "You asked for a seat at this table, Commander Tucker? Would you be willing to do this? Let us use the cell-ship as part of an assassination attempt?"

Trip noticed how the marshal had phrased that—
let "us" use the cell-ship—as if Trip wouldn't be just
as responsible as whoever did the actual killing.

Smart man, Kairn.

"I have to think long and hard about that. And I
have to tell you—the way I'm thinking right now,
the answer would be no. That's just not the way
we do things on Earth." He thought about explaining why—giving a quick history lesson, in effect, talking about how many times that tactic
had backfired, to often disastrous effects, in his
world's past—but nobody looked in the mood for
a lecture. Especially Kairn.

It was the marshall's turn to be angry now.

"I see," Kairn said, and Trip had to give him
credit, he kept the anger pretty well in check. But it
was there to see—in the suddenly too-expression-
less face, the tension in his body, the way he stared
at Trip and yet didn't meet his eyes—no doubt
about it, the marshall was not happy with him.

"But I will think about it," Trip said.

"We all need to think about it," Lind said. "Both
possible missions—rescuing *Enterprise* and this
killing."

"Immediately, I would think," Ella'jaren said.
"Either would impact greatly on the wider plans
we've been discussing."

"Agreed. Either will require substantial planning as well, so the sooner we make our decisions, the better." Kairn turned to Trip and the

Professor. "I think we'll need some time alone. Gentlemen?"

The two of them left the command deck.

"I didn't mean to spring that on you—that change in plan," Brodesser said, once the lift doors shut behind them. "I can guess how important *Enterprise*—and your shipmates—must be to you."

"I appreciate that, sir."

"And we should, without a doubt, plan on rescuing both. As soon as possible."

After the assassination, Trip added silently, filling in the unspoken blank the professor had left.

"I agree," was what he said out loud.

The lift doors opened then, depositing them out onto one of the huge cargo corridors.

They began walking.

"I'm going to the mess, I think. Something to eat." Brodesser smiled. "Third time today. I can't say it's haute cuisine, but it's better than what I've gotten used to."

"I'm sure of that."

"Care to join me? We've hardly had any time to talk, Trip—I'm eager to find out what you've been up to all these years. Besides *Enterprise*, I mean. Your life. Work—I mean it's clear that you've done well, but—"

"I can't, sir," Trip said, and explained about Trant's instructions.

"I see. Well. Why don't we meet on the launch

deck, then?" He smiled. "In fact, that would even work out better. I have an idea about that cloaking device—a way to mimic its function without using the particle generator."

"Really?"

"Yes. I'd love to show you what I mean."

Trip hesitated.

"I meant what I said up there, by the way—about the cell-ship? That is a remarkable piece of equipment. Nothing like any design work I've ever seen. You weren't involved in the construction, were you?"

"No," Trip said.

He hadn't told Brodesser anything about the cell-ship's true origin—Kairn had been right there when they tested the cloak, and there'd been no time after that—but right up until the moment the professor had suggested the assassination, Trip had every intention of telling him all about the Suliban, and Crewman Daniels, and this whole temporal cold war that *Enterprise* seemed to have landed in the middle of. Not anymore.

Something about Brodesser was bothering him. And not just the fact that he'd suggested the assassination attempt, but his whole manner, it was so . . . un-Brodesser-like, for lack of a better word. So difficult to read. Opaque, that was it.

Victor Brodesser had always been so utterly guileless, so transparent in his manner. When he was angry, you knew it. Happy, you knew it. Frustrated, content, depressed . . . you could read the man's mood by reading his face.

Now, though . . .

The professor seemed to have ulterior motives.

Trip didn't like the change.

"I think I'll take a rain check on that, sir." Trip forced a smile. "Trant told me to take it easy, and I'm gonna do that. Go back to my quarters, and rest."

This time he couldn't mistake the look on Brodesser's face for anything but disappointment.

"I do want to catch up, though," Trip added quickly. "I'm sure you're anxious for news about Earth. What's been happening there—there's a whole new Warp Research team, and if you can believe it, they put Sanderson in charge. Unbelievable. And"—he couldn't believe he'd forgotten about it until this minute—"I got a message from Alicia, sir—a couple years ago, now—but she got married. So any day now, you could be a—"

Brodesser frowned. "Who?"

"Alicia, sir."

The man's expression didn't change.

"Your granddaughter?"

"Ah." He smiled. "You mean Olivia."

"Sir?"

"Olivia, Trip. I ought to know my own granddaughter's name."

"Olivia." *Okay,* Trip thought. *Olivia.*

Trant had warned him that portions of

Brodesser's memory might have been affected by what Sadir had done, but . . . it was strange that his granddaughter's name would be one of those portions.

Unless Trip was the one remembering things wrong.

"Olivia. Married." The professor smiled. "Yes. I would like to hear about Olivia. Of course."

They came to a T in the corridor.

"I go this way," Trip said, nodding to the right.

Brodesser paused.

Trip knew what he was going to say before the words left his mouth.

"Trip. Will you do it? Will you fly the cell-ship for them?"

"I really . . ." Trip shook his head. "I can't say yet."

"Of course. I understand. But—you should consider it logically. As Kairn was saying—if they can find a way to use the boy—Sadir's son—then it could end this war all at once." He snapped his fingers. "In a single stroke. The fighting, the killing—it would all end. Which is the important thing, as the Guildsman said."

Trip nodded.

But he had the feeling that Brodesser was much more interested in the assassination than what happened afterward.

"I promised I'd think about it," he said. "And I'm going to. That's the best I can do right now."

"I know you'll do the right thing." Brodesser

clapped a hand on his shoulders. "I'll speak to you soon. Get some rest."

He smiled. Trip forced himself to return it.

He walked the rest of the way to his quarters in silence, feeling nauseated all over again. It had nothing to do with any sort of allergies, though.

When he got there, Trant was pacing in front of his door.

She looked up at his approach.

Not good news. Trip could see it on her face.

"Kairn said you were probably on your way here. I wanted to see you as quickly as possible."

He nodded and pushed opened the door to his quarters.

"Maybe you'd better come in."

There was only the bunk to sit on. Trip gestured for the doctor to take it, but she shook her head.

"I don't need to sit."

She was clearly as anxious to get to it as he was.

"All right." He folded his arms across his chest. "Go ahead."

She nodded. "I'm going to try not to make this too much like a science lesson. So stop me if you need something explained. I just want to make sure you understand—as completely as you can—what's been happening, and why."

"I'll stop you. Don't worry. Just go ahead." He understood her position perfectly. He was usually on the other side in these kinds of discussions—trying to make some complicated engineering process clear without trivializing the underlying science.

"Stereoisomers," she said.

Despite the seriousness of the situation, Trip had to smile.

"You lost me already."

"Stereoisomers. Compounds with the same molecular formula, but a different structure."

"Okay." He nodded. "I got the definition. What's the problem with these stereoisomers? They're causing the reactions—in Hoshi, and me?"

"Yes, but—" She shook her head. "Let me start over. What I found out was that your systems are reacting adversely to a specific protein—a class of proteins, actually."

"Like in the *seela?*"

"Exactly."

"So . . . we just have to avoid those proteins, right? Or is there something you can give us that will—"

"Mitigate the reaction?" She nodded. "That's how I would approach it—normally."

"I get the feeling this is not a normal case, though."

"It's not." She sighed. "The reaction you and Hoshi are having—in differing degrees, obviously—is your body, responding to the presence of these proteins."

"Right." That was basic science. Trip understood that.

"Seeing these proteins as foreign substances. Invaders."

He nodded.

"But they're not."

"They're not?"

"No."

"Right." He shook his head. "Now I'm lost."

"Trip." She walked over to the bunk and picked something up off the shelf behind it.

A ration pack.

"I ran one of these under the microscope, too. The same proteins you're reacting adversely to—they're in here as well."

"Now I really don't get it. How—"

And then it came to him.

"Stereoisomers."

She nodded. "Exactly. The same protein—the same elements, in the same proportions, but a different structure. That difference is causing your systems to react. To attack."

She put the ration pack back down.

"That difference is also behind that metallic smell you've been noticing. Something in your olfactory glands reacting to these proteins." She sighed. "I suspect it's also why the decontamination procedure affected you the way it did, when you first came aboard. Either that, or . . ." She shrugged. "There's something else going on. I don't know."

"So what do we do? We have to avoid this whole class of proteins, I guess."

She let out a small laugh. It was not a happy sound.

"You can't. These proteins—they're ..." She shook her head. "Your body needs them. The foods they're in. The elements they supply—calcium, iron, other trace minerals ..."

"Vitamins," Trip said. "We can take vitamins, right?"

"You can't live on vitamins."

"Okay. We find other proteins that ..."

She was shaking her head.

"So ... so what? What are you saying?" He looked in her eyes, and all at once his throat was dry.

He knew exactly what she was saying.

"No." He shook his head. "No."

"Unless we get you and Hoshi back to your ship—"

"We're going to die?"

"Trip." She spoke slowly, and calmly. "This is not going to happen overnight. There are foods of ours your system can tolerate. *Pisarko* is one of them—we'll find others—"

"*Pisarko?*" He frowned. "That was what made Hoshi—"

"No. Not the *Pisarko*. Minute traces of other ingredients in that particular mix. We'll eliminate those. And your body has reserves. You'll be—"

"Jesus Christ."

Trip sat down. He ran his hands back through his hair.

Trant sat next to him.

"I checked it over—a dozen times. I couldn't believe it. I still can't believe it. It really . . . it makes no sense. It implies the existence of an entirely new universe of compounds—stereoisomers that . . ." She shook her head. "That doesn't matter. We'll get your ship back. Get you and Hoshi to it."

He nodded mutely. That had to be top priority now, he thought, remembering the debate he'd just had with the three Denari commanders and Brodesser. Now they'd have to choose his mission over the professor's, because—

Trip frowned. He looked at Trant.

"Professor Brodesser. What about him? Does his system react to these proteins in the same way, or . . ."

She shook her head. "No. I've done extensive tests on him as well. No reactions like this."

No. Of course not. He'd been here for fourteen years. Duvall too. And both of them were alive, obviously. And in reasonably good health as far as Trip was capable of knowing.

"So . . ." He shook his head. "It's just me and Hoshi that have this problem?"

She sighed. "I know. That seems unlikely."

"Maybe . . . could it be something that we caught—a disease that changed these proteins?"

"No," she said firmly—then threw up her hands in frustration and stood. "I don't know. I shouldn't rule anything out, I suppose."

He looked behind him, where he'd put the ration packs earlier.

Six left.

"I'm sorry, Trip."

"Not your fault." He looked up at her. "At least we know what's happening now."

She nodded, and Trip noticed the dark circles under her eyes. Not a surprise—she'd been putting in some heavy hours on his behalf, he realized.

"You ought to get some sleep," he said, pushing to his feet.

"I will."

He walked to the door and opened it.

"Goodnight, Doctor."

"Goodnight."

She hesitated a moment.

"First thing tomorrow morning, I want you to stop by the ward. I'll have a list of the foods that will be safe for you to eat—and I'll rig up a filter—something like a mask that you can wear around the ship so that—"

"That doesn't sound like sleep to me," he interrupted.

"I'll sleep, don't worry. Later."

"See that you do." He smiled. "You have to take care of yourself, too."

His hand was on her arm before he was aware he'd moved it.

She looked down at it, and then back up at him. There was a question in her eyes.

Trip answered it by leaning forward and kissing her.

She pushed him away.

"Trip," she said. "Don't."

She was right. It was wrong.

And he didn't care.

He was tired of carrying that burden around—to help the Guild, right or wrong to tell them about the cloaking device, to fall in line behind Brodesser's plan, to be with Trant. Especially tonight. Especially after the news she'd just given him. Trip suddenly realized he was tired of thinking about it all.

Or maybe that was just a load of self-serving garbage to excuse his behavior.

Either way . . .

He ran a hand along the side of her face. She took that hand in both of hers, and kissed his fingers.

He pushed the door closed behind her.

Eighteen

THE SOUND OF SOMETHING HARD, rapping on metal. It stopped—the echo carried in the room a second.

The sound started again.

Someone knocking on a door. A metal door. His door, Trip realized, and rolled over in bed.

Which was when he realized something else.

Trant was gone.

"Hold on a minute!" he called out, climbing out of bed.

He had no idea when she'd left. He wasn't sure how he felt about it, either—a little disappointed she wasn't there, but on the other hand . . .

He wasn't sure how he felt about what had happened.

He slipped into his skivvies and walked to the door.

"Yeah?"

"Tucker. It's Royce."

Trip swung the door open.

"You just got up."

"That's right."

The man looked Trip up and down, then shook his head.

"Look at that. You're the same color all over."

"So?"

"Vonn and I had a bet. I just lost."

"Yeah." Trip knew why. The pale Denari skin darkened slightly from the rib cage downward, and then lightened again at the knee.

At least on Trant it did.

"What's going on, Royce?"

"Kairn sent me to get you. He wants you down in the launch bay."

It wasn't hard to guess why. They'd decided on the mission—*Enterprise*, or Sadir. Trip's plan or Brodesser's.

He realized he hadn't spent a single second doing what he'd promised—thinking seriously about whether or not he'd take part in the latter.

"Hang on," he told Royce. "I'll be right with you."

He slipped on his jumpsuit then, churning over the decision in his mind. He didn't have a problem killing people in war—that was what happened. Ships faced off, people faced off, and some of them died. So what was different about this? Why did it feel so wrong?

"Tucker!"

"Coming," he said, and picked a ration pack from the stack behind his bed.

There were five left. Three days' worth, if he stretched them.

Trip frowned and set the pack down again.

He could go without this morning.

The bay was even more crowded today than it had been yesterday. More workstations had been brought in, more personnel—the decoding operation was obviously going full speed ahead.

Kairn was leaning over Lieutenant Fane at her workstation. She was making adjustments—very, very fine adjustments—to controls on the workstation in front of her.

Ella'jaren, Lind, and—to his surprise—Trant stood slightly behind him.

Fane spoke. "Still too faint. I'm sorry, sir."

Kairn was the first to catch sight of Trip.

"Commander," he said. "How are you feeling this morning? You slept well, I trust?"

Out of the corner of his eye, he saw Trant turn away from him.

Trip had to fight the urge to look at her.

"Yes, sir. I did indeed."

He heard footsteps approaching from behind him just then, and turned.

Brodesser was entering the launch bay.

He did not look as if he'd slept at all.

"Ah. Professor. We're all here, then." The marshal turned to Fane. "All right, Lieutenant, we'll leave it for the moment. Let's sit, please."

The table from the briefing room had been moved down to the bay. They found seats around it—all of them, including Fane and Trant.

"Before we start, Commander"—Kairn turned to Trip—"Doctor Trant has informed us of your condition. I want to let you know that we will do everything in our power to see that you and Ensign Hoshi are returned safely to your ship and reunited with your crew."

"I heard as well, Trip," Brodesser said. He'd taken a seat directly across from him, next to Trant. "I'm sorry."

"I appreciate that—all of you." Trip said. At least that explained the doctor's presence here.

"However," Kairn said, "Trant has also informed me that neither of you are in any immediate danger. For that reason—and a number of others—we've decided against rescuing *Enterprise* at this time."

Trip tried to cover his disappointment.

Across the table from him Brodesser straightened.

"We feel the professor's plan holds the best chance of ending this war quickly—and getting you back to your ship, Commander," Lind said, speaking for the first time. "The professor's plan—up to a point."

"Up to a point?" Brodesser frowned. "Meaning?"

The Guildsman leaned forward and rested one arm on the table.

"There will be no assassination," he said.

Trip felt the weight of the world lift off his shoulders.

He'd been sitting at the table for all of five seconds when he realized that he couldn't do it—be party to killing Sadir that way. Never mind that intellectually it made no sense—he'd have no problem if Sadir died because of an attack he launched from *Enterprise*, or *Eclipse*, or in any other battle. But an assassination . . .

At a gut level it just hit him so wrong that he knew if he did take part in that mission, he'd regret it his entire life.

"I'm glad to hear that, sir," Trip said. "Though not entirely sure I understand. Up to a point—what does that mean?"

"I don't understand, either." Brodesser looked not at all pleased. "If there's no assassination . . . what is the plan?"

"Just as you said yesterday, Professor." Kairn steepled his hands on the table. "Capture the king."

Trip and Brodesser exchanged a confused look.

"Capture him? You mean take him hostage?" The professor shook his head. "In hopes of gaining what? I don't understand."

"Bear with me a moment," Kairn said. "And I'll explain."

The marshal passed his hand over the table's control panel.

The surface cleared, and filled with the image of a city—a sprawling metropolis that reminded Trip of late twenty-first century New York. Gleaming towers of steel and glass, a network of highways running up, around, and through them, a monorail, a handful of small ships jetting through the sky—all of it obviously crammed together in a way that suggested organized chaos and yet was—somehow—aesthetically pleasing nonetheless.

All except for a single structure in the center of the image.

A mushroom-shaped building that rose up over that portion of the city underneath it like an umbrella blotting out the sun.

"This is New Irla—Denari's capital. And this monstrosity"—Kairn gestured to that dark building in the center—"is the Kresh. A monument to Sadir's ego. And the heart of his power."

Trip whistled softly. "That is one big, ugly building."

Kairn nodded. "Seven years to construct it, according to our sources. A city in and of itself. And in the Cap"—he pointed to the top of the structure—"more firepower than we possess in our entire fleet."

Trip looked at the top of the building—the Cap—and noticed a series of minuscule bumps, slight, barely visible imperfections, scattered at regular intervals across the surface.

He pointed at one.

"This . . ." He shook his head. "Tell me these are not all weapons placements."

Kairn nodded. "As I said—more firepower than we possess in our entire fleet."

The marshal pressed another button on the panel then, and the image grew.

Trip began to get an idea of just how big the Kresh was.

There were two towers flanking its central stem—and as they came into clearer focus, Trip saw those towers were the equivalent of fifty- or sixty-story buildings on Earth. Perhaps the size of two *Enterprises*, laid end to end. Yet their tips touched only a quarter way up the Kresh's central stem.

Which also gave him an idea of just how thick that stem was—probably twice as big around as a deck from *Enterprise*'s saucer section. Monolithic not just in its size, but in appearance. As far as he could tell from this view of the building, there were no windows at all in the lower half of the structure. It was a featureless, smooth, unbroken surface—a solid wall of unbroken gray metal. Only as his eyes traveled over the upper half of the stem did he note slight irregularities in that surface—slightly different shades of gray, some flashes of reflected light that could have been windows or ornamentation of some kind. At the very top of the stem, just as it disappeared from sight, there was a ring of metal, or some other

kind of a polished surface that caught the light—
what little light managed to reach that portion of
the tower.

He focused on the Cap.

In the far view—the one Kairn had first shown
them—what had struck him was how big across it
was, how much of the city beneath it overshadowed. Now what he noticed was its thickness—
roughly the same height of those fifty-story
towers below. A city unto itself was no exaggeration—Trip would have bet money you could have
fit a hundred thousand people in there without
breaking a sweat. Monumental engineering was
not to his taste, but you had to admire the archi-
tect who'd figured out a way for the tower to support the millions of tons of building above it.

Its upper surface was gently angled, sloping
down to the rim's edge, but the very top was flat
and sunk into the metal. There, the gray metal became a lighter-colored surface of a clearly different texture (concrete, perhaps, though it was
hard to be sure of anything at this resolution). A
half-dozen structures of varying shapes and sizes
were built up on that lighter surface.

Moving downward toward the rim, the
weapons placements he'd spotted before were un-
mistakable. The minuscule bumps revealed themselves as massive gun turrets (more likely firing
explosive charges of some kind than phased-
energy weapons, from what he could see of them)

placed in two parallel rings around the outer rim of the Cap. There were slim, needlelike towers—communications antennae, he guessed—scattered across the surface as well.

The underside of the Cap was hard to see from the perspective he had, but he could tell that the rim-to-stem angle was far steeper than that of the upper surface. He saw weapons placements—though nowhere near as numerous as those above—and countless other metal structures and irregularities on this surface as well, all of which he was certain had some strategic function or another.

"Seven years to build? Only that?" Brodesser shook his head. "That in and of itself is quite a feat."

"The general spared no expense," Kairn said. "It is—as I said—the seat of his power. Literally. The weapons you see are just the beginning of it. The Cap serves as living quarters and training facilities for his troops, and in the stem—the administrative and support offices for his entire government. But what we are interested in at the moment are these buildings—here."

He pointed to the flat, white area at the very top of the Cap.

"These are residential quarters—reserved for the use of the general, his family, some more important members of the council. There is also a communications center here that enables Sadir, when he is on Denari, to run virtually the entire war from this location."

"When he's on Denari?"

"One thing I will grant Sadir," Kairn said. "He fights with his troops. He is rarely far from the war. But we've intercepted a series of transmissions from Kota Base to the Kresh. Sadir's forces are planning a major new offensive against the last of our positions in the Belt. Seven days from now the general plans to meet here with the council in order to finalize strategy."

Kairn looked around the table. "We plan to kidnap him before that meeting can take place. At a minimum, that will force them to change their strategy. In an ideal world . . . they would abandon the offensive altogether. At least long enough for us to mount an attack of our own."

Trip frowned.

"With Sadir out of the picture—aren't you afraid that'll just start this civil war you're worried about?"

"There is always that risk," Lind answered. "But now it's a risk we have to take. Even with the advantage the coding algorithms give us . . . at this point in time we would be able to do little against an attack on this scale."

"Okay." Trip sighed. "How—exactly—would this mission work?"

"The residential complex includes a landing pad—reserved for use by Sadir and the council. That will be your entry point."

Trip nodded. "And from there . . . ?"

The marshal frowned.

"From there," he said, "your path is yet to be determined."

"Excuse me? Yet to be determined?"

"Our source for all this information on the Kresh does not, unfortunately, have access to the residential complex. We're not sure which of these buildings is Sadir's actual residence."

Trip couldn't believe it. He had to laugh.

"Well . . . I mean, how do you expect to kidnap him if you can't even find him?"

"We'll find him."

That was Lieutenant Fane.

"Sir. May I . . . ?"

"Go ahead," Kairn nodded.

"We've been attempting to triangulate the exact location of Sadir's communications center. From this far off, it's close to impossible to do. Nearer the Kresh, however . . . it will be a relatively simple matter. Once we have that location, we can plan our route."

"We can't be certain Sadir's going to be in the com center though," Trip said.

"No. You miss the point. Once we find the com center, it'll be easy enough to locate the general. He's in constant communication with his staff."

Trip smiled. "So we won't know where we're going until we get there."

Blank faces all around the table.

"It's a joke," he said—and then, "Never mind."

Lind cleared his throat. "I assume from your

questions, Commander, that you'll fly this mission for us?"

Trip nodded. "I will. Who else is going to be on it?"

"Lieutenant Fane, obviously, to man the communications gear. Royce. One other person, yet to be determined. Vonn, perhaps."

"We talking about a lot of gear?" he asked Fane.

"A fairly substantial amount."

Trip frowned. "It's not a big ship. We're gonna be a little tight."

"We can't go with fewer than four, in my opinion," Kairn said. "The residential complex, while isolated, is not undefended. You have to be prepared—and capable—of dealing with whatever happens."

Brodesser cleared his throat.

"Excuse me," the professor said. "I have an idea about that."

Nineteen

OVER THE NEXT FEW DAYS the mission took shape, modified by the changes that Brodesser had suggested.

Trip learned to eat—if not enjoy—*pisarko*. He and the professor got that chance, at last, to catch up with each other, and even if Trip was still a little uncomfortable around him, for reasons he couldn't quite put his finger on, that was still a good thing. He even learned to call him Victor without feeling strange about it.

Most important of all, Hoshi came out of her coma.

He'd been in the launch bay, preparing for the mission, when Trant summoned him down to the ward.

When he saw the smile on the doctor's face, he thought for a moment she'd discovered a cure for their problem.

Instead, she led him through the ward to the

isolation chamber where Hoshi was sitting up in bed, eating a bowl of *pisarko*.

Trip couldn't say that he and the communications officer had been the closest of friends aboard *Enterprise,* but the sight of her without diagnostic sensors and feeding tubes, looking awake, alert, and as healthy as possible given the circumstances had him blinking away tears.

"Hey."

"Commander."

"You look about a million times better."

She nodded and set down her spoon.

"I wish I felt that way." She was looking at him a little funny. Trip followed her gaze and realized why.

He was wearing a Guild uniform.

Not that they didn't do laundry aboard *Eclipse*—though certainly not with the regularity they had aboard *Enterprise*—but the uniform he'd been wearing since coming aboard the Denari vessel had seen more than its fair share of use—and abuse—over the last week.

"Time to retire that, Trip," Trant—who he'd finally gotten used to calling Neesa, at least when the two of them were alone—had told him the other morning while he was getting dressed.

Hence, the new uniform. The first time Trip had seen himself in it, he'd felt a little funny, too. Like he was changing sides—even though, he felt that Starfleet and the Guild were on the same side, at least until Sadir was gone. And it was only a temporary thing—it had to be only temporary, because if he and Hoshi didn't get back to *Enterprise* . . .

Which reminded him of something else.

Trant had left it to him to break the bad news. To tell Hoshi the real reason for her "allergic reaction"—and the fate that might be in store for the two of them if they couldn't get back to *Enterprise*.

He sat down on the edge of the bed.

"I know," he said, grabbing the shirtsleeve of the Denari coverall. "Feels a little funny, too. But when in Rome . . ."

"I suppose. Anything would be better than this." She gestured to the hospital gown she was in.

"I know how you feel." They shared a smile.

"The doctor said you'd gotten sick as well. Had the same kind of reaction?"

"That's right."

"So . . ." She looked from him to Trant. "It's not just me, then. What's happening?"

Trip cleared his throat.

"Hoshi," he said. "You have to brace yourself for some bad news."

And then he explained as best he could—about their common protein sensitivity, the stereoisomers—Trant pitching in as needed. One thing they did not have in common—Hoshi had to stay isolated. In the ward. Her sensitivity was so acute that Trant was afraid even the slightest exposure to those proteins might send her back into a coma.

The doctor did promise to bring in a workstation so that Hoshi could access the Denari archives and begin working on a design for the transmitting device they hoped to be able to reach Starfleet with.

Still, the ensign was not a happy camper when Trip left the ward that morning. He had promised to visit her as often as he could, a promise he kept to the best of his ability over the next few days. But as the mission grew closer, his free time shrank. There was a lot to do, and little time to do it in.

Fane's communications gear—the equipment that would let her find and fix Sadir's location once they got close enough to the Kresh—had to be modified to interface with the Suliban systems. A course had to be plotted for the cell-ship, and their initial insertion point determined as well—tasks Trip had thought would be relatively easy, but became more complex as he learned the extent of the defenses protecting the Kresh. Because Sadir's complex was not only well-defended from within, but above as well—a heavily armored geosynchronous orbital platform with fixed gun placements and ships that patrolled far beyond what Trip would have considered a necessary distance.

There were also details to learn about the Kresh itself. They had a fairly complete picture of the systems that ran the Cap—power, communications, etc.—and the thinking was that those systems would be duplicated in Sadir's residences above.

Kairn also wanted the three of them flying in the cell-ship—Trip, Royce, and Fane (Brodesser's changes had allowed them to eliminate the fourth person, which pleased everyone once they saw how much room Fane's equipment would actually take up)—to do at least a minimal amount of combat training—weapons and hand-to-hand—which Trip had initially been glad of.

But not after the first few sessions, after Royce and Fane both trounced him thoroughly in the hand-to-hand. It wasn't that either of them was necessarily better—faster or stronger.

It was more like Trip's reflexes were not responding the way he expected them to. The way they had in the past.

After the second day of sessions he asked Trant about it.

They were in his quarters—Hoshi's old quarters, which Trip had taken over with only a modicum of guilt after Trant made it crystal-clear that Hoshi would only be leaving the ward in an EVA suit to go back aboard *Enterprise*.

The two of them had been spending a lot of time in each other's company—surreptitiously, for reasons they were both dancing around for the most part. Trip rationalized what they were doing like this: after this mission, he was going to *Enterprise*. And sooner, rather than later, after that, *Enterprise* was leaving the Denari system altogether. Trant would go back to the life she had and, after a while, forget that he'd ever existed.

He didn't know—exactly—how she was rationalizing it.

"And you've been noticing this problem for how long?"

"The last day or two."

She sighed. "We should do some more tests."

"No." He shook his head. "No more tests. I'd just like to know that it's probably being caused by this protein thing."

"I can't answer that without doing the tests."

"Guess."

"I don't like guessing."

"Speculate."

"It would be uninformed speculation."

Which Trant did not indulge in. She was like that, he'd come to realize. Vulcan-esque, when it came to her discipline. And as un-Vulcan-like as he could imagine in other ways.

"There are other foods we can attempt to incorporate within your diet. More variety might make a difference."

"More variety would be fine with me," Trip said, running his spoon through the bowl of *pisarko* in front of him. So far, it—and the *fossum*—were the only Denari foods he could tolerate. Not just because of the proteins—because of the taste. Every other dish Trant had put in front of him had made him gag.

"I'll do some more research, then."

She pushed back her chair from the table and stood.

"You don't have to do it now," he said. "Stay awhile."

"I can't. Too much else to do."

"Don't you have a staff?" Trip asked. He stood then and came up behind her. She had her back to him. He put his hands on her shoulders. "Let them do some work, for once."

She shook her head.

"It's not just that. I told Ferik that I would eat with him. Up in the mess."

"Oh." Trip nodded. He hadn't seen Ferik in several days, busy as he was—but he knew she had. The man spent most of his time around the medical ward. That couldn't be a lot of fun for Trant—not right now, especially . . .

"Sure," he said, letting go. "Come back later."

"If I can."

"Try."

She took a deep breath. "This is hard for me sometimes, Trip. You understand that?"

"I understand. Ferik."

"Not just Ferik. Every time I go down to that ward, and I see the door to Hoshi's room, I'm reminded that you can't stay here. You have to get back to your ship, and the sooner the better."

"I will. Once we have Sadir, we're going after *Enterprise*."

He had, in fact, already begun making plans to

do just that. Had made one choice for his team to recapture the ship that seemed so obvious in retrospect that he wondered why it hadn't occurred to him immediately.

Victor could handle the engines. In his sleep, probably.

"That's another thing," Trant said. "The mission."

"The mission?" He frowned. "You're not gonna start in on that happy-pill thing again, are you?"

Though he'd thought about it himself, more than once, over the last few days. Now that he'd spent so much time with Kairn and Lind—it wasn't just his skin at risk if he got caught. There were things he knew about the Guild—the fact that they had the coding algorithms, for one—that could cripple their war effort if Sadir caught him, and made him talk.

"No." She smiled. "I know better now. But . . . it's risky, Trip. Much more risky than the last one, in a lot of ways. What if you can't locate Sadir?"

"It's in the plan." They'd gone over it several times. "If Fane can't find the communications center, we abort. Simple as that."

"And you'll do it? Abort?" She shook her head. "Last time it was just a prison break, and you pushed the mission well past the safety margin."

"Not to worry. If we can't find Sadir—we're not sticking around very long."

"You promise?"

"Oh, yes. You have nothing to worry about on that score."

The more he learned about the Kresh, in fact, the more nervous he got. Multiply redundant sensor systems, pulse weapons that if what Kairn was saying was true, were at least as powerful as their photon torpedoes. . . .

No. He would have second thoughts about sending *Enterprise* herself up against the Kresh. If even the slightest indication appeared that things were going wrong. . . .

"Good."

But she still had something on her mind. He could see that.

"What?"

She took a long time before answering.

"I've been thinking," she said. "About what might happen. Afterward. When you go back to *Enterprise*. I thought . . ." She smiled. "You don't think your doctor would need an assistant, do you?"

Ah.

She caught the expression on his face, and her smile—ever so slightly—cracked.

"I didn't think so."

He sighed.

Trip had made his choice about what kind of life he was going to live long ago. Back when he first joined Starfleet. Not a settled life—at least, not for a long, long time.

"I'm sorry," he said.

She nodded. "It's just—you think that part of you is dead. And then all at once—" Her voice broke.

Trip took her in his arms. "It's all right."

"No." She looked up at him. "It's not all right. But it'll have to do."

The com buzzed.

"Ferik to Trant. I'm in mess hall."

She stepped back, and opened a channel.

"This is Trant. I'm on my way."

She smiled—as forced a smile as he'd ever seen—and then she was gone.

Trant did not come back that night.

Probably a good thing, he decided. He needed to focus. Needed his strength.

Probably just what she'd been thinking.

He ate the last ration pack, one he'd been saving just for this morning, just for that little extra boost of energy he hoped it would give him. He put on not his Starfleet uniform, or the Denari one, but a black coverall—an exact copy (or as close as they could make) of the ones worn by the maintenance engineers who worked in the Cap. Fane and Royce wore the same thing.

Eclipse had moved as close as they could get to Denari itself—farther away from the safety of the Belt than they'd been in years, a precise maneuver through Sadir's positions made possible only by extensive study of various fleet intercepts. As close as it was, though, when the cell-ship dropped, they had a four-hour journey ahead of them.

Halfway through that journey they engaged the cloak.

From this point onward, they were on subspace silence.

Fane powered up the gear she'd brought and went to work.

Her gear took up all the space behind Trip's seat and barely left room for Royce at all. He'd flipped around her chair so that she faced to the side of the ship, the equipment surrounding her on either hand.

The first step was finding the transmissions she was looking for. She and Trip had modified the cell-ship's transceiver to route all intercepted messages to a specially programmed computer, which was set up to listen for certain key phrases. Sadir. The general. Major offensive. A half-dozen others they'd decided on.

Thousands came in. The computer deciphered all of them. Fane picked a hundred at random and routed a third to listening stations in front of each of them. This was drudgery—no way around it. No computer could do the work of deciding what mentions of the key phrases were relevant to their search.

Trip picked up his earpiece, and cued up the first message.

". . . policy directive as per General Sadir, no additional funds authorized . . ."

Nope. On to the next one.

"... General Makandros wants ..."

Next.

"... I don't know whether or not he was deliberately trying to be offensive, but when he told me ..."

Trip rolled his eyes. Definitely not.

Nor did he find anything relevant in that entire first batch. Neither did Royce, or Fane.

He checked his sensors. An hour, traveling at this rate, until they reached Denari. He frowned. They might have to slow down a little. Not good. That would throw off everyone's timing.

"Next group coming in," the lieutenant said, and Trip picked up his earpiece again.

Royce straightened almost at once.

"Got something," he said.

"Let's hear it," Fane said.

Royce punched a button on his station.

"... additional security in residence, during the general's stay. Confirming arrival of twenty-four more guards to the—"

Fane switched it off.

"That's it. That's from the com center," she said, and smiled.

Then she got down to work.

This part was all on her shoulders. Now that they'd ID'd a message from Sadir's com center, she had a frequency to listen in on. A way to fix its location. Every signal that came over that channel let her hone in a little closer.

They were near enough to Denari now that she could begin using some of the satellites orbiting the planet—those that predated Sadir's rise to power—to help in the process as well. Access their reception protocols, see when the signal from the com center reached them, and use that information to triangulate a fix.

She was also able to pick up some of the other signals that those satellites were receiving.

"Got a visual," she said abruptly, and all at once, the main display filled with an image of Sadir's residence atop the Cap. A bird's-eye view, a much more precise look at it than they'd had before.

The complex was shaped like an oval. There were six buildings scattered across it. Two towers, at opposite ends of the oval. A long, low building next to one of them—two smaller, squarish buildings flanking the other. A circular structure in the center.

"Could be any of them," Fane said without looking up. "No way to tell yet."

The sensors beeped softly, and Trip glanced down at his work screen.

"Incoming," he said. "Six ships—five small ones, one big. Very big."

Royce, who had the seat just behind him and to his right, leaned forward.

"Isn't that a little soon?"

"Yeah." Trip frowned. Based on the transmissions they'd intercepted, and what sensor data they had been able to gather from *Eclipse*, he would have thought they were at least half an hour from any of the patrols. Not that it made a difference, cloaked as they were.

He moved to clear the data from his screen— and his heart leapt into his chest.

The big ship. He knew those readings like the back of his hand.

It was *Enterprise*.

"That's my ship," he said.

"What?"

"That's *Enterprise.*"

He watched the screen a second.

She was moving on impulse, heading almost directly toward them. On a vector away from New Irla—Sadir's shipyards. Heading to where? He had no idea. There hadn't been anything in the transmissions about this. And who was flying her? What about the engines? Who was on them? Had Sadir trained a crew— kept on a skeleton crew from *Enterprise?* Was he moving the ship into position to attack the Guild?

Trip's first impulse was to break off their approach to Denari, and head after her. He shot that down immediately—not likely just the three of them could seize control. And there were those five ships flanking her. They wouldn't stand by while he tried.

His second thought was to break radio silence, and let *Eclipse* know she was coming.

But they'd see that soon enough for themselves. In time, he trusted, to get safely away.

What could he do? Nothing.

"Something's happening," Royce said, leaning over his shoulder and looking down at the screen.

Trip looked, too. He was right—something was happening.

Enterprise was going to warp.

Her signal on the display wavered, and then disappeared from sight. A second later the other five signals did the same.

Trip stared at the empty screen and shook his head.

"Sonuvabitch," he said.

What now? he thought.

"Got it." The sound of Fane's voice shattered his train of thought.

She pointed to the circular building, in the center of the residential complex.

"The com center."

Trip nodded. He put *Enterprise* to the back of his mind.

Out of the corner of his eye he saw Fane send a burst transmission—that was the signal. The mission was a go.

He focused on the controls in front of him. Royce was on sensors.

"Let's bag ourselves a general," Trip said, and punched firing thrusters.

Twenty

DENARI WAS a green-and-white soccer ball—all cloud cover and ocean. From the briefing, Trip knew the planet had two continents—one the size of Africa, covering the planet's northern pole, the second, far smaller one—not much more than an island, really—near the planet's equator. That one was their target. He couldn't spot either from this distance, though they were only fifteen minutes from the Kresh, and closing fast.

"First sensor barrier approaching," Royce said.

The outer range of the orbital platform's detection range. Passive and active detection systems. A wide-band jamming frequency as well, designed to interrupt communications between any possible attacking vessels.

That was all right. They were on subspace silence anyway.

Trip was flying by sight as much as by sensor now—coming in to such a heavily trafficked area, he had to be able to react instantaneously. The computer could have done it for him, he supposed, but the autopilot was one Suliban system he'd never entirely understood. Now was not the time to start depending on it.

The orbital platform came into view. It looked like a coin, spinning slowly in space. A coin with raised surfaces, on both sides. Weapons emplacements. There were ships too—dozens of them, exactly like the ones that had attacked *Enterprise*—hovering nearby. Deadly little gnats, ready to attack on an instant's notice.

Trip had found time during the week to rewrite code yet again, so that he could punch the shields on while they were cloaked. He did that now. Not that it would do much good if they were spotted—not even Suliban technology, he guessed, could hold up to that much firepower for very long. Still, it made him feel better.

"Nervous?"

Royce had spoken. Trip replied without turning.

"Aren't you?"

"Absolutely. I didn't even really believe this cloak thing would really work until now."

"Hey . . ."

He did turn in his seat slightly now, and smiled.

"Didn't we talk about having a more positive attitude?"

Royce smiled back.

The proximity alarm sounded.

Trip turned just in time to avoid missing a huge transport, rocketing up toward the platform from the planet below.

"Sorry," he said. "One of the disadvantages of being cloaked."

Neither Royce nor Fane said a word.

Trip suspected that if he turned around again, they'd both be several shades paler than usual.

But he didn't. He'd learned his lesson.

He kept his eyes glued to the viewscreen.

"Ten minutes," Fane announced.

"Moving out of range of the orbital station's sensors . . . now," Royce said. "We are in Kresh airspace."

Which meant they were being swept by a far more extensive series of sensor scans. A far more sensitive series as well.

A beep sounded. One of the many audio feedback circuits the Suliban had incorporated into this ship—Trip wasn't sure what this one meant, but most of them did not generally sound to announce good news.

Had Sadir's sensors just picked them up?

Trip's heart leapt up into his throat.

"Royce?"

"Yeah—not sure what that was yet."

"Send the incident data to my station."

"Tucker, concentrate on flying. Give me a minute, and I'll figure it—"

"Send it to my station," Trip said again.

Royce did.

Trip took a quick look and couldn't make heads or tails of it. Still . . .

"Fane," he said. "Any indication of increased com usage?"

"No." Her reply was almost instantaneous.

"Royce, anything on sensors? Ships powering up? Any indication they spotted us?"

He took longer to respond. "No," he said finally. "Nothing."

The beep meant something, though. But if Sadir hadn't picked them up . . .

He stayed on course.

The planet filled the viewscreen now. The cloud cover cleared for a second, and Trip saw the smaller continent. A flash of brown, and more green—a darker shade than the oceans. Shaped like a crooked finger. At the very tip of it there was a dark spot. Gray, almost black.

The Kresh, he realized. Hell, you could see it from space.

His pulse quickened, just a little.

The clouds closed up again.

"Five minutes," Fane announced.

Trip kept one eye on their approach vector, one eye on Denari.

"Entering the atmosphere," he said. "Now."

They dived down through the clouds.

The cell-ship wobbled. Turbulence, some friction from the reentry. Hull temp at . . . three K.

The general's sensor techs were going to pick that heat signature up, and there was nothing that could be done about it. When they didn't see a ship accompanying that heat, they'd write it off as a meteor, burning up as it entered the atmosphere.

At least that was the thinking.

They shot through the clouds into wide open sky.

Proximity alarms sounded instantly.

There were ships everywhere—smaller patrol vessels, like the ones that had attacked *Enterprise.* Even smaller ships shaped like daggers—fighter ships, most likely. And big ships, too—transports, like the one they'd almost run into earlier, and what had to be fighting ships—long, lean cruisers with obvious weaponry and sensor equipment.

Heart of Sadir's power was right.

"Shutting down active sensors," Royce announced.

Trip nodded. This close in, they didn't want to risk a stray E-M probe being picked up and queried. Even if Sadir's people couldn't match a source to it, they'd be on alert. And if they were on alert . . .

The plan wouldn't work at all.

They were over the ocean now, heading toward New Irla. The sea was greener than it had looked from space—a deep forest green unlike any of Earths oceans.

Denari's curvature slowly revealed the approaching city to them. A megalopolis that covered the horizon.

But all Trip could see was the Kresh.

The images aboard *Eclipse* hadn't done it justice. Not its scale, and especially not the way it overshadowed the entire city. From above you could see the majority of New Irla looked up to open sky. From here though—and certainly from anywhere within the city, he was sure—the Kresh dominated. A more obvious—and ominous—reminder of Sadir's power he couldn't imagine.

Trip wondered what the Guild would do with it, if the mission they were on was successful. If they won the war. Hard to knock a thing like that down. Harder still to imagine anyone looking at it and not thinking of Sadir.

It filled the viewscreen now.

"One minute," Fane said.

Trip nodded and slowed their approach.

The central trunk of the building came into view—Trip had a better view of the upper half of that trunk and the portions of it that had gleamed from space in the satellite captures he'd seen.

They were windows, all of them. Thousands and thousands of windows, looking out on the city below. He realized then how far off his previous estimate of how many people could fit into the Kresh had been. A hundred thousand?

A million. And more, perhaps.

They were close now—the central stem slowly

disappeared beneath the viewscreen. The rim of the Cap approached.

They cleared it, and Trip was staring right down the barrel of one of the weapons turrets. It had to be sixty feet long if it was an inch.

If he'd been nervous before . . . well, he couldn't think of what he was right now.

Trip swallowed hard as they passed over turret, and then almost immediately approached another. A second ring of weapons placements, and these, he saw, were different from the first. Barrels significantly narrower and shorter. Laser guns, he guessed, as they passed over them.

The residential complex came into view. He fired braking thrusters.

They passed over one of the towers, the long narrow building . . .

And there was the com center itself. The white surface near it was marked with yellow lines—proscribed landing areas for Sadir's ships.

Trip flew past them and eased off completely on the forward thrusters. The cell-ship slowed.

He set it down right next to the com center—as close to their target as he could get without hitting it. Three feet shy of the exterior wall.

They settled down with a slight bump.

"Right on target," Royce said.

Fane nodded. "Right on schedule."

Trip powered down the engines and looked through the viewscreen, across the complex. Deserted, just as they'd expected. Just as it had been on every image they'd seen of the structure. Not a surprise. Access to the complex was from beneath—as was all travel between those buildings.

He turned in his seat.

Fane had eased out from the crowded com station and was loading the pockets of her coverall with equipment. Royce was checking the charge on his weapon.

"All set?" Trip asked.

Both nodded.

"Then here goes nothing," he said, and opened the airlock.

The wind whipped the hair away from his face.

It was a cold wind—bitterly cold, and blowing loudly enough that he couldn't hear himself think for a second. Again, not a surprise—they were several thousand feet off the ground.

He pushed himself into the face of that wind—through the airlock, and out onto the complex's surface. Royce followed a second later, then Fane. The three of them crouched down in the shadow of the com building.

Trip pulled the door override from his pocket and pressed a control. The airlock slid shut, and the little bit of ship that had showed for just a second disappeared.

Royce stared at the spot where the ship had been.

"I'd like to know how that works," he said, shaking his head.

"Ask the professor when we get back."

"Tucker! Royce!"

Fane had circled around the building and was standing next to an airlock. Writing covered the door.

" 'Maintenance access only.' " Royce smiled. "That's us."

There was an access panel next to the door. Keypad controlled. Fane ran a sensor device over it.

"This is getting to be a habit," Trip said. "Breaking in through the service entrance."

"That it is, Commander." Royce smiled.

"Maybe you two should go in for a career change," Fane suggested.

Trip shook his head. "Why, Lieutenant."

"What?"

It was his turn to smile. "You have a sense of humor."

"Don't tell anyone." She snapped the sensor device shut.

"Just like the ones on the lower levels," she said. "Seven-digit access code. Standard maintenance override should work."

Which their contact in the Kresh had given them—a code that opened all airlocks on the Stem and inside the Cap itself.

Fane punched in the digits. The door slid open, and the three of them stepped quickly inside.

A standard airlock—a room about four feet wide, a dozen feet long. There was another door at the far end. Another access panel. Fane punched in the code again, and this door opened as well.

Onto a corridor fully as large as the oversize cargo halls on *Eclipse,* only far better maintained. The walls, the ceiling, even the floor—all the surfaces Trip could see gleamed. Power conduit, bunched together in neat, precise bundles ran along both sides of the corridor, at knee height. Com piping, tinted a light blue on the wall in front of them, a red just shy of pink on the wall behind them, ran at shoulder level.

Fane traced the piping down the corridor, Royce and Trip a step behind her. The corridor bent, and the pinkish-red piping climbed the wall and ran across the ceiling to join with first the blue, and then a half-dozen other colors of similar tubing. They all formed a massive bundle that disappeared into the wall—into the com center beyond.

Without a word Fane pulled out the hand-sensor again, and an earpiece. She held the sensor up to the blue piping and listened for a moment, then shook her head.

"Nothing on this one," she said, and moved the sensor to the red piping.

Each color piping represented a different building in the complex. She was eavesdropping on com traffic coming to and from each, listening again for clues that would lead them to Sadir's residence, and the general himself.

"Hey."

He turned to Royce. "What?"

"Let me see your weapon."

"It's charged, don't worry."

Royce held out his hand, and then his eyes widened, and just as quickly, he took it back.

Trip heard the footsteps then, and turned.

A half-dozen soldiers, weapons drawn, were heading toward them at a jog.

Twenty-one

"DON'T MOVE—any of you!"

The lead one got right in Trip's face.

"What are you doing here? Who are you?"

"Who do we look like?"

The soldier frowned.

"I didn't hear anything about this."

"Well." Trip smiled. "You're not maintenance, are you?"

The man hesitated. Trip could almost see his mind working.

"We had a com outage below. We're trying to trace the fault back," Fane added.

The soldier frowned. "I'd better check with Central anyway. You wait here."

"Sure thing," Trip said, smiling.

His hand reached into his pocket and closed on one of the knockout pellets that Royce had used down on Vox 4. This was sooner than they'd hoped to use them, but better than that—

"Never mind!" Fane called out to the lead soldier, stepping past Trip. She pocketed her sensor. "It's not up here, anyway. We'd better check back farther down the line." She looked at the soldier. "Where's the nearest lift?"

He nodded, still frowning, in the direction they'd come from. "Back that way."

"All right. Thanks."

Trip gave the man a thumbs-up, and the three of them turned around and started walking.

"He's still watching, right?" Trip asked when they'd gotten twenty feet down the corridor.

"You can bet on that," Royce replied.

Fane made a show of checking one of the com light-pipes on the corridor wall. As she did so, Trip noticed, she also checked on the soldiers.

"Still there," she said. "But not moving."

They rounded a curve in the corridor, and there, just like the soldier had promised them, was the lift.

"Safe now, I think," Trip said. He turned to Fane. "You find what we need?"

"The green one," she said, nodding towards the wall on their left, and the light pipe that ran along it. "A lot of com traffic. Half of it I couldn't decipher."

Trip and Royce followed her as she traced the pipe back.

The corridor began sloping upward slightly. Royce had taken his weapon out, Trip saw. He followed suit. They had no more false I.D.s, or papers, or explanations, or excuses left. Anyone they met from here on out—and he had no doubt these corridors were regularly patrolled—would have to be physically taken down.

They rounded a sharp corner, and the green piping disappeared into an outlet in the wall.

Ahead, the corridor ended abruptly, in a door with big red letters stamped across it.

"I don't suppose that says 'maintenance access,' " Trip said.

Royce shook his head.

He stepped to one side of the door. Trip moved up just behind him.

Fane stood on the other side of the entrance, next to the access panel.

"Masks," Royce said, and they all donned them.

Trip's hand tightened on the little glass knock-out canisters they'd used in the prison, and he pulled two out of his pocket.

Royce held two as well.

He nodded to Fane. She punched in the access code, and the door to Sadir's residence slid open.

Royce slid quickly into the airlock, raised his arm to throw . . .

And stopped.

Trip moved up right behind him.

The room before them was empty.

There was a workstation directly in front of them—its screen was dark, unlit. Hanging on the wall was a large LCD screen that was blank as well.

Royce drew his weapon and stepped forward.

Trip followed. The floor was carpeted—a thick, gray-black pile that his shoes sunk into without making a sound.

"Fane," Royce said quietly, his voice muffled by the mask. He waved her forward.

She pulled a small transmitter off her equipment belt, and pressed a button on the side of it. A single, quick data burst, after which she snapped the transmitter back in place.

Trip looked around the room.

It was an office, he decided. Sadir's office, most likely. The workstation, the LCD screen—he saw a com console to the left of the station as well. This was definitely where the general did his work.

He frowned and slid the mask down off his face.

"Hey," he said softly to Fane. "Didn't you tell me there was a lot of activity going back and forth from here to the com center?"

She took her mask off as well.

"There was . . ." She frowned, too. "A few minutes ago."

"You'd think it was coming from this room," Trip said. "Wouldn't you?"

Fane nodded. "Probably. But there could be stations elsewhere in the residence."

"Could be, but . . ."

He walked forward then, and touched the seat in front of the workstation.

It was warm.

All at once he had a bad feeling. A sinking-in-the-stomach, let's-get-out-here kind of feeling.

"This doesn't feel right to me," he said. "Where is Sadir? His guards?"

Royce nodded grimly.

"Let's stay alert," he said. There were doors on either side of the room. He pointed to the one on the left. "You two, that way. I'll go right. No heroics, remember. If you find Sadir, use the knockout gas, and then come find me. I'll do the same."

"Right." Fane nodded, pulling out a weapon of her own.

She and Trip slipped masks back on and stepped into the next room.

It was empty as well. Not an office, but a living room of some kind, Trip guessed. A long, low couch—a table in front of it—several chairs . . .

A single large photograph on the wall just behind the furniture. Trip walked closer to examine it.

Two dozen or so Denari, in military uniform. There was a caption under the picture. He waved Fane over, and asked her to read it to him.

"First Expeditionary Force—this picture's about twenty years old," she whispered.

First Expeditionary Force—it sounded familiar to him, and a second later the memory came rushing back. The article that Hoshi had found—this was the force that Sadir had led against Lind and the Guild twenty years ago. The one that the Guildsman had defeated, despite being outnumbered.

"There's Sadir," Fane said.

Trip looked at the figure she'd pointed at. The general looked much as he had in that article, save for one thing. The smile on his long, thin face looked genuine.

The photo's presence on the wall spoke of an old grudge, never forgotten.

He stepped back from the picture. This room had a door leading off to the left, and another going straight. Fane gestured toward the latter and walked toward it.

Trip made for the other door.

He pushed it open, knockout gas at the ready . . .

And stopped.

The room before him was made of glass.

And it looked out over the edge of the world.

Trip blinked and tried to get a handle on what he was seeing. Just beyond the glass wall in front of him—some twenty feet away—there was nothing but space. Not the sky of the outside world, but a pitch-black void. A shaft of empty space, ringed by rooms like the one he was in.

He stepped to the wall, pressed his nose against it, and looked down.

The shaft went on farther than the eye could see. Down to a bottom that was so far off he couldn't even conceive of a number to apply to it.

It was the Stem, he realized. He was looking down through the Stem itself.

The shaft was suffused by a dim, golden light.

Every level, as far down as he could see, had a balcony of some sort peering over the edge of the shaft. There was movement down there as well—people or machinery, he couldn't tell which.

Hell of an observation deck, Trip thought. Though this was not the time to play tourist. There was a job at hand—Sadir. Where was he?

Trip turned around. There was nothing here of interest. Doors led out of the room to either side—he chose the one that would keep him moving in the same direction as Fane and pushed it open.

Another office—almost identical to the first one they'd found. A workstation, a com console, an LCD screen—a chair that was not warm to the touch. No Sadir.

There was a long, low piece of furniture along the far wall—a chest of some kind—and just beyond it another door. Trip headed for that.

And stopped suddenly.

His eye fell on something on top of the chest. Something metal, the size and shape of a cufflink. Something that looked vaguely familiar to him.

He picked it up.

It was a rank insignia. A Starfleet insignia. *Duvall,* he thought.

He set it back down and looked around the room again.

Could this be Duvall's office?

Only one way to find out.

He slid one of the chest drawers gently open.

Definitely Duvall's office.

The drawer was filled with things from *Daedalus*.

One of the old Fleet laser pistols. A communicator. A facsimile of the initial *Daedalus* proposal. Photographs—dozens of them, mostly pictures of people Trip didn't recognize, posed against various Earth backdrops.

He shut that one and opened a second drawer. More of the same. A folder with Cooney's name on it, containing pictures of him, personal items that could only have come from his quarters. Other folders, with other crewmen's names on them.

It wasn't just Duvall's things in here, then. These had belonged to everyone aboard *Daedalus*. But after what she had done . . .

Why had Duvall saved them?

He heard a soft thump from the room ahead of him.

Just as two Denari soldiers walked through it, weapons drawn.

Trip froze.

A third man walked into the room.

A man in a simple gray uniform, medium height, medium build. An innocuous, harmless-looking man.

General Sadir.

He looked at Trip a moment and smiled.

"Commander Tucker," he said. "We meet at last."

Twenty-two

TRIP MIND RACED. Where was Royce? Fane? How did Sadir know who he was?

"I almost didn't recognize you." The general looked Trip up and down. "The uniform."

"How do you know my name?"

"I know a lot about you, Commander Tucker, chief engineer of the *Enterprise*. I've been studying you for a long time—since we first ran through the ship's personnel records and found you missing. You and the communications officer. She's not with you now, though—is she?"

Trip didn't say a word.

"All right," Sadir said, nodding. "Never mind her. I'm far more interested in the ship. The cloak. Where is that?"

Trip tried to keep his mouth from falling open. How did Sadir know about the cloak?

"I suspect it's somewhere on the landing pad above," the general continued. "I don't think you came all the way through the Stem to get here—despite the uniform. Save me some time, and I'll be far more inclined to treat you kindly."

"Cloak?" Trip asked. "What do you mean, cloak?"

Sadir shook his head. "Please don't waste my time."

Trip's mind raced. *Steady*, he told himself. *He can't know anything for sure*. It had only been a week since he'd revealed its existence to Lind and Kairn, and . . .

His heart leapt into his throat.

Trip just realized he'd made a big, big mistake.

Of course Sadir knew about the cloak. He'd known about it since the day of the attack on *Enterprise*, when Trip used it to escape his ships.

He had detailed readings of that escape, no doubt. Of the ship cloaking and decloaking. Sensor records his scientists had been pouring over for close to two weeks now, studying the—

That beep that had sounded just when they'd entered Kresh airspace.

"You knew we were coming," Trip said. "Your sensors—"

"Not sensors. A special E-M probe we had installed in the Kresh's defense systems. It appears to work very nicely." Sadir smiled. "I've been waiting for you to use that ship again. Waiting to get my hands on it. An invisible ship?" He shook his head, and smiled even more broadly. "The strategic advantages . . ."

"You'll have to find it first," Trip said.

Sadir nodded. "We will—though again, it would go quicker with your help."

"Sorry," Trip said quickly. "Can't oblige."

"Let me try one more time to change your mind." The general nodded to one of the soldiers, who barked out an order Trip couldn't understand.

A second later Fane and Royce were marched into the room. Both looked worse for the wear—Royce had a huge black-and-blue bruise on one cheek. Fane was favoring her right leg.

The general walked over to one of the guards and held out his hand.

"Your weapon, please."

The guard gave it to him.

Sadir turned and pressed it to the side of Royce's head.

"I'll give you a moment to reconsider your decision. Then I fire."

No doubt Sadir would do it, too. Without a second thought.

Trip thought that seeing him in person would somehow bring the non descript man from the photos to life—that he'd look in the general's eyes and discover what made him tick. He'd been wrong. There was nothing in Sadir's gaze—no cold light of calculation or cruelty, no repressed anger, no smoldering hatred, or resentment, or anything at all, in fact. The man was unreadable—a cipher.

"Commander," the general said again, pushing Royce down to his knees with the barrel of the weapon. "Where is that ship?"

Trip met Royce's eyes, and saw the man was prepared to die.

"Don't tell him anything," the Denari said.

Sadir nodded. "Laudable. You have ten seconds, Commander Tucker."

"Ten seconds or ten years—it doesn't matter. Fire away," Royce said.

But he was wrong, Trip knew. A few seconds might make all the difference in the world.

"If I give you the ship," he said to Sadir, "what happens to us?"

"You I have plans for. They—" Sadir gestured to Fane and Royce—"die quickly."

"Not good enough."

"This isn't a negotiation."

"Then why should I—"

"You're stalling," Sadir said suddenly, straightening up. He looked Trip in the eye. "Why?"

"Stalling?" Trip shook his head. "I don't know what you mean."

"I think you do." Sadir turned to one of the guards. "Go check the—"

That was as far as he got.

Something sparkled in the air . . . then hit the ground and shattered. A light greenish smoke filled the room.

Trip barely managed to slip his mask back on. Royce and Fane did the same.

Sadir's guards weren't as lucky. They fell to the floor. The general fell with them.

Marshall Kairn and three other Guild soldiers walked into the room and surveyed it with grim satisfaction.

Royce rose to his feet and smiled.

"Sir!"

"You're all right?" Kairn spoke to all three of them, turning his head to take them in under his gaze.

"We're fine. Now that you're here," Trip said.

Kairn's presence had been Brodesser's addition to their plan—the professor had figured out the cloak, how to build it—and installed a duplicate device aboard *Lessander*. Kairn and the others had followed in that vessel, just behind the cell-ship— had landed just on the other side of the com building. When Fane had signaled them from Sadir's quarters, they knew where their target was.

Finding this particular room had just taken a little longer than all of them would have liked.

"Get Sadir," Kairn said to one of the men with him. "Quickly."

The marshal turned back to Trip.

"We ran into another patrol. We took them out, but we don't have much time before they're missed."

"We'll have to hurry, then," Trip said.

The Guild soldier slung Sadir over his shoulder, and turned to go.

What happened next seemed to occur in slow motion.

The general's eyes snapped open. In a heartbeat he had ripped the Guild soldier's weapon from his belt and done a flip right over him, landing up and on his feet again.

He raised his weapon in one smooth motion, aimed it at Kairn—

And Trip, who'd been moving the second Sadir's eyes had opened, kicked it out of the general's hand.

There was life in the old, malnourished reflexes yet, Trip thought with a smile.

The general stared at Trip—the useless guards—in disbelief.

"You're coming with us, Sadir," Kairn said, raising his own weapon. "This way."

"You're Kairn," Sadir said. "Lind's lackey."

"Guildsman Lind, yes," Kairn said. "We work together."

"That old fossil's still alive, is he?"

"You'll see for yourself, soon enough." Kairn smiled. "He has some questions for you—about this new offensive you're planning. . . ."

The general shook his head.

"I don't think I'll be answering those questions," Sadir said. "In fact, I don't think I'll be answering any of your questions."

Trip took his arm. "It's not like you have a choice. Just—"

He happened to look up at that second and see Sadir's eyes.

And then—somehow—he knew exactly what was about to happen.

"Poison pill!" Trip shouted. He grabbed Sadir's neck with one hand and tried to reach his mouth with the other.

The general turned away and bit down.

Froth collected at the corners of his mouth.

"Medkit!" Kairn screamed. "Hurry!"

Trip let him go: Sadir slumped to his knees. His head shook violently.

He began making noises—deep, guttural noises in the back of his throat.

It was over in seconds.

"He's dead," Royce said, as he knelt next to Sadir's body. Trip saw the general had died with his eyes open wide . . . they were as unreadable in death as they had been in life.

"Idiots," Kairn said quietly. "We're all idiots. We should have suspected—" He sighed. "The whole mission, for nothing." He holstered his weapon.

"Move—everyone! Back to the ships."

Trip turned to go—

And his eyes fell on the open drawer. Duvall's *Daedalus* collection.

There was a book sticking out of it. He hadn't noticed it before.

But it looked somehow familiar to him.

"Tucker." Royce was at the doorway, frowning. "Come on!"

"A minute."

Trip pulled the book the rest of the way out of the drawer.

It was an oversize volume, with a brown leather binding, and gilt-edged writing on the front of it.

The Song of El Cid.

The book that he and *Daedalus*'s engineering staff had given Brodesser the night before the launch.

Except it couldn't be. Because that book was back in his own cabin, back aboard *Enterprise*.

Impossible.

Another copy, then. Someone else had given Brodesser a copy. Easy enough to check. He flipped it open. The inside front cover was covered with writing.

Victor:
Next stop, Andromeda!
> *J. G. Cooney*

Professor:
Second star to the right, straight on till night, and never mind the naysayers.
Warp speed!
> Steve Y.

And his own inscription:

Professor:
Thanks for the best year of my life.
Charles Tucker III

Inscriptions from the engineering staff. This was the book they'd given Brodesser. But how could that be?

Sadir. That was it. He'd gone aboard *Enterprise* and somehow found it. Brought it back here, and stored it here among the things from *Daedalus*.

That was what had happened. That had to be have been what happened.

He went to close the book . . . and frowned.

So far. His inscription. It was supposed to say "Thanks for the best year of my life *so far.*"

"Tucker!"

He turned.

Royce stood in the doorway. "What in the hell do you think you're doing? Grab what you need and let's go!"

"Give me a minute."

"We don't have a minute!"

Trip ignored him and looked at the inscriptions again.

That was his handwriting, but not what he'd written.

Impossible.

So he was remembering the inscription wrong.

323

Except he'd just looked at it, not much more than two weeks ago, back aboard *Enterprise*.

So this was a different book. A copy. Brodesser had a copy made to take with him, a copy that was messed up somehow, and he'd left one with Alicia, and that was the one—

No. Not Alicia.

Olivia. His granddaughter's name was Olivia.

Except it wasn't. Trip was suddenly as certain of that as he was of his own name.

But there couldn't be two granddaughters.

Just like there couldn't be two books.

His heart was hammering in his chest.

Two books, one slightly different from the other.

Two granddaughters, with slightly different names.

Stereoisomers.

Compounds with the same molecular formula, but a different structure.

Trant's words came rushing back to him.

"It makes no sense. It implies the existence of an entirely new universe of compounds . . ."

His mind raced.

And all at once, he had it.

Trip was a practical engineer, not a theoretical physicist. But you had to know some theory to be an engineer—he'd taken his share of courses at the Academy, knew the big concepts and how they applied to his work. Warp fields. Superstrings. Black holes.

Parallel universes.

The idea that all possible realities existed at once. That the space-time continuum was literally infinite—that somewhere out there was a universe containing every possible you, the you who had decided to wear the blue shirt that morning, had chosen to be a teacher, marry your high-school sweetheart, go away to college, join Starfleet. A universe where Zephram Cochrane hadn't discovered the warp engine, where the Klingons had been the ones to make the first contact with humanity, where A. G. Robinson commanded *Enterprise*.

Where *Daedalus* hadn't blown up seconds after launching.

He should have seen it before. That had been a major disaster. There was an exhaustive investigation. No doubt about it, the report had concluded. The ship had been destroyed—thoroughly, completely. No talk of the impulse deck flying off, or any possibility of survivors. *Atomized*, was the word the investigators had used. Finding Victor alive had pushed those realities to the back of his mind, but that was what had happened.

In his universe.

Not in this one.

In this one the ship had exploded—but here that explosion had not destroyed it but had, instead, ripped the very fabric of the space-time continuum. Had created the anomaly, a doorway between universes.

And *Enterprise* had flown right through it.

That moment in the shuttle bay, when the light had changed. When his world had turned upside-down . . .

They had crossed over.

And now that he realized that, everything else—*Enterprise*'s failure to detect the mine field, or the ships at Kota Base—it all made sense. Those things only existed here, because of *Daedalus*. The single mine that had crippled *Enterprise* must have been a stray that passed through the anomaly. It didn't belong there.

Like he didn't belong here.

"Tucker!"

Royce was standing in the doorway.

"Last chance."

"Coming," Trip said.

He grabbed the book and ran.

**Coming in May
the conclusion**

Daedalus's Children
by Dave Stern

One

JONATHAN ARCHER clenched and unclenched his fist. Once, twice, several times . . .

There was definitely something wrong with him.

An ache in all his joints, not just his fingers. A weariness in his bones, an exhaustion that just wouldn't go away, no matter how much he rested during the day, how many hours of sleep he got at night. It went beyond a simple adjustment to prison life, he was certain of that, even though Rava One's doctors dismissed his complaints as bellyaching.

"Archer!"

He looked up from the cot he sat on.

Tomon—one of the prison guards, Archer's least favorite guard, in fact—stood outside his cell.

"Up!" he yelled, brandishing his weapon—a long, thin metal rod akin to an old-fashioned taser. Primitive, but highly effective. If he touched you with it, you got a debilitating electric shock. Archer knew this from hard-earned experience—

the first time he'd been a little too slow in obeying Tomon's commands, he'd gotten a taste of that shock. It had left him twitching on the ground for what felt like hours.

It had left Tomon with a nasty smile on his face.

Archer remembered that smile as he rose from his cot and locked eyes with the guard. Tomon was small, and slight—almost a foot shorter than the captain, a good twenty-three kilos lighter—with a nasty streak Archer was sure he'd adopted in an attempt to compensate for his size. Over the last couple weeks—since the crew had first been imprisoned here on Rava One—he'd turned that nasty streak on the captain more than once.

Archer was looking forward to a little payback—sooner, rather than later.

Some of that attitude must have shown in his eyes.

"You want some more of this?" Tomon asked, raising his weapon.

"No," Archer said with as much humility as he could muster, gazing down at the ground.

"Then wipe that look off your face. And fall in." Tomon stepped to the side of the cell doorway then, and deactivated the ion field.

The captain of the *Enterprise* shuffled forward, stopping just outside his cell.

A metal wall rose before him, stretching up a good three stories. High at the top of that wall, a single porthole—a piece of glass perhaps two meters square—looked out onto the stars.

Rava One was a satellite—location unknown. Archer and his crew had been trapped here for two and a half weeks.

"Eyes front, Archer," Tomon snapped.

The captain lowered his gaze and stared at the blank wall in front of him.

"Good."

Tomon moved on, to the cell to the captain's left. Archer risked a quick glance to his right.

O'Neill stood there, hands clasped behind her back, in front of her cell. She wore a drab, gray one-piece coverall. The same coverall Archer wore. Beyond her the captain saw Dwight, and Carstairs, and Duel.

The captain nodded briefly to all of them.

Dwight looked worse, he saw. Pale, thin, hunched over like an old man. Archer frowned and shook his head. The young ensign had been in the infirmary most of the last week, unable to keep any of the food the Denari were giving them down. He wasn't the only one, but he'd been by far the most seriously affected. An allergic reaction—anaphylactic shock, Phlox had called it—that had almost killed him the first day. Dwight had been sick almost every day since. More than the rest of them, he'd had to be very careful about what he ate. Which last meal, had been almost nothing.

Archer locked eyes with him now and offered what he hoped was an encouraging smile.

Hang in there kid. D-Day—D for "deliverance"— is coming soon.

"What did I say, Archer? Hey?"

The captain heard Tomon's yell and felt the jab of his weapon at the exact same second.

His brain exploded in agony.

He was vaguely aware of falling, the back of his head slamming to the floor, his hands and feet, arms and legs, twitching spasmodically, over and over again. Mostly, his world was pain. White-hot daggers of it, shooting up and down his spine, through his nervous system as the electrical impulses from brain to body overloaded.

"Back!" the captain heard Tomon yell. "Or you're next!"

Archer had no idea who exactly he was talking to—one of the crew, obviously—but he silently urged whoever it was to do what Tomon said. No incidents. That might mean a lockdown—no exercise period. They couldn't afford that now.

The thrashing subsided. Archer got control of his body back, and lay there a moment. He tasted blood in his mouth—he'd bitten his tongue again. The backs of his hands were bruised, where he'd slammed them into the hard metal floor.

He looked up and saw Tomon looming over him.

The guard pressed the rod—deactivated, for a second Archer had been afraid Tomon was going to shock him again, and he'd tensed up—against Archer's chin, forcing his head back against the floor.

"Now. Why don't you get up and do what you're told. Captain."

As usual, the Denari guard put a sneer into that last word.

Archer forced himself not to react.

"I will," he said, and climbed to his feet.

All around him, he sensed his crew watching. Four men to his left, thirteen others to his right.

Stay calm, everyone, he willed silently.

Tomon stepped back then, and ordered everyone to form a line. Then he marched them down, in formation, to an open space by the exit door, where he lined them up again, in a single row.

Archer heard the rest of A block fall into formation behind them.

Two more rows of eighteen prisoners. Blocks A–1 (his) through A–3. All *Enterprise* crew. B block, next to them, held the rest of them. C and D blocks—the remainder of those on the prison satellite—held other prisoners. Denari prisoners. With whom *Enterprise* crew was not allowed to mingle.

Nonetheless, the captain had been able to learn a few things about them. Most of his information came through Doctor Phlox, who—out of all of them—seemed to be having the easiest time adjusting to life in Rava. Not physically—he suffered, albeit to a lesser degree, from the same problems as *Enterprise*'s human crew, an inability to (as the doctor put it) "tolerate" some of the Denari foods, a general malaise, a growing stiffness and soreness in his body that he attributed to certain chemical deficiencies—but mentally. The doctor seemed, by and large, to be his usual, good-natured self. Though the captain knew that with Denobulans, appearances could be deceiving.

Phlox—who had one of the two Universal Translator modules the prison authorities had allowed them to keep (Archer, of course, had the other)—had managed to convince those authorities to allow him to work with the medical staff on Rava, to help figure out what exactly was affecting the *Enterprise* crew. And while he'd spent the vast majority of his time in the prison infirmary doing just that, he'd also managed to find time to speak with some of the other prisoners—the Denari—and glean a few pieces of information that Archer had found more than helpful.

Rava held some two hundred prisoners, *Enterprise* crew included. Most of them had been there for years—more than a decade, in some cases. Political prisoners, by and large, moved off-planet to avoid any possible rescue attempts. By the same person, apparently, who had ordered the attack on their ship. General Sadir—a dictator who ran Denari with an iron fist. Who was in the final stages of a war designed to crush his sole remaining opposition, a group of former government officials and miners collectively known as the Guild.

The prison was run by a minimal staff—forty guards, all equipped with the taserlike rods Tomon so eagerly used on him, as well as hand weapons eerily identical to the old Starfleet laser pistols, half a dozen administrators, three medical workers, with a Colonel Gastornis—a military man whom Archer had never met—in charge.

No one had ever escaped from the prison satellite.

But almost since the day they'd arrived, two and a half weeks ago, Archer had thought of nothing else. Escaping, and getting back his ship. After the first few days, after talking with the crew in B block, he'd learned the guards' schedules. After a week he thought he'd spotted a weakness in the system.

Another few days and he'd come up with a plan. Not a perfect plan—he'd had too few opportunities to speak, unobserved, with his crew, for that—but a plan that could, should work, if—

"All right everyone. March!" Tomon and the other guards stepped aside then, and the huge door leading from A block to the central prison complex beyond opened.

It was the same door they'd marched through that first day, when they'd been led out of the transport to their cells. Archer had still been in shock, then, or something close to it. Everything that had happened from the moment the explosion had crippled *Enterprise* right up until then had seemed more like a dream, a nightmare really, than reality. One minute they were cruising toward the anomaly, everything going according to plan, everything on schedule, T'Pol and Lieutenant Duel ready to board the cell-ship for a week-long scientific study—and the next, there was a hole in the bottom of the saucer section, and they were being boarded by two dozen ships whose existence, according to T'Pol, was "an impossibility."

There had been so many of the Denari troops—hundreds, he'd guessed—that their presence, the sight of them swarming every deck aboard his ship, had seemed like a bad dream as well. His, and his crew's helplessness—the ship was crippled, the armory inaccessible—had only added to that feeling of unreality.

They'd been escorted off *Enterprise* then, and onto a single crowded transport vessel. A day's journey that had ended here, where they'd been marched off to identical, featureless cells.

Only then had the realization of what had happened sunk in. *Enterprise* was in enemy hands.

And Archer and his crew were prisoners of war.

They stepped from the cell-block proper into the corridor beyond.

It was slightly wider and significantly taller than those on *Enterprise*. The additional height was for a pair of walkways that ran at shoulder height, and to either side of the main corridor.

The guards proceeded down those, toward the door at the far end of the corridor. Five on either side, weapons drawn, eyes glued to the prisoners on the path below.

Archer heard the door behind them slam shut.

He coughed.

Up ahead, Ensign Dwight suddenly stopped and bent over double.

The prisoners behind him came to an immediate halt. Those ahead continued to march.

"Halt! Everyone!"

That was Tomon—up above them, to their left and almost directly parallel with Archer.

"You!" He pointed to Dwight. "Stay in formation! Keep moving!"

The ensign gasped and let out a moan. He waved a hand at Tomon.

"Oh, God. Please. Give me a minute."

He sounded as if he was in agony.

"Keep moving!" Tomon said again. "Now!"

"Here—let me through, please. Let me through."

That was Phlox, coming up behind the captain. Archer turned and saw the crew making way for him.

"Stop!" A guard on their right yelled now and raised his laser pistol.

Phlox froze, steps behind Archer.

The captain tensed.

Dwight moaned again and collapsed on the ground. All eyes went to him.

Phlox took another step forward, and passed the captain.

As he did so, he slipped Archer an ampule he'd stolen from the medical ward.

"Stop!" the guard on the right yelled. "No more warnings."

Phlox glared. "For God's sake, let me see what's the matter with him."

The guards exchanged reluctant glances.

"All right," one of the guards on the right said. "Quickly. The rest of you, keep moving."

The prisoners around Dwight began to back away from him—a movement that rippled through the entire line.

The movement, subtle and precise, put prisoners near every one of the guards, save for the two farthest away.

Archer jumped into the fray.

"Let me through, too," Archer said, and began walking forward.

"You stay where you are," Tomon hissed. "Captain."

Archer froze in his tracks.

Right next to Tomon.

He craned his neck and looked up at the guard.

Tomon had his taser out. The captain saw the weapon was charged and ready.

But so was he.

"You have to use that word," Archer said, "with a little more respect."

Tomon's eyes blazed fire.

He jumped down to the main corridor and advanced on Archer.

Predictable, the captain thought. *So predictable.*

"You're going to need a week in the infirmary," the guard said. *"Captain."*

He jabbed the taser at Archer.

The captain might have been weak, a little tired, not entirely up to snuff, but the day hadn't come when he couldn't outfight a twerp like Tomon in his sleep.

Archer dodged right.

The weapon—and the guard who held it—slid harmlessly past him.

As Tomon tried to recover, Archer's right arm shot out, and he jabbed the ampule into the guard's arm.

"Hey!" Tomon stopped moving, and rubbed his arm. "What—"

His eyes rolled back in his head, and he passed out.

That was A block's cue.

The prisoners who had maneuvered next to the guards above them attacked. Archer heard, rather than saw them move.

He was too busy pulling Tomon's laser pistol from his belt.

The guards at the end of the corridor were already moving too. One of them toward the fray—the other, obviously more savvy one, toward what could only be an alarm button on the wall.

Archer targeted him first.

A single shot from the laser pistol—and it was uncanny, how identical these were to the ones Starfleet had stopped using a dozen years ago, right down to the colors and feel of the hand grip—and that man went down. A second shot, and the other guard followed.

And when the captain turned around, it was over.

The ten A block guards had all fallen—as had some of his own crew, though a quick check by Phlox revealed none of them seriously injured—and Archer's people were gathering the guards weapons. Changing into their clothes, some of them, for the next phase of the plan.

Archer nodded as he watched, a grim smile on his face. It wasn't an escape yet.

But they were well on their way.

The captain found Dwight and clapped him on the shoulder.

"Nice work, Ensign. You should have been an actor."

The young man smiled. "It wasn't entirely an act, sir—but I appreciate the compliment."

Archer nodded. No, it wasn't entirely an act. The young man's illness, and the sickness the rest of the crew was suffering from—both were all too real. Not the least of the reasons they needed to get back to *Enterprise* was to get Phlox to sickbay, to his equipment, so the doctor could get them all well again.

But first things first.

Archer turned to the door at the end of the corridor.

The main complex, where they'd find the rest of the crew—B block—waiting to take their exercise.

No, the captain corrected himself silently.

Not the rest of the crew.

Not Trip, nor Hoshi—who'd never even made it with the rest of them to Rava. Archer didn't know where they were—Reed had been of the opinion that they'd taken the cell-ship and escaped. The captain thought that likely at first—but as the days passed, his certainty waned. He knew Trip. *Enterprise*'s chief engineer would have come looking for them—would have found them by now. If he could.

So something had happened along the way. Either that, or . . .

Archer wouldn't think about the *or* just now.

Other members of his crew were missing as well. Reed. T'Pol. Travis. Hess and Ryan from engineering. They'd all come to the prison with them, been on A block up until the third day after their arrival. Then all of them had been marched away, and not heard from—since. Archer had only a rough idea of the prison complex's size—but it was certainly big enough for them to still be here, somewhere. He intended to find them, if they were.

"Captain." O'Neill, dressed in one of the Denari guard uniforms, approached. "We're ready."

Archer nodded. They had to move quickly.

"All right everyone."

He looked around at his crew.

"You know the plan. Let's move."

They took up positions then—the "guards" on the walkways above, the prisoners on the corridor below—and began to march.

ACKNOWLEDGMENTS

Like the old saying goes . . .

  Some days you eat the bear.

  And some days the bear eats you.

  On this particular book, I got devoured whole.

  Never mind days, on this project entire weeks flew past without the story progressing in any substantive form. I finally typed those two magical words—THE END—in mid-June 2003, leaving the Pocket Books staff a scant two and a half months—as opposed to the usual year—to make their planned publication schedules.

  That they succeeded in doing so, and producing the book you now hold, is a tribute to the hard work and professional capabilities of many people—to whom I would like to offer (in the words of the wonderful wizard himself) both a testimonial, and heartfelt thanks. Specifically: Donna O'Neill, Joann Foster . . .

  And most especially, Margaret Clark, whose

saintly patience and words of wisdom kept me on track toward a finish line that at times seemed impossibly far away. . . .

Thanks are also due to: Paula Block, for adjusting her own schedule to make this happen; Janet Holliday, for giggles and protein deficiencies; K. P. Ryan himself; and Scott Shannon. And my family, who are always happy to see the end of this writing process.

I return now to the K'Pellis Cluster, and the knotty problem of parallel universes. . . .

Dave Stern
June 2003